ABOUT THE AUTHOR

Lexie Winston has been an astronaut, rock star, princess and time traveller. In her dreams. But none of the dreams have lived up to what becoming an author has been like. She gets to live in a world of pure imagination, and her heroines get to do the things she's always wished she could.

When not writing books, Lexie is a mother of two gorgeous teenagers and the wife to a patient and understanding man. They live in Western Australia and are lorded over by a black toy poodle. She loves camping, reading and if her iPad was stolen, her world would explode. (It has the kindle app on it.)

And you can find all links at

www.lexiewinston.com

PERFORMER

LEXIE WINSTON

NEIGHPALM PUBLISHING

ALSO BY LEXIE WINSTON

First published by Neighpalm Publishing in 2023

Performer - Galaxy Circus Series

Mobi format: 978-0-6455262-4-0
Print: 978-0-6455262-5-7

Cover design by Raven Ink Covers
Editing by Elemental Editing

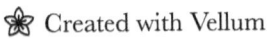 Created with Vellum

AUTHOR'S NOTE

Performer is the fifth Galaxy Circus novel, a fast-burn RH series that contains some adult situations which may be triggering, such as dub-con.

Galaxy Circus will also contain MM and male appendages of a somewhat interesting nature.

CHAPTER ONE

Lila

"Help, help!" The muffled shouts have me dropping what I was doing in the kitchen and running at Vilaxian speed through the house. When I arrive, it's all I can do not to burst out laughing. I find the warlock, one of the most powerful beings in the universe, being smothered by one very enthusiastic child. It looks like something out of an alien movie. Cordelia, who is using her favorite move, has latched herself around Xavier's head and is placing little kraken kisses all over his face, which are going to leave marks—I know from experience. He's going to look like he was attacked by a hickey monster.

My gaze moves down, and I find Jack and Calypso wrapped around each of his legs, not allowing him to move anywhere. Of course he won't use his powers against our children, so for now, he's stuck there. They adore their other fathers, but Xavier is certainly a favorite because he's a huge softy and he gives in to them all the time. I can't imagine what he's going to be like when they can actually talk and ask for things.

"Were you thinking about helping him at all?" I ask the children's biological father, who is sitting on a nearby sofa with a tablet in hand, scrolling through something.

"Nah, I figure he's one of the most powerful beings in the universe, so he's got this," Cas says without even looking up, snickering under his breath.

"Xav is going to make you pay for this," I caution, and he looks up and shrugs.

"Makes things interesting, and it's good practice for when he has his own." He winks at me, and I roll my eyes. Like hell we are having any more children anytime soon. One day, sure, but at the moment, it's all I can do to keep these three alive. I can't imagine adding more to the mix.

It's been two weeks since we left the ocean, and the children still haven't shifted out of their kraken forms. I'm still feeding them live fish and crustaceans, which is what I was programming the replicator for in the kitchen. I'll herd the three of them to the swimming pool and release the fish and crustaceans, and then they will practice their hunting skills. It's been so cute watching Caspian's kraken teach them how to catch their food. For such a big, fearsome creature, he is completely besotted with our children. My own kraken often insists on joining them, but I'm also desperately waiting for the day they shift so I can hold warm little babies in my arms, not wriggly little squirming krakens.

"Cordy, honey, please let Daddy X breathe. He's no good to me if you starve him of oxygen and he becomes a vegetable." I take a seat on the sofa next to Caspian and lean in, trying to get a look at what he's doing.

"Malik has decided that he will take over my spot in the circus," Cas tells me, pointing to a message from his brother. A huge grin crosses my face, and Xavier, who has finally gotten Cordelia to let go of his face, glares at me.

"Thanks for the help."

I wave off his pretend annoyance. I know he freaking loves it. He cradles the offending baby kraken in his arms like she's the most precious thing in the world.

"You were fine. I knew you had this," I tell him before turning back to Cas. "I can't wait to introduce him to Magenta. She's going to take one look at him and be infatuated."

Xavier shuffles his way over to the couch, bringing Jack and Cally along for the ride. I'm pretty sure if they were in human form, they would be giggling madly. I'm not sure how old they will be when they shift, but they have grown so much in two weeks.

"Isn't she in a thing with Hale, Velorina, and Nixie?" he asks as he takes a seat. The two children attached to his legs make their way up his body until he has all three of them cradled in his arms. He places absent-minded kisses on each of their little domed heads, and I feel my heart pitter-patter with love. I can't wait to get my memories back and be able to seal the warlock intimate bond. As soon as my children shift, we are going to make plans to leave Skarr again. We need to go to Rilu and find the flower we need to heal Grandpa J, and then our next destination will be Westalin before we resume the circus tour.

"I'm not sure, to be honest. I think they were messing around, but you saw how funny the Vilax-ians were about my and Saxon's blood rose bond. They are not even blood roses, and as far as I know, they are just using each other for mutual gratifica-tion. Magenta will have to move on if she doesn't want to start the Skarrian bonding process, and I don't know about her and Nixie. Someone told me Aquilians don't have any kind of fated mate, so maybe she and Magenta will work out, but I haven't had a chance to ask her. We were going to have a girls' night once I got back to the ship." I sigh, thinking about how my normal life has gone out the window—not that I regret any of what's happened, but it's so different from where I was not so many months ago, drifting with no purpose or destination in mind.

"And you can still do that. The guys and I will watch the kids. What's the point of having so many mates if you can't have time to yourself?" Cas presses a kiss to my head much like Xavier had done with the children.

"Alright, I guess it's dinnertime for the little slime balls," I say, standing up. "Can I leave it to you two to get them to the pool while I grab their meal?" I look between my two mates, and Cas eagerly throws his tablet to the side, his eyes flashing to the black of his beast for a moment before switching back.

"Of course." He stands up and holds out his hand to Jack and Cally, who eagerly move from Xavier to Caspian.

"Come on, are you going to swim with us?" he asks Xavier, who quickly shakes his head.

"No, as much as I like you and I'm interested in…" He trails off and looks at the kids before continuing. "Playing with you guys in the bedroom, I do not like to be probed while swimming, and your damn kraken does it to me every time I get into the water with him." Xavier frowns, and Cas runs a hand through his hair, grimacing slightly.

"Yeah, sorry about that. It's weird because he has been dead set against any males. I've had relationships before in the past, but now that Lila has had our babies, it's like it gave him permission to enjoy himself and, well, he's as horny and reckless as Lila's kraken at the moment. It's like the two of them are ready to start a baby factory, and they don't care if it's them having the babies or any others in this relationship."

He's not wrong. Those fuck me vibes, which were supposed to ease off completely once I had the babies, are still riding me hard. Every time the lightning cats walk into the room, Maxsim turns around and walks back out again. Echo assures me he is trying, but my pheromones are just too much for him to handle, and it's playing with his emotions. Poor Maxsim is confused. Although he doesn't want to hate me anymore, he can't decide if he wants to fuck or fight me. I know how he feels. I have the same problem. I want to pin Echo to the ground and fuck him until he can't see straight, and at the same time, I want to roll over and show my ass to Maxsim and beg him to knot me. We can't keep going on like this, but I refuse to do anything with them until I've locked down Link and Xavier, and Link is being a stubborn motherfucker.

He is going out of his way to avoid me. He is annoyed that I still haven't mastered Alien 101. He says I'm putting my life in danger by not becoming an alien expert overnight. I mean, he's probably not wrong, but there is only so much of me to go around, and I have devoted all my time to my babies in the last two weeks. That's going to have to change tomorrow. William, Eric, and Link have found an old mimic who is coming by to give me a talking to. Apparently there is a real possibility of me splicing my body into a number of different species if I'm not careful, which really doesn't sound like fun and could kill me. I know that Link's being an asshole out of fear, but that really doesn't work for me. I'm a stubborn bitch and likely to dig my heels in if he's going to be like that.

I hold my hands out for Cordy, but she snuggles down into Xavier's arms and stubbornly wraps her little tentacles around him so she will be hard to remove.

"Come on, baby, let's leave Daddy X for a moment and go get something to eat. I bet you're hungry," I coax my daughter, but she really is from my genes. She is stubborn and determined, and there is not much that will get her to change her mind once she's made it.

"Cordy, honey, come and swim with me and your brother and sister." Caspian finally decides to get involved, and now it's Xavier's turn to smirk when she doesn't listen to him.

"What if I find Daddy Sax and ask him to swim with us?" I bribe her with the promise of Saxon, who is not going to be happy. He really does not like to swim. He hates not being in control of his body like he is on the land. His Vilaxian strength and speed is hampered by the water, and of course he can't breathe under it like we can.

There's a flash of light, and Xavier yelps with surprise. All of a sudden, there's a pretty, pale blue skinned toddler with purple spiky hair sticking up all over her face. She has perfect pouty lips, and her matching blue eyebrows are set in a stubborn frown.

"No," she says, wrapping her arms around Xavier's neck and snuggling into his side. I can practically see the damn warlock melt into a puddle of useless goo. Some help he is.

"Oh wow." I stare at my beautiful child with amazement. We did that. My fingers itch to reach out and snatch her from him, but I control myself. "Did you know they wouldn't be babies?" I ask Caspian, who is still staring at her with his mouth wide open in shock.

He slowly shakes his head. "No. When Clove and Calvin shifted after a couple of weeks, they were probably the size of a six-month-old human baby." His words send panic shooting through my body, and my heart starts to race.

"Link!" I call before shouting even louder and more insistently. "Link!" I don't care if he's pissy, I want him to take a look at my baby and tell me that I did not damage her in any way. Blood rose bonding, being hit by lightning, and activating my Skarrian powers caused an incredible amount of pressure on my body, so I wouldn't be surprised if I hurt them in some way, and I will never forgive myself.

Everyone in the house must hear the urgency in my voice, because within the next few minutes, our living area fills with the rest of my family. William, Eric, and Saxon all appear from separate areas of the house. The lightning cats, both in their cat forms, come bounding in from outside. They really do love the cold weather and can be found there most days if not in Echo's nest. Finally, Link arrives. I'm not sure where he was, but if I could guess, it was anywhere that I'm not. His attitude has surprised me, and I really need to sit down and talk to him because we can't go on like this. The attraction mark is still on my shoulder, but I worry that maybe he's changed his mind, and that he would be happier with a smarter, more organized cyborg like himself. Saxon did tell me that he is getting pressure from his mother, but he refuses to tell her whom he is involved with. I wonder if he's embarrassed about me. It's been a lot these last few weeks, and I've been tumbling into bed, exhausted, as soon as the kids are settled into the wonderful cribs he got them. I need to do better.

"What's wrong?" His mouth rounds out into an O as he catches sight of the naked little girl in

Xavier's arms. "She's a toddler?" He turns his surprised eyes back to me as Echo and Maxsim belly crawl over to Xavier. Cordelia squeals with excitement, clambers out of his arms, and reaches for the fluffy cats. Suddenly, the two in Caspian's arms flash, and gone are the other two kraken babies, and in their place are two more naked toddlers. Jack has blue skin and blue hair that sticks up at all angles just like Cordy, but Cally is a mix of my and Caspian's coloring. Her skin is mottled blue and purple, and she has longish pink hair. They squeal and reach for the cats.

"Kitty," Jack shouts, clapping his hands together as Caspian does his best to juggle the two squirming toddlers.

"Whoa." William and Eric are bug-eyed as they stare in awe at our children.

"Daddy Link!" Cally smiles brightly at my cyborg fiancé and holds out her hands. "Kisses." She puckers her lips and blows raspberries. Link stumbles slightly as he steps toward Caspian and takes Cally into his arms.

"Daddy Sax." Not to be outdone by his sisters, Jack waves his arms at my Vilaxian, and the brave general's already pale skin pales even further and he actually steps back. Huh, I never would have guessed a baby would scare the brave warrior.

William just puts a hand on his back and gives

him a shove. "No you don't. You get in there and hold your child."

Saxon swallows nervously, but I see the moment he decides to commit. His back straightens, and a determined glint replaces the sheer terror that was there previously. He steps up to Cas and holds out his hands. Jack leaps, but Saxon is there to catch him, and he tucks him safely into his chest. Jack grabs Saxon's face and uses his little hands to push Saxon's lips into a kiss before smacking a big one on his lips. Saxon looks like he could be knocked over with a feather for a moment, but then out comes that sexy as fuck grin, and he beams as he blows little raspberries against Jack's naked tummy.

"Well shit. Now I feel even more like chopped liver," I grumble as I watch my children make nice with the men in my life. Cas puts his arm around me and gives me a side hug.

"Don't feel like that. Just be happy that our children love all the men in your life. It would have been tricky if they didn't." He is smiling so widely I'm surprised his face doesn't split in two as he watches our little family. I am happy, but I'm also dying to get my hands on the adorable, chubby little babies.

I also want Link's opinion first, so I will be patient.

CHAPTER TWO

Lila

"So why are the children toddlers? From my guess, I'd say they are about two." William's eyes are narrowed as he reaches out and tickles Cally in Link's arms, distracting her while Link does a hand scan of her. "That's not what you were expecting, was it?"

Cas shakes his head. "No, I was expecting them to be a little younger." We all watch as Link finishes his scan of Cally's body. He then passes her back to Xavier and untangles Cordy's little fingers from Echo's fur and does the same thing to her. She bats at his hand, whining slightly because she was taken away from the soft kitty. Echo grumbles too, but Maxsim just headbutts him gently, and they sit and wait patiently while their baby is examined.

Link is giving nothing away with the blank expression on his face, and I feel the urge to shift and bite his fucking head off. My fangs click down, and I start to growl. Saxon hands Jack off to William and comes over to me.

"When was the last time you ate?" he asks, gripping my arms and making me look him in the eye.

"I can't remember, okay? What with the kids and trying to learn everything Link wants me to learn and just trying to remember to put my underwear on the right way every morning, I may not have had any blood for a couple of days," I snap at him, and his eyes soften, but he purses his lips.

"Come on, Lila, you need to do better. When you don't drink blood, your temper gets shorter, and you would feel very sorry if you attacked one of us out of bloodlust."

"Fine, but if Link doesn't hurry the fuck up and tell me what's going on, it's his vein I'm going to drain." I glare at my cyborg fiancé, who slowly looks up from Cordy and finally pays attention.

Frowning, he drops his hand away from her naked body. "Xavier, can you put clothes on the kids? Now that they've changed, their bodies are having trouble trying to regulate their temperature, and I don't want them to get sick," he asks, still looking at me with that same, infuriatingly blank look.

Xavier waves a hand, and all three of the kids

are instantly clothed in adorable matching onesies. They are all black and covered in stars, with the Galaxy Circus symbol on them. Xavier then waves another hand, and a playpen appears over in the corner of the room. It's filled with toys and soft mats, and he stands up, goes over to it, and places Cally inside before waving his hand and telekinetically floating Jack and Cordelia over to it as well. They clap and squeal with delight. Cally pulls herself up on the railing and waves as her siblings float to the mat.

"There, that will keep them occupied while we talk about them."

Echo and Maxsim move to the playpen, where both stretch out in front of it and put their heads on their front paws, listening but guarding the babies as well. I've seen how Echo looks longingly at them when he's in his bipedal form. I think he's dying to have a litter, but it hasn't happened for him and Maxsim yet. I mean, it wasn't really a stable environment for breeding with Natalia always gunning for him, but maybe now that she's gone, they will be able to conceive with his next heat. I would be so happy for them.

"Lila, stop growling," Link snaps at me, and I flip him off, but I take a deep breath and sit down, waiting for him to give me the results of his scans. He just frowns and shakes his head with disappointment. "I would like to do more tests back on the ship, but as far as I can tell, they are fine. It is possible that you bonding with Saxon may have had something to do with their accelerated growth. They are showing a few Vilaxian markers, and as far as I know, Vilaxian growth is faster than most." He turns a questioning gaze to Saxon who nods.

"Yes, our children grow rapidly until they hit their teens, and then their bodies practically freeze and growth slows completely."

"As far as I can tell, that's what happened to the babies. Their growth will be quite rapid. Caspian says he was expecting six-month-old babies, whereas these three are probably closer to two. That seems to be an accelerated growth rate four times that of a shifter baby."

"Once our children shift, their growth rate is probably twice as fast as a human's, so within six months of hatching, they are roughly the size of a one-year-old from Earth," Caspian explains, and I feel like my head is about to explode with all these different numbers.

"So you are saying that by the time they are four years old, they will look like teenagers?" I ask, trying to wrap my head around it all. "Do they mature mentally at the same rate, or is it just physically?" My panic has not eased. I thought I had plenty of time to get this parenting thing right, but it seems like I only have as short period of time to try not to fuck up their lives completely.

"Again, I'd like to run a few tests, but considering the fact that they are talking and can recognize each of us, I'm going to go with yes, they seem to be."

My gaze leaves the damn cyborg and flits toward my babies, who look to be entertaining themselves just fine inside the playpen. Cordy and Jack appear to be building something out of blocks, but Cally has a little cardboard book in her hand, and she is turning the pages, her little pink eyebrows furrowed in concentration. Frustration and fear and worry all batter at my emotions, and I feel angry and unstable and I have no idea how to fix it.

"So basically you really don't know anything, and this is all going to be guesswork?" I snap unreasonably at the doctor, my worry and hunger getting the better of me.

He just shrugs, still wearing that damn blank look on his face. For fuck's sake, why can't I get him to react to anything? I'm deliberately being a bitch in the hopes I can get some kind of reaction out of him, but nope, nothing besides continuing blankness.

"Yes, Lila, I am just guessing. I'm not sure there has ever been a case of children like yours before, but I will look through the Skarrian databases again, as well as the notes that the Vilaxian queen sent me."

I feel all out of sorts. I think the thing that hurts

the most is that none of the kids wanted hugs or kisses from me. I mean, in their kraken form, we've barely been apart, but I thought maybe once they shifted, things would be the same. Maybe they don't really need me anymore now that I've hatched them. Maybe that was my job, and now I don't have anything to do with raising them. I have no idea how Fluxxians raise their children. Mira and Murphy both seemed to have good relationships with all of their kids, but they have proven to be the exception on Fluxx.

Fuck me, I really need to do better at my research, especially all the species that are in my bond group, but I fucking hate learning via book. I am so much better at learning through practical means. I have the attention span of a goldfish, and every time Link puts that damn tablet in front of me, I find something better to do with my time. There are some pretty cool galactic games on that tablet, and I get distracted by pretty, shiny things.

A big sigh leaves my mouth, and I stand up. "I guess I need to go replicate them something different for dinner," I say, feeling my body sag with weariness. Cas grabs me and shakes his head, pushing me in the direction of the stairs.

"No, you go take care of your need for blood and leave dinner to me. Between all of us, I'm sure we can work out a meal for them. Right, guys?" He turns to the rest of the males in the room, and my partners all look like deer caught in headlights, but Eric and William are nodding with confidence.

"Of course we can," William assures me. "We had plenty of experience with Marcus. We've got this."

"That would be awesome, thank you." I feel tears of gratitude and frustration well in my eyes. "Are you coming?" I ask Saxon, and he looks between me and Link before shaking his head.

"No, I think Link should be the one to go. I don't think it would hurt for him to have a look at you too. Since the five of you stepped out of the ocean, your emotions have been all over the place." Saxon is a brave man, bringing that up out loud, and I take a step toward him, my hands clenched, but Xavier stands up and steps between us, his hands held up in a placating way.

"Now stop, Lila. He is only saying what we all think. I can feel how chaotic your emotions have been, and even I'm having trouble keeping up with it all. I try to siphon off the most that I can, but it's all so confusing. There's exhaustion, guilt, and frustration, not to mention overwhelming lust which really should have settled by now according to Fluxx shifter notes for krakens. You should be feeling joy and happiness at the birth of your babies. It's there, but only briefly." My warlock mate looks worried, and when I look at everyone else, they have the same expression.

"We have been talking, and we think maybe you might be suffering from a little postpartum depression. Will you please let Link take a look at you too? And for God's sake, can the two of you sort out what is happening between you? Tiptoeing around you is exhausting." Cas glares at us.

"Yes, fuck or fight, but enough of this avoiding one another crap," Saxon says dryly. Echo lifts his head and yowls his agreement, and Maxsim just blinks his nonjudgmental eyes. Wow, for once, the big guy is on my side, and I kind of appreciate his silence.

"Fine, I guess you better come too," I tell Link and start heading to my bedroom, but when I turn around, he hasn't moved.

"Link," Xavier growls, and I see Link's shoulders slump. My stomach plummets. This is it. He's going to reject me. I feel no burning sensation where our attraction marks are, though, so I still have a little hope.

"Please." I finally cave and hold out a hand. I won't beg, but it doesn't take much for me to give a little. At my words, his head comes up and he blinks in disbelief. Holy crap, have Link and I completely miscommunicated? Does he feel like I've been rejecting him? I totally haven't, but I hate being nagged. Maybe I'm just as much to blame for this situation as he is.

I make an executive decision. I hurry over to the

playpen and, one by one, I lift my babies up. My heart just about melts when they wrap their arms around me as I smother them all with kisses. "Mommy needs to do something tonight, so your daddies and grandpas are going to feed you and put you to bed. Mommy will see you in the morning, okay?"

"Bye, mommy." Jack waves his hand, and Cally and Cordy follow suit.

"We love you," they call out, not concerned in the least, which I'm incredibly grateful for. I grab my wayward cyborg fiancé by the hand and tow him up the stairs to my bedroom. We are going to take Saxon's advice, but by the time we leave the bedroom, we will either be bonded or broken up.

CHAPTER THREE

Link

Lila's hand is cool and clammy in mine as she drags me away from the rest of the family. My heart rate, which I can normally keep steady and constant, starts to race on its own in anticipation of what's to come. I feel like things have gone massively sideways for Lila and me since she emerged from the water. When I heard about her losing her bracelet, shifting, and having sex with that blasted merman, I felt some small amount of hurt but mostly all I felt was panic—panic that her mimic powers were now unbound, and she would be out of control, and something would go horribly wrong, and she would die before we could ever be joined. My life would be over then. I don't think I would ever be able to find someone quite like Lila again. I don't think I would want to.

I admit that maybe I went into panic mode and became a little insistent about her learning the various alien species in the hopes that it would help her get a handle on her abilities. Maybe I kept putting the tablet in front of her every time she had a free moment, and maybe I got a little pissy when she didn't put all of her attention on the task. I guess I kind of lost sight of the fact that unlike me and all cyborgs, who only have to read something once before we assimilate it into our knowledge, Lila takes more than that—not to mention her incredibly short attention span. I hadn't thought about the fact that she was also learning to be a mother to three baby krakens she knew nothing about either, so maybe I owe her an apology, but instead of being so abrupt, maybe she could have just said it was too much. Maybe we are both to blame.

The air is loaded with tension as we enter her bedroom and she closes the door behind us. She flops down onto the bed and holds her arms out. "Have at it, Doc," she says dryly and slightly sarcastically.

We weren't kidding about the postpartum depression. With all those hormones riding her hard as well as the changes in her own DNA and her body, she must be feeling topsy-turvy. Her emotions really are all over the place. When I look down at her, I feel a rush of sympathy wash over me.

"Lila, enough. Look, I'm sorry, okay?" I drop to my knees at her feet, looking up at her. We can't go on like this anymore. It kind of feels like we've gone backward instead of forward, and that, combined with my mother's continuous video calls which I have been ignoring and my uncertainty over our relationship, is kind of causing me to lose my cool. "I'm sorry I've been nagging you, but shit, so much has happened in a short period of time, and I'm worried about your mimic abilities and the changes you've already made. Your body has been through so much stress, and I worry you're going to be exhausted and mess up. I guess I let my own emotions rule my actions instead of using logic and reason. Can you forgive me?"

She sighs and lowers her arms, dropping her head onto her chest. When she finally lifts it, tears flow down her face. "I'm so sorry. It's been so much. I thought you hated me because of what happened with Nikos, and you wanted me to learn all the species, and it was all I could do to keep my head above water while trying to look after three kraken babies who just don't fucking stop."

I grip her arms and lean my forehead against

hers. "Aww, baby, no. I admit I had a slight moment of jealousy because that damn can of tuna fish got to you first, but I don't blame you nor am I upset. I always knew you were attracted to him despite your denials. It's literally written on your skin, so I got over that quickly. I just didn't want anything to happen to you. But now that I think about it, you actually haven't had any problems with holding your form, have you?"

I watch her think about it, and her eyebrows jump in surprise. "No, actually. I've been fine with you for obvious reasons, since I can't actually shift into a cyborg, but Saxon and Cas are the same because I already had those traits, and I haven't felt the need to shift into warlock mist because Xavier hasn't, nor did I feel the urge to copy his powers when he used them earlier for the kids."

She sounds as surprised as I feel, and I sit back on my heels and think about what I've learned. "Maybe because you already shifted into a warlock when you first got hit by lightning, you've assimilated that form, so to speak."

"But I haven't felt the need to shift into the cats either," she argues.

"Yes, but what if that is because of your whisperer abilities? You are a match for them anyway, whether in this form or if you shifted into lightning cat form," I suggest, and her eyes widen and she nods.

"Yes, you could be right. Apparently I am supposed to be a perfect match for either of them, so there is no need for me to shift into their form. I'll be grateful when I meet the old mimic tomorrow and can finally get some real answers. I can't believe that the Skarrian databases have hardly any information about mimics."

We were all surprised to learn this. According to William and Eric, there should be huge databases on each ability so nothing comes as a shock if a child starts exhibiting certain traits, but to our surprise, both the whisperer and mimic abilities had been redacted. It's almost like the Skarrian council, or the people on it, would be happy if those abilities disappeared. I guess both of them are incredibly powerful and unique gifts.

"Look, how about I do a quick checkup just to make sure everything is sitting well, and then you can feed from me and get a good night's rest. I know it's been a while since you've really slept well. I can give you a sedative if you want. The guys will be fine looking after the babies tonight without your help," I suggest, and her eyes narrow and she leans in.

"Link Tesla, do you still want to bond with me?" she asks point-blank, and I startle a little. I hadn't been expecting her to ask.

"Of course I do. I'm sorry if I gave you the

impression that I didn't," I assure her, and a slow grin crosses her lips.

"Well good then. I don't know about needing a good night's sleep, but I've heard a couple of mind-blowing orgasms can make a person tired. How about we try that instead of a sedative?" She reaches for me, but before she can grab me, I scramble to my feet and hold my hands up. Her shoulders droop, and her smile drops.

"Just let me do the scan first, and I promise I will have you seeing Jesus," I reassure her, and her smile picks up again.

She scrambles back on the bed and lies down for me. I climb up next to her and activate the scanner in my hand, carefully watching the screen built into my arm as I run it slowly over her body. It logs all of her vital information, assimilating and comparing it to previous scans I've taken from her. Everything looks pretty good. All her organs are functioning as they should be, but I can tell her body is flooded with hormones and there is a chemical imbalance in her brain. That would explain why her emotions are all over the place. She's having trouble regulating her moods. I'm wondering if it's something we can medicate or if it's something that will settle on its own. Seeing the old mimic is hopefully going to answer a lot of questions for all of us.

I drop my hand and turn my attention to the beautiful woman waiting patiently on the bed for my results.

"Physically your body is in amazing condition. You're healthy and everything is functioning at a hundred percent capacity."

"But?" she asks, frowning.

"Emotionally you're a little bit of a mess," I say frankly, and she shrugs.

"That's really not news to anyone."

"No, but what do we do about it? I can medicate you, or we can wait and see what Oshan says about it tomorrow."

She thinks about it carefully before shaking her head. "Let's wait and see what Oshan says about it. I don't want to do something that is going to make it worse."

"That's a good idea. I hadn't thought about the possibility that the medication wouldn't work."

A grin crosses her lips, and she pounces.

"Oof." I find myself on my back with Lila straddling me, leaning over me with twinkling eyes.

"And to be honest, what I feel at the moment is total horniness, and I'm almost certain you can take care of that for me." She waggles her eyebrows, and I purse my lips. "What, are you changing your mind?" she growls, and I quickly shake my head.

"No, no, of course not."

"Good, because I don't want to wait any longer. Link, please bond with me, right here, right now." She sounds a little nervous despite the lust flashing in her eyes, and I know how she feels. I've waited patiently for today.

"Lila, I would love nothing more than to bond with you. Will you take some of my nanobots as a token of my affection and love?" I ask her formally. It's the way two cyborgs join. It's kind of like the human tradition of exchanging rings.

"Yes, I would love to have a part of you permanently inside me." She giggles at the suggestive words. "What do we need to do?"

I lift my hand and extend my pointer finger, then I activate the needle that allows me to inject her with some of my nanobots. Her eyes widen, and she bites her lip nervously. "I just need to inject them into you. Where would you like me to do it?" I ask, and she whips her shirt off. Her luscious breasts are not bound by a bra, and I'm momentarily distracted by her rosy pink nipples. My mouth waters, and my cock, which has been semi-hard since she leaped on top of me, hardens fully.

"Right here." She points to the space between her breasts just above her heart. My own heart lurches, and a feeling of warmth rushes over me.

"This may hurt, but only for a moment," I warn her as I press the tip of my finger between her breasts. Once it's resting against her skin, I allow the needle to come out and slide in, and I see her wince with the slight prick of pain. "Almost done," I say as I inject some of my nanobots into her. In a rush, they come flooding out of me and into her. I try to hold back the amount, since traditionally it's only a small exchange, but these seem to want to be in Lila. Finally, the flood diminishes and my finger retracts. As I pull my hand away, I see a ring of scars around Lila's nipple that I hadn't noticed before.

"What's this?" I ask her, brushing my finger lightly over the nipple, and she frowns as she looks down.

"That damn can of tuna bit me when he lured me out of the cave to swim with him." She doesn't like to admit out loud that they had sex. She always uses the words *swim with him.* "It took forever to heal, even with my accelerated Vilaxian healing."

My heart skips a beat, and I try to hide my frown from Lila. I don't want to stress her out any more than she already is, and I will have to talk to the guys about this. To me, it looks like a mating bite. Although Aquilians don't have fated mates, they still bite their partners when they form pods, usually in a spot where someone else can see and know they are spoken for. Aquilian women don't cover their breasts when in mer form, which is ninety percent of the time. If I am right, then she is going to kill Nikos when she eventually learns what he has done.

"Are you ready for me to blow your mind and seal you to me forever?" Lila looks a little nervous, but I forget about the bite mark for now and reach up, dragging her head down to mine and kissing her thoroughly.

"Yes please," I tell her when we pull apart, breathless from the kiss. She grins and lifts my shirt over my head, tossing it to the side before running her hands up and down my chest.

"I love your body. It's so freaking sexy, just like your mind," she mutters distractedly as she leans in and nips one of my nipples before doing the same thing to the other. "I love that I have a part of you permanently inside me, but right now, I want another part of you inside me."

She scrambles to her feet and drags her pants and underwear down, tossing them off the bed in the same direction as both of our shirts. She's completely naked, and my mouth waters, wanting to taste some part of her body. She bounces onto the bed on her knees and undoes my pants, dragging them down my legs as I lift my hips to help her. My cock pops free, and her gaze locks onto it. She licks her lips, and it bobs in anticipation.

Lila tosses my pants off the bed before wrapping her hand around my hard length, leaning in and licking the tip like a lollipop. I can't stop the groan from slipping out of my mouth.

"Do you like that?" she asks with a teasing glint in her eye.

"Yes," I mutter as she slides her hand up and down the length of my dick, her firm grip feeling amazing as she spreads some of her spit across it.

"Please, Lila, suck it. Stop teasing me," I beg her, and her smile broadens.

"Oh, I do love hearing you beg, Dr. Tesla. I believe you deserve a reward." She bobs her head again, and this time she fully engulfs my throbbing length, taking me deep into the back of her throat. The suckers lining her throat latch on as she slides her mouth up and down, and I feel my orgasm barrel closer.

"Ugh, stop," I call out. "Please." I lift her off and drag her up my body as she giggles at my obvious lack of patience.

"The first time I come, I want it to be in your pussy," I growl as I settle her above my cock and thrust up into her. She's wet and hot and tight, and it takes a couple of thrusts. Her head drops back as she moans, but finally, I'm fully seated.

I did some research on Earth women's physiological makeup since the last time we had sex. I want to make this as good for her as possible. Their G-spot is in the upper wall of their vagina, so I activate my nanobots and create a small nub that will brush against it with every thrust. I test it out, and her eyes roll back in her head as she gasps, pressing her hands against my chest.

"Oh my god, what was that? It felt so good." She starts to bounce up and down on her own, her suckers deep inside tickling and teasing my cock as her tight pussy walls grip it.

"Ugh," I groan and grab her hips and start to thrust harder. "This is going to be a quick one to take the edge off for both of us. I will do better next time," I tell her, and she giggles.

"I thought you could control your body," she teases as her hands slide up to massage her tits. She looks like a wanton goddess riding my cock, and it's no wonder I'm not going to last.

"Normally I can, but I love you and you feel so good," I mutter, and she smiles like I said the best thing in the world. My movements speed up, and I feel her getting tighter. I slide my finger down and brush her clit, and she stiffens before throwing her head back and screaming, her orgasm and pleasure triggering my own. I thrust twice more before I, too, come hard. My own guttural groan and pants join hers as we both ride out our pleasure.

It takes us a few moments to come down from our orgasms, and we're both a little sweaty and breathing heavily, but her grin says it all. "That's one. Only a couple more until you're all mine."

"Luckily I have good recovery." My cock hasn't

even softened as I flip us and kiss her hard, ready for round two.

"God, I love you," she murmurs, running her hand up and down my back, and I feel like I could rule the world.

"I love you too, my beautiful girl. Now how about we get to seeing Jesus?"

CHAPTER FOUR

Lila

Being bonded to Link feels different than my mating with Caspian and my blood rose bonding with Saxon. Because it was the men who triggered the bond, we are bound in the way of their race. With Link, though, we are bound in the way of my race, or I guess my original race because apparently now I am all races, but I digress. There is a heaviness that sits in my chest. I'm not sure if it's a part of his soul or what, but I know that it is Link, and with it, I am able to tap into how he is feeling.

Right now, he feels smug, loved, and well fucked. I smile to myself as I roll over and look at the gorgeous, naked, shimmery man. His silver eyes are closed, and his silver hair is sticking up all over the place. His chest rises and falls, his breathing heavy in his slumber. The sex was mind-blowing, and when we hit that fifth mutual orgasm, it was like my body and his merged momentarily. I could feel what he felt and vice versa. I was flooded with the most intense love and happiness that my eyes filled with tears. Never again will I be alone, because I carry a part of this gorgeous man inside me—both metaphorically and physically. Apparently him giving me his nanobots is nothing but symbolic. I can't actually do anything with them, but it sure would be fun to be able to change my body parts to whatever I want them to be. Imagine being able to make your boobs bigger or your waist skinnier, or I could even grow a dick and know what it feels like to pee standing up. I look down my naked body and think about what a dick would look like on me. Of course it would be a perfect length and girth, and it would be a pretty pink, even when erect.

A tingling sensation starts to happen in my groin, and my mouth drops open in surprise as my skin starts to move down there. My mound flattens slightly, and my clit starts to enlarge, growing bigger and bigger until there is no denying what is happening. My vagina is closing up, and a heavy weight sits between my legs as testicles grow in place of my lips.

"Argh!" I scream, but I can't look away. It's like a car wreck, and my eyes are glued to the action.

Link sits bolt upright next to me and looks around for the danger. "What's wrong?" he asks drowsily when he doesn't see any immediate threat. "Are you okay? Did our bonding do any damage? Let me check you out." He raises his hand to scan me, but I just grab hold of his chin and turn his head to look at my groin.

"I would say something went wrong. I have a cock."

"Holy fuck." The swear word falls out of Link's mouth as his eyes bulge in surprise. "You have a really big cock."

"Why do I have a really big cock, Link?" I demand, grinding my teeth. It lies against my thigh and twitches when I think about it, but it seems to have stopped growing.

"Ah, I'm not exactly sure." He runs a hand through his messy hair, sounding bewildered. "Did you wake up like that?"

"No, Link, I didn't wake up like this. I woke up with a perfectly functioning, albeit well-abused, vajayjay."

He smirks slightly, knowing he was the one who abused it, before shaking his head and focusing on the problem at hand. His hand leaves his hair and runs down his body to his own groin where he gives himself a little scratch while considering my new drama.

"So what were you thinking about before this happened?" He points at the offending member before leaning closer to get a better look. His warm breath brushes across it, and when he lifts it, I moan at the strange new sensations that feel kind of awesome. We watch in interest as my cock starts to fill with blood and grow.

"Wow." He pulls his hand away, and the thing stands at full attention. "So it's sensitive like the real thing?" he asks, and I have a sudden, wicked thought. Well, it's there now, so I may as well take full advantage of it.

"I'm not sure. Maybe you should give me a blow job so we know for sure."

He frowns and narrows his eyes before chuckling. "Ah, let's work this out first, and if you still want me to show you what a blow job feels like, I'm sure we can figure something out." Did he just agree to blow me? Does Link swing both ways? Is this something I knew? I know Xavier, Saxon, and Cas all do, but I can't remember if Link is bi as well. I mean, he must be if his mom set him up with a male fiancé. I think I remember him or someone saying cyborgs aren't particularly fussy. My heart races with anticipation, and I quickly explain what happened.

"I was lying here thinking about the nanobots

you injected me with, and how nice it was that you could share a part of yourself with me. And then I thought wouldn't it be cool if I could use those nanobots like cyborgs can? Suddenly, I got a really big dick, so that seems to work."

"Well, shit, it seems that you got your wish. It's the only thing that would explain it. My nanobots seem to have assimilated with your body and are actively working instead of just being a benign presence. You obviously feel sensation in it." He waves at my dick, which bobs up and down at his attention.

"Ah, yeah, but it's kind of painful." I reach down and give it a tug. "Like all the blood is stretching it to its limit."

He grins wryly. "Welcome to having an erection."

I run my hand up and down the length and groan at how good it feels. "Oh wow, that feels really good." I keep stroking with one hand, and I pinch my nipple with the other. "Oh yeah, fuck."

When I look at my new husband, his wry grin is gone, and in its place is more heat. "You should spit on it. It feels even better with lubrication," he suggests, and I remove my hand and lift it to do exactly that, but he stops me and gives me a kiss, his tongue rolling with mine before pulling away. "Or I could do it for you." He pushes my hand away from my tit and takes one of my nipples into his mouth, biting on it and causing my cock to throb before sliding his way down the bed. I stare down my body as he settles between my legs, a much different view from what I am used to. He takes my dick into his hand, and I feel a bolt of lightning in the base of my spine, and I arch my back. His hand is bigger and more calloused than mine and feels completely different when he strokes the length of my cock.

"Oh yes," I sigh, unable to take my eyes away from the sight before me.

Link leans in and runs his tongue up the length of my cock, and I grunt as pleasure rolls across me. "Oh wow. Can you suck it? I want to know what it feels like, but I can't guarantee I won't come down your throat. I think I'm pretty close already," I tell him, trying to think of things other than what my beautiful husband is doing to my new appendage.

Before he can do anything, though, the door opens, and Xavier pops his head in. The two of us freeze, and I pray that none of my children are with their warlock father.

"Hey, guys, Oshan is here..." Xavier's voice drops away as he catches sight of what is before him. He slowly blinks before stepping farther into the room, pulling the door closed behind him, and turning the lock. He moves over to the bed, his eyes not leaving Link's hand that's wrapped around my new dick. "Well, it certainly looks like you guys had fun last night. Why does Lila have a dick, and what are you doing with it, Link?" he asks casually, though his loose lounge pants make it obvious that he is not unappreciative of the sight.

I thought maybe Link would get embarrassed and stop what he was doing, but he just moves over on the bed and pats the empty space. "I'm giving Lila her first blow job, want to help?"

Holy fuck, this is not how I thought my morning would go, but before I can say anything, Xavier snaps his fingers and is naked. He climbs sinuously up on the bed and lies down next to Link. "I'd be delighted to, but I want all the details when we are done, and like I said, the mimic is waiting and, well, I don't think we should keep him too long." He reaches out and trails a finger up and down the length of my cock. "What a pretty dick. How does it taste?" he asks Link conversationally before leaning in and pulling Link's head toward him. He kisses him, licking and sucking his mouth before pulling away. "Hmm, she's delicious."

"Oh, uh," I grunt and try desperately to think of non-sexy things. That's what guys do when they are trying not to come too quickly. Fuck, why can't I think of anything horrible? Oh, I know, that Madova snake woman. She was gross as fuck. Yes, that works. The tingling recedes. Phew, crisis averted.

I swear the guys are ganging up on me, though, because no sooner than I think I'm okay than they both wrap their lips around either side of my dick in a coordinated attack. My fingers tighten in my sheets and my legs stiffen as my head thrashes back and forth. "Oh my god, please, it's so good," I beg, and Xavier chuckles and moves south toward my testicles while Link moves north toward the head of my dick. I'm writhing in pleasure, unable to keep track of who is doing what. Link's mouth engulfs my cock, and I can't stop my hips as they thrust up and into the hot, wet warmth of his mouth. At the same time, Xavier fondles one testicle while licking the other before going even farther south. I freeze, not sure how I'm supposed to feel about his tongue probing my asshole. It feels incredible, but am I allowed to like it? That's kind of super taboo.

"If you have time to think, then we're obviously doing something wrong." His musical voice sounds amused as they both double down on their assault, but it's a battle I've already lost. I can't help myself, and I start thrusting my cock in and out of Link's mouth just as Xavier slips a finger into my asshole.

"Holy fuck!" I scream as he strokes something deep inside me, and I lose it. My cum floods Link's mouth, his throat constricting around my dick as he swallows, and my mind splinters into a million little fragments at the sensations battering my body. He takes it like a champ, and this is obviously not the first blow job he's given.

As my orgasm subsides, Xavier removes his

finger from my ass and gets up, going over to my bathroom. I can hear the tap running, but Link is still paying special attention to cleaning up my dick, and I can't bring myself to look away. Seeing his pink tongue licking up the remnants of my cum makes blood rush into my cock once more, and it starts to harden again.

He blinks in surprise before chuckling. "Yeah, those nanobots are definitely at work. You have the same kind of recovery time as I do." He's not wrong. The damn man is like an Energizer bunny.

Xavier returns with a glass of water and hands it to Link, who takes it and downs the liquid while Xavier uses a cloth to clean the rest of me up.

"No time for anything else. We need you to speak to Oshan, but can someone please explain what just happened here?" He tosses the cloth back in the direction of the bathroom before sitting down on the bed. His naked lavender body makes my mouth water, and his own thick length is at attention too. Link sits up and joins us, and his dick is also hard. I kind of want to challenge them to a sword fight. Do you think we could have a three-way blow job? Or what about running a train? I wouldn't mind knowing what it was like to actually fuck someone, and I'm not interested in a female. I wonder if Link can change his dick to a vajayjay. I would happily fuck him.

"Lila!" Xavier snaps, and I startle. I really was

lost in my fantasies. Link is explaining about the nanobot exchange.

"I didn't think she would be able to use them," Xavier says, and I can't stop myself from reaching out to touch his dick. I am so crazy horny, and not even the blow job or all the sex from last night eased anything.

Xavier slaps my hand away and waves his hand, clothing both him and Link while leaving me naked.

"Lila, honey, do you think you can picture what your body looked like before?" Link asks gently, and I pout because I'm definitely not going to get a train now, but I do as he asks. Just like before, things start to change but in the opposite direction. My balls retract, forming my lips, and my vagina reopens at the same time my cock shrinks back into itself, leaving behind my clit and mound once more.

"Huh," Xavier grunts as they stare, fascinated with the process, but I'm just sad I didn't get to play with it a little more. Shit, I didn't even get to do a helicopter.

"Did she actually come fluid into your mouth?" Xavier asks Link clinically, and he nods.

"Yes. I probably should have thought to take a sample. I'd love to know if she was actually fertile or not."

"Well, she definitely has a prostate. That's what

I massaged when she came," Xavier adds helpfully, and Link's eyes widen with excitement.

"This is so fascinating, I'd love to see what else she can do with them."

Xavier sighs and stands up. "Well, it's going to have to wait. Come on, let's get this meeting over with. We may get some answers, or we may have just as many questions, but I don't think we are going to be bored, that's for sure," Xavier says, waving a hand and cleaning and clothing me. I guess the two of them have finished talking about me. I probably should be annoyed, but I'm too busy sulking about the lack of orgasms.

"What do you mean by that?" I ask, climbing off the bed with the help of Link's offered hand. He presses a kiss to my forehead, and I smile at him. "Thanks for my first blow job." I kiss him on the mouth before turning to Xavier and pressing a kiss to his mouth too. "You too, it was fun."

Xavier rolls his eyes playfully. "I can feel how horny you still are, *phoeall*, but this is important. I promise if you're a good girl, we can come back up here and play some more, okay?"

"Okay, but you better make good on that promise, or your ass is mine." I slap his ass and walk out of the room, leaving them both a little speechless. "For real," I call back over my shoulder, and I hear Link chuckle as they follow behind me.

"It's okay, *phoeall*, I like a thick dick up my ass."

Xavier has caught up to me, and he whispers in my ear, turning the tables on me. I groan. Fuck, that's not fair. Now I'm even hornier. I feel sorry for everyone I'm about to meet with, because my pheromones are not going away anytime soon.

CHAPTER FIVE

Lila

When I reach the main living area of our house, I'm surprised to find it empty except for an old man who looks like Professor Dumbledore from *Harry Potter*. He has a long gray hair and beard and sparkling blue eyes, and he's wearing a robe—a robe, for fuck's sake. All he needs is a pointy hat and a wand. He stands up as I enter, and we both take stock of one another. He doesn't look all that special except for the fact that he's the first old person I've seen since joining the circus—or the first one who actually looks their age.

"Lila?" he asks, and I nod. A smile spreads across his lips. "Please join me." I step into the room, followed closely by Link and Xavier, but Oshan shakes his head. "Just Lila, if you don't mind. I have no problem if she shares all this information with you later, but it really is a discussion she and I need to have privately for now."

They both frown, but I assure them with my eyes that I'm okay and that I need this probably more than I've needed anything, except for maybe dick in a while.

"Go check on the babies for me please, Link," I request, and that is enough to distract him. Xavier narrows his eyes but doesn't argue, instead following the cyborg on the mission I've now assigned him.

I take a seat on the sofa opposite Oshan and cross my legs, trying to resist the urge to squirm as he studies me closely. "How are you feeling?" he asks, and I shrug noncommittally. I'm not sure if I'm ready to admit exactly how I'm feeling to this stranger.

He sighs and waves a hand, and we are surrounded by a warlock bubble of privacy. My eyes widen, and he smirks.

"Alright, I'll do the talking, shall I?" He doesn't wait for an answer. "I found out I was a mimic in my late teens. I hadn't really been showing signs of any kind of Skarrian powers, unlike all of my peers, and I was considered to be a dud. I was a real disappointment to my parents, and I didn't have a lot of friends. The few I had were solid, and one day we attended a recruiting expo for soldiers to fight for the Una's against the Aaz'axians. Their race had been decimated, and they needed help, and we weren't about to let the Aaz'axians get their hands on the orb that could wipe us all out. Many planets sent volunteers. I was sent to training camp, and it was there that I changed for the first time, surrounded by so many different races. Back then, mimics were still remembered, and I was able to get some much needed help, but I had to work out a few things on my own."

"Such as?" I ask, leaning forward, fascinated by this man's story.

"Assimilating each mimic race was fairly easy. Once I assumed a new form, it was like it became a part of a database inside my mind, and I only had to picture it again, and I could become it."

I nod. I've avoided thinking about other forms because I had a feeling this was the key to my abilities. I hadn't wanted to play around with anything without definitive answers.

"But it must be clear. The easiest way to do it is to have a mirror, and when you assume another form, you examine yourself down to the smallest detail and lock that into your mind." I wrinkle my nose, and he frowns. "What's wrong?"

"I'm not good with details," I tell him, and his frown clears, replaced with a look of understanding.

"I wasn't either, but it quickly became second nature. I have a database of thousands of creatures inside my mind and can access each one of them easily." My mouth drops open in shock. "I think it's part of the mimic skill. You should be able to do it too, but you have to see it clearly in your mind. Don't try to think of two forms at the same time, because it will not work. I was cautioned that if I tried, I could either get stuck or my body would just explode because they weren't ever meant to be combined."

Holy shit! A shiver runs down my spine at the thought of blowing myself up.

"Okay, so let's get to your hormones and emotions. Are you feeling the desperate need to constantly fuck?" the old man asks bluntly, and I feel my face flush red before I answer him.

"Yes. I thought it was my pregnancy vibes from when I was carrying the babies, but it hasn't stopped, and my emotions swing from happy to sad to angry with the snap of a finger."

He nods with complete understanding on his face, and I feel this immense sense of relief. Finally, someone who gets it and isn't judging.

"Mimic powers use an incredible amount of energy, and the way we refuel that energy is through sex. I assume you've noticed you are attracted to a lot of men as well?"

"Yes. I have three husbands, a fiancé, two cats I won in a mate challenge that I'm not sure what to do with, and a merman I did the wet tango with when I really wasn't sure I wanted to."

"That is normal. The more races you assimilate, the more people you will add to your harem. I currently have twenty members in my harem, both women and men. My friends whom I mentioned earlier were the first I added to it, and it just grew from there." My eyes just about bug out of my head when he says this. "Your harem contains some incredibly powerful men already, though, so I'm not sure if you will need that many, but I thought I would warn you. Every time you find yourself feeling out of sorts, just find one or more of them and let them give you a couple of orgasms, then you'll soon feel normal again."

He is so matter-of-fact about it, but I'm still trying to wrap my head around the multiple mates thing, and now I'm being told there could be more.

"But I just spent the night fucking my cyborg's brains out, and I'm still horny," I argue, and he sighs.

"That is because you haven't filled your harem with the right amount of people yet. I suggest you bond with the cats. Your body will keep riding you until it deems you have the right number of people, and then it will even out somewhat, and you will only get horny if you have used or need to use your powers. Most days, I don't use them anymore except to keep my family safe. My warlock powers of glamour come in very handy. I'm able to keep us all disguised so no one really knows what we look like." He gestures to his own body, and I realize he doesn't really look like Professor Dumbledore.

"Safe?" I ask, not even wanting to touch the idea of mating with the cats at this moment.

His eyes become shadowed, and his lips turn down in a frown. "Yes. Mimics are rare, and legend has it, they only appear in times of great turmoil, hence why my powers revealed themselves when I joined the war efforts. I was able to help the Una's get away from the Aaz'axians, but it came at a great cost to the Una's and their race became extinct. I have an Una husband, and something you may not be aware of is not only can a mimic change race, but they can also change sex if needed. I was able to assume female Una form and have a baby with my Una husband. I'd like it very much if I could introduce my son to you if you don't mind. The fate of the Una race is at stake."

I'm speechless at his attempt at matchmaking and his revelation about being able to change sex, but he doesn't wait for me to acknowledge his words.

"After that, I was approached by all manner of species wanting to hire me to do things for them. Some of them were legit, and some were a little shady. When I said no, they tried to use my family as a bargaining chip. After that, we decided to relocate. Much like your family, we don't have a permanent base, and instead we move from home to home on various planets in an attempt to keep our secret, never staying anywhere longer than we have to."

"That sounds exhausting. What about kids? Are they half and half of whatever their other parent is and Skarrian?" I want to know if I have to watch for the babies to start exhibiting Skarrian powers as well.

"No. They will be fully whatever their other parent is. So your kraken babies will stay shifters. My three original harem members were Skarrian, so I have some Skarrian children, but the rest are whatever their other parent is, so if you have a baby with the warlock, it will be pure warlock. Same with the Vilaxian. The only one I'm not so sure about is the cyborg. I don't have a cyborg mate, and as far as I know, we can't mimic them because they are not completely organic."

I bite my lip, wondering if I should tell Oshan about what just happened with Link, but I decide to keep it to myself. He can't help me with it anyway.

"Unfortunately, it is widely known that you are a mimic. That gossip spread throughout the galaxy faster than any before it. It's how I knew to contact your grandpas to offer my assistance. Now, do you have any questions?"

"How old are you?" I ask now that I know he was in the war between the Una's and Aaz'axians.

From what I understand, that was hundreds of years ago.

"I've recently celebrated my seven hundredth birthday. My partners, children, grandchildren, and great-grandchildren all came together and threw a huge party for me." He smiles broadly, and I find myself speechless. He must see my confusion, because he allows his glamour to drop, and sitting before me is a handsome, blond-haired and blue-eyed man in his late twenties. "Mimics are ageless, and our mates will be the same. It is hard watching your children, grandchildren, and great-grandchildren age. I have lost a few over the years, and it's probably the hardest thing about being a mimic, but most races are generally long-lived, so it could be worse. And sharing all the love and grief with your mates makes it all bearable, though we have stopped having any more children."

My heart sinks when I consider what all of that means. I'm going to outlive all of my children. One day, I'm going to have to say goodbye to Cordelia, Calypso, and Jack. That's enough to not want to have any more, but could I really deny my other mates the chance to be a parent just because it will eventually be hard to say goodbye? It's not really a decision I should make without discussing it with them first.

"Oh, I can feel that I've made you sad. Don't

think of it like that. Think of it as a blessing for all the time you have in their lives."

"Vilaxians don't age, right?" I ask him, suddenly thinking of something.

He shakes his head. "No, the blood they drink makes them regenerate, so they remain practically ageless, like mimics."

"Well, I changed into a Vilaxian before my mimic powers were active. Technically, I'm a Skarrian-Vilaxian-shifter hybrid, and my babies were in my womb when that changed. Link said they showed some Vilaxian DNA, but wasn't sure how that would manifest."

"I think I can see where you're going with this. You may very well pass the genetic trait onto all of your children. I have no idea. You will be the first hybrid mimic, so everything that happens to you will probably be slightly different than what I experienced. Your children may very well be ageless as well, though whether or not they pass that onto their own children and so forth, only time will tell."

My enthusiasm dies down at his words, and I'm back to feeling sad.

"Lila, the best advice I can give you is to live your best life. Love and joy and happiness always come with a side of sadness and pain, whether you're long-lived or not. Parents frequently outlive their own children throughout the galaxy. Don't let fear stop you from having everything you deserve.

Now, I don't know what turmoil has seen the need for another mimic in this world, but if it is linked to the orb again, then all I can say is that it cannot get into the wrong hands. Your family was chosen to protect the orb because they are true of heart with no self-serving desires, and I can tell that still stands with your grandfather's generation."

What the fuck? I thought the knowledge of us protecting the orb was limited to my direct family.

"You know that we protect the orb?" I ask, and he nods solemnly. "I was one of the Una's who descended to Skarr and selected the Adams family."

"My grandpas said the orb absorbed the remaining Una's," I argue, remembering the story they told me.

"It did, but because I am not strictly an Una, I was left behind. I was also tasked as a last resort safety net. If the Adams family ever became corrupt, I could retrieve the orb from them."

"What would happen to it then?" I ask, and he shrugs.

"My harem and I would probably find a way to destroy it. Although it can do much good, it can also cause much destruction."

His words are heavy, and I can't help but ponder what the ramifications of doing that would be. Surely if it had been destroyable, the Una's would have done that in the first place.

CHAPTER SIX

Lila

"But wouldn't destroying it wipe out half the galaxy, not to mention yourselves?"

"Yes, which is why I am grateful your family has been incorruptible up until now. I'm hoping that will continue, and from what I can tell from you, it will. There is no deceit or hubris in you, Lila. You will be an excellent choice to carry on the protection of the orb, but there are rumors of a faction that has been searching diligently, and they are getting closer and closer to discovering the whereabouts of the orb. They must not get their hands on the orb."

"Yes, we discovered a performer, a Madovian stripper, on the circus ship, who was working for a faction called the Syndicate, and she admitted they were searching for the orb."

Oshan shudders. "Madovians are a nasty race. Your mind becomes very primal when you assume their form. I've only done it once so I would have it in my database, and I really wouldn't want to do it again."

I lean forward. Now this is interesting information. I'd like to pick his brain a little more, because I have not let go of my plan of assuming her form and returning to the Syndicate so we can learn more. "Would you be able to assume that form, and then I can mimic it, or does it need to be the real thing?" I'm kind of regretting that we killed her now. Maybe we should have held her for questioning.

"No, you will need to mimic a real one first. I asked much the same thing of the mimic who taught me everything. When they were more common, there was a school for them, and they would bring a volunteer from each race through so they could all assimilate at the same time, but then people realized how dangerous mimics could be and started hunting them, much like Skarrians with your whisperer power. It's an age-old problem. People are scared of others who are more powerful than them. Mimics started appearing less and less in Skarrian society. You are the first, or the first to be public about it, since me." Crap, that's worrying. "I would suggest that you get your warlock fiancé to help you. He can trance people and then make them forget everything that has happened. I think it would be better if you made a big deal out of the fact that people made a mistake. You aren't a mimic, just a regular Skarrian. Maybe push the fact that you have the whisperer ability."

"It's too late. The grandpas already registered me," I tell him, and he sighs heavily.

"Well then, we can say that you are a low-powered mimic and can only assume the forms of those in your harem. That was known to happen too. Hopefully that will keep you a little safer."

"Is it true that I am the perfect mate for any species now?" I still can't wrap my head around this fact.

"Yes, you will be able to have babies with any race, and that baby will be born of that race. It's why I want to introduce you to Utaz. If you had children, it would be a way to revitalize the Una race."

I shake my head. "But it won't really, because any child we have would still be mateless, and that would be a fate worse than death."

His enthusiasm dims. "I'm hoping there are still some Una's somewhere throughout the galaxy, hiding, or even another mimic who could also help repopulate. They are such a kind and gentle species, and so incredibly intelligent. They are also highly enlightened, much like the Celestians."

"Well, I guess if we can find an Aaz'axian on Earth, then anything is possible," I tell him, and his eyes almost bulge out of his head at my announcement.

"You found an Aaz'axian? Wow, most of them perished in the war, and the ones who didn't fled to the ends of the earth and assumed glamours to hide. They would look at you as a breeding blessing too. All of their women died of a mysterious illness."

"I haven't seen Brannock again since I found out I was a mimic, so I'm not even sure he knows. I haven't asked what became of him when we came back to Skarr. For all I know, he's gone."

I think back to the pretty but deadly looking man we found in the jail on Earth. There was something that just didn't sit right with me about his capture, and once everything else has been dealt with, I think Area 51 and Agent Smith deserve a more intensive investigation. I do wonder what happened to him though. Xavier said that he seemed resigned to the fact that he couldn't return to Earth, but he wouldn't put it past him to try. If the Jelliads can get down there, then there must be a way. I guess Aura would be the person to approach.

"Well, my dance card is kind of full at the moment. My poor warlock wants my memories unlocked and the intimate bond returned before we mate, which I understand, and he has been really patient. I'm not all that sure about the cats either. Do I need to add their form to my database even though I am a whisperer?"

"Well, not to mate them, but don't you think it would be handy to have another animal form if you need one? If you could shift into a lightning cat, then that's just one more weapon in your arsenal."

His words make sense, and I think about what Maxsim and Echo look like in bipedal form—the softness of their fur, the twitchiness of their tails, and the way their ears flick back and forth on their heads when they hear things in different directions —and just like that, my body shimmers and I change. Although I'm still in a basic bipedal form, my ears shift to the top of my head, and my skin starts to sprout blue fur. Large fangs form inside my mouth, and my eyesight changes. Something wiggles under my butt, and I jump to my feet. Long talons extend from my fingers, and a growl escapes my mouth. Holy crap, that was my tail. That scared me.

I look down my body and notice my clothes are gone, and there is a naked patch over my breasts and down to my pubic mound. The skin is a light pale blue color, and my nipples are the same bright blue as my fur. I yowl and swipe my hands over my naked bits, shielding them from Oshan, embarrassed to expose myself to the man, but he just chuckles and waves a hand, and the same dress-like covering Natalia used to wear covers my body. Thank goodness for his warlock conjuring skills. That would have been awkward if anyone had come in.

"For some reason, clothes always disappear when you change forms, so you either need to have some on hand if the race you assume needs them or have your warlock conjure them."

"Can you use two different powers at the same time?" I ask, and it comes out all mangled due to the two new massive fangs in my mouth, but Oshan seems to understand.

"No, you need to be in the right form to access the specific powers." With those words, he conjures a loincloth and lays it on the table in front of him, and then his body starts to shimmer. It's almost a mist similar to what Xavier uses to cover himself, but unlike the opaqueness of his, this one is more translucent. I can see something is happening within the mist, but I can't make out exactly what. When it clears, Oshan has assumed a lightning cat form. Much like me, he has a bare patch of skin that runs the length of his body, exposing nipples and a long, thick cock. I quickly avert my eyes from his nakedness, and he puts on the loincloth he conjured before changing.

"So that previous form was a warlock glamour?" I ask, even though I think that's what he said earlier.

"Yes. I don't have glamour powers as a Skarrian, so I wear my warlock form most of the time, but that is what I look like in my Skarrian form."

My mind whirls with all the information, and I start to crackle with agitation. Oshan holds up his hands. "Now, Lila, think calm thoughts. Just like any new powers, it takes a little bit to get used to each individual form, and lightning cat lightning is deadly to all but other lightning cats, and then it depends on their strength."

"Agh, this is so frustrating and overwhelming," I whine, and he starts to purr the same kind of sound I've heard come from Echo before.

"Easy does it. I'm not sure what designation you will be. The cat that I mimicked was an alpha, but with your whisperer abilities, it might interfere with what form you took. Who were you thinking about when you assumed this form?"

I feel my tail twitch back and forth in agitation, and the need to move rides me hard. "Ah, uh, I guess I was thinking about both Echo and Maxsim."

Oshan grimaces, and his cat nose wrinkles

adorably. "Well, do you want to fight or fuck me?" he asks, and I recoil.

"Definitely not fuck, but I don't really feel like fighting you either. I'm kind of indifferent. You feel more familial than anything else."

Those words only just finish leaving my mouth when an almighty roar rips through the room, and Maxsim appears in the doorway with his fangs bared and claws unsheathed.

"Now that's how I would expect another alpha cat to react." Oshan points at the agitated male who stalks into the room, followed by Echo. Maxsim's gaze moves between me and Oshan as a rolling growl rattles his chest and his tail flicks behind him. Lightning crackles around his body, and my fur stands on end. I ignore the fact that my nipples become hard and a throb develops low in my body.

An enticing scent of peppermint and fresh snow reaches my nostrils, and my mouth starts to water. I just want to rub myself all over his body.

"Ah, I see now. A mated alpha and omega. No wonder you are confused." He quickly returns to his old man form and dresses himself again, and the rattling growl from Maxsim cuts off abruptly, though he does place himself between Oshan and me, pushing me backward with his tail until I fall into the seat behind me. I just stare at the back of the big cat in amusement as the end of his tail caresses my leg. Echo jumps over the sofa and joins me on it, his eyes shining with admiration as he reaches out to run his fingers through my fur. I shudder with how good it feels and lean into him.

"Easy now, Alpha. I am not competition for Lila or your omega." Oshan holds up his hands, trying to placate the angry cat between us. "Lila, I would take my advice and deal with this before you go any further, but I will leave my information for you, and you can contact me at any time if you have questions."

I'm so completely distracted by Echo and his scent of frost and crisp apples, I only send a wave of my hand at the old mimic. My tongue darts out, and I swipe it over Echo's cheek, and he starts to purr before butting his head against mine and rubbing his cheek on my own.

"Thank you, Oshan, for everything. I'm not sure how I can repay you," I call, finally getting my act together, not wanting to insult the man who has taught me so much.

"By meeting my son one day. That's all I ask." Without waiting for me to protest, he disappears from the room. Fuck! That is not good. I don't really want to be pimped out as a baby maker, but I guess I do owe the man.

"Lila, you are such a pretty lightning cat," Echo whispers in my ear as he nuzzles further into me. I'm so turned on, but I'm also worried about Maxsim's reaction if I return Echo's affections. This omega has slowly wormed his way into my heart, and I desperately want to lick him all over. In fact, I push him back and clamber into his lap. Our furry legs rub against one another, and I purr at the sensations.

"I want to kiss you, but I can't with these." I point to the fangs in my mouth, and he grins and pulls my mouth down to his.

"I like a little pain with my pleasure." He nips my lips, and I feel him break the skin before lapping at it with his tongue. "And I like the taste of blood, and yours is delicious. You can will your fangs away. Just think of your mouth as normal, and they will retreat so they are not as sharp," he says in his rumble that hits all the right spots, and I grind down against the thick length below me. Suddenly, there is a hand in my hair, yanking my head back.

"What are you doing to my omega?" Maxsim demands, and a whine slips out of my mouth unbidden. He leans down and clamps his teeth around my neck and bites down. He doesn't break the skin, but I feel myself get wet, very wet, and I shudder with a rush of desire.

"Do it again, Max," Echo orders. "She just leaked slick all over my leg. I think our pretty pussy needs a knot to ease the ache deep inside her."

Another keening cry leaves my mouth as Maxsim does as instructed. Echo's hand drifts under my skirt, and he runs a finger through the wet mess I'm making on his lap. He brings a finger up to his lips and runs his tongue over it. I watch as his eyes roll back in his head, and he shudders as my taste coats his taste buds.

Maxsim releases the grip he has on my neck with his teeth but keeps hold of the hair on my head. He strokes his hand over my tail as he leans in and whispers, "Do you want me to knot you, pretty little omega?" His words are a rough grumble, and I close my eyes so I don't have to look at either of them. I'm so indecisive. Despite the need that is riding me with a force that makes me want to beg, I don't know where we stand. Are we going to mate? Does he even like me? Is Echo okay with any of this? It's so hard to focus on anything, and a sob escapes my mouth before I can stop it. Both cats freeze.

"Oh, pretty girl, it's okay." Echo throws his arms around me and squeezes me tight, and I feel some of the tension in my body drain away. "You have questions, and you need them answered before we can do this. How about we go to my nest, and we can talk about this a little more? You will feel safe and secure and more comfortable surrounded by all the lovely things, I promise."

I'm at a loss for words, and all I can do is nod my agreement. Echo looks at Maxsim and nods his head. The big alpha cat swoops in and lifts me off the sexy omega's lap, his nose twitching when

Echo's wet lap is exposed to the air, but Echo doesn't look upset, instead he looks thrilled.

"You go, and I will let the others know what is happening. Hopefully they can keep the little ones entertained for a little while longer."

CHAPTER SEVEN

Maxsim

The little Earth girl in my arms smells like a mouthwatering omega at this very moment —one who has my alpha instincts riding me so very hard. I just want to drag her into my den and stuff her full of my knot and tear my fangs through her neck, marking her as mine, but that would be disloyal to the omega who already wears my mark, so the guilt is making everything taste bitter.

Although, from the looks of my omega, he is not against any of that happening, which is strange because normally omegas fight for an alpha's attention. Maybe it's because she is a female omega, or maybe she smells like an alpha to him. Who knows what the whisperer abilities are doing? Maybe it means having more than one omega in a pack.

There is often more than one alpha, but dominance fights usually play a part in establishing who will be the lead alpha. I don't feel like asserting my dominance over Lila in any way other than inserting my cock deep into her warm pussy.

She sniffs the air as I hurry upstairs to the large living area she and Echo like to spend their time in —the one that overlooks the pounding winter seas where Xavier kindly placed a nest for Echo.

She moans and turns her face into my chest where she snuffles, breathing deeply. "Oh my god, you smell so fucking good. It makes me ache deep inside. Fuck, what is that feeling? It hurts but feels good. Did I pee myself? Everything is so wet down there." She sounds embarrassed, and I run a hand over her fur, hoping to reassure her.

"No, little girl, that is your slick. It is preparing your tight pussy for my alpha knot." The words come out of my mouth in a rumble I can't help. I'm feeling so incredibly primal at the moment. It's a wonder she hasn't thrown me into a mating rut with how wet she is and how much she is perfuming the air. It's almost like she's in heat, and if the scent of Echo was anything to go by, I'd say she has accelerated his as well. I may have to take care of two omegas in heat, and I'm not sure if I am capable of that.

She groans again and shivers in my arms, and I hasten to get to the room. There are things we need to talk about first. She and I aren't sure where we stand. I'm almost certain she feels affection for Echo, but he and I are a pair, and I will not allow him to be mated to her unless I am as well. I came to feel a sense of affection for the pretty Earth girl once I took Echo and the guys' advice and let go of my preconceived notions and resentment toward her. We watched over her during her pregnancy mostly in cat form, but I saw how she treated each of her mates and potential mates as equals and lavished as much affection and love on each and every one of them. No one was left out or neglected, and she proved she is the kind and caring, not to mention sassy and silly, individual Echo told me she was. And seeing her with her children—baby krakens, which must have been weird for the Earth girl—only solidified that. She could have been grossed out or repulsed by the fact that her children were animals, but she wasn't. In fact, she loves them.

I must admit my affection is quite real, but I have always had trouble expressing how I feel. Even when Echo and I first mated, it took him being bold and daring to get me to admit that I wanted him and loved him. We had been friends first, and I worried changing that relationship would mess everything up, but it hadn't. It had only made it better, and my cock throbs as I think about him and Lila spread out before me.

When I reach the large room, I stride over to the nest and leap down, barely jostling the slick-soaked girl in my arms. I place her onto the deep cushions, and she starts to purr and roll around, spreading her scent all over the lush bedding. She grabs a pillow and inhales deeply, her eyes almost rolling back in her head, and the scent of her perfume floods the air. I just hope this doesn't set off Echo's possessiveness. It is, after all, his nest, and I'm not sure how he will feel about sharing it with another omega, because that is all she is presenting as at the moment. There isn't a hint of alpha pheromones.

I'm so busy watching Lila, mesmerized by her actions, that I don't notice Echo has entered the room until I feel his warmth on my back. He nuzzles my neck, peering over my shoulder at the girl rolling around in his nest.

"She smells so good," he mutters, and I feel him push his hard cock against my backside and grind. His arms slide around my waist and, pressing his chest to my back, he brushes his fingers across the front of my body, making my fur bristle with desire.

"Did you let the others know what is happening?" I ask him absently, and I feel him nod his response against my shoulder.

"Yes, they will keep the little ones occupied a little longer. I told them that I thought Lila might be experiencing a heat brought on by her whisperer powers, and the fact she mimicked an Iceen form. They are, of course, worried, but they trust us to look after her." His chest puffs out as he says this, and I smother a grin at his pride that her mates would trust us to take care of her.

"Max, it hurts," Lila sobs, grasping at the soft furnishings below her, and I feel a growl rise in my chest at the use of my nickname.

"Did you hear that, Max?" Echo giggles, whispering in my ear. "Your other omega needs you to ease the ache inside her." He grinds his dick against my backside again, and his hands drift down my front.

I grab his hands, stopping them from going any lower, and tug him in front of me, putting a finger beneath his chin so he will look me in the eye. "Are you okay with this?" I ask, completely unsure of everything. I don't want to hurt my omega, but the other one is calling to my inner alpha. If I'm really honest with myself, she has from the very start, and I guess it confused me. Why was I having such visceral reactions to another person, a non-lightning cat and Earth girl at that, especially when I was already mated? It's the omega in the relationship who controls who joins a streak, and I guess I was feeling guilty for being disloyal to my omega.

"Oh yes, so okay. I can't wait to lick her slick from your cock," Echo says and starts to whine. "But when you finish knotting her, the two of you might have to take care of me. My heat is starting too." I look down. His cock has lifted his loincloth, and I can see how red it is, signaling he's ready to be bred.

I can't help myself, I roar loudly, and it echoes around the room, causing both my omegas to whine, and their perfume fills the air. I'm not sure how I am going to satisfy both of them on my own, but I'm certainly going to try.

I take Echo's hand and leap down into the nest, dragging him with me. Lila has removed the dress the old mimic gave her to cover her nudity, and her hand is stroking her clit, trying to get relief from the deep ache, but nothing is going to fix that for her except an alpha's knot and my cum deep inside her, especially now that she has shifted into lightning cat form.

Her nipples and folds aren't pink, so if she is in heat, it's not a breeding one like Echo's is. The first one usually isn't. The two of us get down next to her, and she reaches for us, but Echo grabs her wrists and holds her down. Her feline eyes dilate, making the dark pupils large as she looks up at us with wonder and no small part of confusion.

"Lila, do you know what is happening?" I ask her, grabbing her chin so she will look at me. I like having her in my control.

She tries to nod, but I hold her firmly so she has to use her words. "Yes, you're going to fuck me now, knot me, and make the pain go away," she whines as the rest of her body writhes, her legs crossing as she tries to ease the ache.

"Yes, and then I am going to bite you and make you my mate. Are you okay with that?" She seems to regain a small amount of lucidity at my words and sits up, her breasts jiggling with the motion, drawing my attention for a moment.

"Yes, Maxsim, I know now that we are meant to be. My mimic abilities are drawing you all to me, which I kind of feel takes away your choice, but I don't think we can deny it. I think it will get harder and harder for us if we keep ignoring it." There's a hint of guilt in her voice and in her eyes when she looks at Echo. "Are you okay with this? With Maxsim mating me?" she asks, and I feel a twinge of growing love that she cares enough to ask him.

He quickly nods and rubs his cheek against hers, purring loudly, before knocking her back over and crawling between her legs. "Yes, as long as I can help, and then you will have to help him with my heat and bite me too. I need you as my mate, and Max and I are a package." Echo is flat-out demanding, and Lila's eyes widen with surprise as he parts her legs and bends down, swiping his tongue through her slick-soaked folds.

She moans and shudders, her eyes losing all focus as her need swamps her. "Yes to it all. I want you both now, please. Please stop the pain," she begs.

Echo laps at her pussy, and she moans, reaching down to run her hands through his mane. His rumbling purr is loud as it vibrates against her clit, working like a human vibrator. It doesn't take long before she screams out her first orgasm as I watch my omega get her ready for me. She's going to need a couple more before she's properly prepared to take my knot. It's very large, so I will let him fuck her first before I have my turn, but that doesn't mean I can't have some fun while I wait for my turn. While Echo concentrates on stretching out our new streak member, I lean in and lap at her nipples. She gasps, and her hands leave Echo's lush white mane as she reaches for mine. Her fingers grip the long hair tightly, and I feel a shudder skate down my spine to my balls at the pinch of pain. My knot starts to inflate, and my own slick starts to drip from the tip of my cock in preparation for her pussy. Her nipples are taut and perky as I roll my tongue around them. The spikes that are designed to rend flesh from bone stand up slightly, giving a small amount of friction, but not enough to do any damage. Goosebumps break out across her small patch of skin down the front of her body, and the rest of her gorgeous soft fur stands up.

"Yes, oh yes, shit, that feels so good!"

I pull away, and she cries out in disappointment.

Smiling, I press a tentative kiss to her mouth, still a little unsure if she really wants this or if it's her need talking, but she slides her tongue into my mouth and mashes her lips to mine in a breath-taking kiss. I'm a little dazed myself as I pull away and look down at her. She has this small, sexy, secretive smile as she runs her finger across her lip, looking pleased with herself, and I feel a sense of relief as I slide down her body to join my omega mate in teasing her soaked cunt.

He lifts his head, his eyes glazed with lust, his whiskers and mouth glinting with her slick. I swipe my tongue over his face, wanting to taste Lila, and what better way but from my omega's lips? A growl rumbles from my mouth when her taste rolls across my tongue. Fuck, she's sweet and a little salty, and I can tell she's ripe for knotting.

"Why don't you fuck our omega and stretch her out a little for me?" I say to Echo, who is slick drunk. It's amusing, and I can't help but smile as I help him up. He's never had this before, since he's usually the one that makes me slick drunk. His dick is covered with his own slick, but I lean down and take it into my mouth, coating it with spit. A moan rolls through the nest, and when I look up, Lila is watching us with big eyes, and her fingers are furiously rubbing her clit.

"Do you like what you see, pretty omega?" I ask her as I stretch Echo out on his back, his erect red dick a blaring beacon against his white fur. I keep my eyes on her as I run my tongue up and down his long length, and she whimpers. "Echo's dick is so long, it's going to touch all the right places. It's going to feel so good inside you," I croon to her, and she gets up on her hands and knees and crawls toward us, kneeling on the other side of him before running her own tongue along his length. It's Echo's turn to moan, and when I lean in and do the same, our mouths meeting with his dick between us, his groan is long and guttural as he pants.

"Oh, oh shit. Ugh," he mutters incomprehensibly as Lila and I lavish attention on his dick, but it's not his turn. First Lila, and then both of us will make sure he is well taken care of. I push Lila off his dick, and she glares at me. Her pheromones change marginally, becoming slightly bitter to me— the mark of another alpha. Echo gasps and lunges for her, but I hold him back before turning my attention to our willful new mate.

"You first, Lila. Let me knot you and fuck my cum deep inside of you. It will ease the ache, and then you and I can love Echo long and hard, I promise," I croon reassuringly to her, and it seems to mollify her. Her pheromones change back to sweet omega, and I tuck that information away in my mind to consider later. Lila presents as both depending on her mood.

Echo reaches for her, pushing her back into the

nest as he spreads her legs and climbs between them. I lean forward and grab his cock, guiding it toward her tight pussy. They both moan loudly as he slides into her without any resistance, both of them covered in slick from our attentions.

I watch on with smug satisfaction as my two omegas pleasure each other, knowing my turn isn't far away.

CHAPTER EIGHT

Echo

I'm so incredibly worked up from my heat and both Maxsim's and Lila's tongues that it's all I can do not to embarrass myself by coming immediately. Thinking about Natalia stops me from painting Lila's cervix with my own cum after one stroke. Her cunt is tight and warm and so slippery. It feels amazing, and it's been so very long since I wasn't the one being knotted. I won't admit it to Max, but I missed this. I'd been hoping for a female in our streak, but there wasn't anyone my cat and I had been drawn to until Lila.

Max caresses my hips, and I shudder as his claws dig in slightly before he draws them back, encouraging me to move. I've settled enough to allow it to happen, and I stare deep into her beautiful cat eyes as I lazily stroke my cock in and out of her tight channel. Her claws dig into my back as she pants and moans and thrashes around, her need for Max's knot building. He's a big cat, though, and I need to help stretch her out a bit. I'm longer than him, but he's much wider at the base where his knot is, and it always hurts slightly when he slams it through my tight ring. It will for Lila too, but not as badly if I help prep her first.

My hips start to move faster as I lean in and lap at her pretty blue nipple. I'd love to see them as red as my dick, telling me she is ready for breeding, but that hasn't happened this time, and who knows if it will in the future. Once I've paid them enough attention, I bring my mouth to hers, stuttering slightly as I feel Max's hand drift from my hips to fondle my balls, which are slapping against Lila. I feel them tighten at his touch before he reaches between us, gathering some of the copious amount of slick. He then parts my butt cheeks and slides his finger into my ass. My eyes roll back into my head, and I pound harder into Lila. She's practically begging now, and her cunt pulses as she screams when her orgasm rolls through her body. I can't hold myself off any longer. With Maxsim's finger stroking the part inside of me that feels so good and her own orgasm rippling around me, it triggers my own release, and I feel my cum explode from the tip of my dick, filling her with my seed. I roar loudly, my head thrown back as stars explode behind my eyelids.

"Oh yes, oh God, Echo, fuck," Lila mutters loudly as we ride the waves of mutual pleasure.

Maxsim withdraws his finger, and he nuzzles into my neck. "Good job, my omega, you prepped her for my knot so beautifully. Why don't you slide out and let Lila taste your combined release while I fill her with my knot?"

I shudder at his words, which are said quietly enough that Lila doesn't hear, but it makes my cock throb deep inside of her, my own heat keeping me perpetually hard until I can get an alpha knot. It's painful, but I can wait for Lila to get hers first. It will just make it that much sweeter when they get to me.

I lean in and kiss her softly, and she returns the kiss with equal affection, her now clawless fingers stroking the blood-soaked fur on my back. I don't think she realizes what she did when she clawed my back while coming, but I feel like a fucking stud. I guess this is how Maxsim feels every time he fucks me. It's intoxicating, but I think maybe I'm pussy and slick drunk. I allow Maxsim to help me disengage from Lila, then I crawl my way to her head. My red cock is still standing at attention. She turns her head and blinks at me before a sexy smile spreads across her lips. She shuffles closer and opens her mouth, her tongue, which looks to have the same kind of spikes as mine and Max's, flicks out. I hadn't seen it earlier, but sure enough, as she runs it up the length of my slick-covered cock, I feel those spikes lying flat. Thankfully that came naturally without us having to tell her about them. If they were up, they would strip my dick of skin within a couple of tongue lashings.

"Echo, choke Lila with your dick while I fuck her onto my knot," Max commands, and both of us shudder from his growly voice.

Lila is so fucking responsive, and it makes me want to shove my cock down her throat. Without any hesitation, she takes it in her hand and licks up and down, tasting our combined juices. I stare down at her as her eyes roll back in her head at the taste before she wraps her plump lips around it and takes me deeply. I squeeze my own eyes shut at the feel of her hot mouth engulfing my length, and it's only her gasp that has me opening them to see what Max is doing to her. He's flipped her around so she presents for him and lined his cock up with her pussy. I hold my breath to see if he's going to ease her into this or if he's going to force it in hard and fast. Our eyes meet, and I can see by the vicious glint that it's going to be the latter. Sometimes it's easier that way, and once she gets over the initial pain, she will be soaring on pleasure, and it will no longer matter.

He slides in slightly, and her gasp becomes a

long, drawn-out, guttural moan. Max is wider than I am, and that's just the tip of his cock. He slides in and out a couple of times, letting her get used to the stretch, his knot pushing against the tight rim of her pussy. It's designed to stretch around his knot, but it would be easier if it wasn't already halfway inflated, so there is only one option now. I struggle to focus on what he's doing, since Lila's ministrations to my cock double down as she revels in the pleasure he's wringing from her body. I see exactly when Max decides to slam his knot home, and when he snaps his hips back, I surge down Lila's throat, hoping my cock will help distract her and praying she won't bite down when he does.

Maxsim slides in just like they are two pieces of a jigsaw puzzle who are meant to fit together. His eyes widen with awe as his knot inflates, triggering her second orgasm, and his animal instincts take over. His fangs lengthen as he leans in and bites Lila's shoulder, sealing himself to her as her mate forever more. Lila disengages from my cock, throws her head back, and roars her pleasure, lightning crackling all around us as Maxsim pulls free and laps at the bloody bite mark, a smug purr rattling from his chest.

Mindless with lust, Lila returns to sucking my dick like it's her favorite lollipop as sparks of lightning bounce between the three of us, enhancing our pleasure. Seeing her between us is nothing short of magical, and I can tell by the look of pure pleasure on Maxsim's face that he feels the same way. I can't hold back any longer, and my seed pours down her throat. Lightning now bounces in a continuous loop between all three of us, but it's not painful, instead managing to drive the sensations of bliss higher. Max is locked in, and all he can do is move with small thrusts, but every time he does, it triggers another mind melting orgasm. I should know, because it does that for me too.

Lila finally finishes swallowing me down, and she collapses onto her front, panting and twitching with the never-ending cycle of pleasure. I throw myself down next to her, panting as well, my throbbing dick still as hard as can be. I stroke her sweaty fur back from her face and kiss her, swallowing her moans of pleasure much like she swallowed me down. Max rearranges them so she is lying on her side, with him cuddled around her, firmly knotted for a while. That gives me perfect access to the front of her body, and I position myself so I can play with her pretty titties and lap at her clit. Lila is never going to forget this mating, and I can only hope it's the first of many to come.

After about an hour, Max's knot suddenly deflates, and he pulls free of his now sleeping mate. Although she didn't bite him, I can faintly feel her in our streak link. I feel a little jealous that he has that connection with her and I don't, but hopefully that is something we will eventually rectify.

He runs a gentle hand down her back with a sweet smile of affection on his lips and adoration in his eyes. That's exactly how he looks at me, and I couldn't be happier, but now I am impatient. I've held off for as long as I can, and now I am a needy, sweaty, slick-soaked mess. I prowl down to where he just disengaged from Lila and lean over, using my tongue to clean up the mess he made of her pussy. I want both of them involved in my heat, and I won't settle for anything less.

My eyes roll back in my head as I lick Lila's cum-filled pussy, their combined release spicy and addictive on my taste buds. I hold Maxsim's gaze in challenge. He growls, and I see his cock harden again. My pheromones flood the space, signaling it's my turn to be knotted.

Hands slide into my mane and yank my head so that I have to look up. I find Lila looking down at me with a feral intensity in her eyes. Gone is the begging, submissive omega, and in her place is a snarling, aggressive alpha.

"Such a good boy, cleaning up the mess your

alpha made of my pussy, but I think you forgot something." She gets up on her knees and shuffles over to Maxsim, dragging me with her. "You should clean up your alpha's cock too." She pushes my head down onto his thick length, and I gag slightly before my throat relaxes and I take him down. That same spicy taste coats his cock, and I feel slick leak from me, preparing me for my alpha's cock.

Lila lets go of my hair and grabs Maxsim's face, dragging his mouth to hers. Their kiss above me is forceful and combative, and both of them are using fangs and claws. Alpha loving is neither gentle nor sweet. It's a battle of wills, and I can't wait for these two to turn their aggression and attention to me. I'm sucking at Maxsim's cock, cleaning him up, when I feel a claw scrape down my back, and when I look up, they are looking at me like I'm a meal they can't wait to devour. An unbidden whimper escapes my mouth, and I feel more slick drip from me.

"Lie down on your back, Omega, so that your alphas can fuck you together," Maxsim growls as Lila helps me onto my back before climbing over me, running her hand up and down my cock before notching it at her pussy. It's dripping slick, and she slides onto it with ease as she lowers herself down. My eyes close at the sensation, but they soon pop open as she leans forward and kisses me, her beautiful breasts rubbing against my chest. Her tail curls around and caresses my arms and anything she can reach with it. She's distracting me for Maxsim much like I did for her.

I feel his finger, now claw free, probe at my slick-soaked ass. "Such a good omega, all wet and ready for your alpha." He pushes my knees back, and Lila grabs onto them, holding them up and spreading me wide so Maxsim has full access to my dripping hole. He pushes in, and I can't keep my eyes open against the onslaught of pleasure. Lila bounces up and down on my cock, still holding my legs up.

"Such a good omega," she croons as Maxsim pulls back and surges forward again. Tears leak out of my eyes, and my whine is almost constant. The pleasure is too intense, and they are both keeping me right on the edge, teasing me when I need them to lock and knot me.

"Please," I sob, my hands clenching the bedding beneath me. "Please."

"What is it you want, Omega?" Maxsim growls. "I want to hear your words."

"Make me come," I pant, and a smug smile crosses Lila's face as she reaches back and pulls Maxsim's lips to hers. I watch as the two of them kiss while their bodies do such wicked things to mine. Lila's pussy pulses, and then the base of it starts to inflate, tightening so it's like a ring around the base of my cock. She can no longer bounce up and down, and I feel suckers attach themselves to my cock. Holy fuck, that's awesomely weird.

At the same time, Maxsim slams his knot home, and I come like I never have before. Pure white lightning flashes through my body as indescribable bliss shatters me into a million pieces. I hear the two of them roar, but I am so lost in the sensations coursing through my body that I don't care. Wave after wave of pure pleasure assaults my senses, the three of us locked together in carnal bliss. I feel Maxsim's cum painting my cervix deep inside at the same time I feel something happening inside Lila's pussy. I think my mating spike is sucking Lila's eggs from her womb. Fucking hell, we didn't discuss breeding. She only just had Caspian's babies, so she is going to freak out. I try desperately to stop it, but there's nothing I can do, Maxsim rocks his knot inside me, and Lila leans down and latches onto my neck on the opposite side of Maxsim's bite. The pain is exquisite, but at the same time, she squeezes her ring again, and once more, I'm soaring, all other thoughts floating away as our mating link clicks into place.

CHAPTER NINE

Lila

And just like that, I have two more husbands. We spent all night loving Echo through his heat, and all of us ended up with each other's marks. Fucking hell. I'm kind of embarrassed now that I am no longer foggy from the scent of all our pheromones, but the nest is fucking full of it. The bedding is soaked with the remains of our releases, and if I stay, I know I'm going to beg the two of them to use and abuse my body like a rag doll. My neck and shoulder ache where both of their marks now sit, and as my eyes roam over their sleeping sexy bodies, I get a thrill from seeing my own fang marks bruising their skin. I know that when they heal and fade, a silvery mark like the one they have for each other will remain.

I'm both amazed and horrified, but Oshan said it would continue to happen until my mimic powers were satisfied. My fingers itch to reach out and stroke both males, who are so different from one another. Maxsim is bulky and tall, and I instinctively know he is my alpha and will protect me anyway he can, but looking at Echo, I have a different feeling. His lithe, lean, somewhat feminine body calls to something deep and primal inside me —that same part that made me fuck his brains out, my pussy locking him to me while Maxsim did the same behind him. Apparently if a male and female alpha lock an omega at the same time, their heat is quick and relatively painless, because this morning, Echo lies there with a small, secretive smile on his sleepy face, completely satisfied, which usually takes Maxsim days to achieve.

I bite my lip and slowly roll away from Echo's side. He was sandwiched between the two of us when we finally fell asleep last night, but I desperately need to escape so I can take a moment to breathe and think about what happened. I also need a shower, because I reek of sex, and I want to find my babies and give them cuddles and reassure my other husbands, especially Xavier, that they are just as equally loved by me. Saxon must be starving, and I hope he and Xavier have been making use of one another while I have been preoccupied by the others. Thank goodness they are all bisexual. I'm not sure if I could physically handle having all of them rely solely on me for sex despite what Magenta says about resilient Skarrian pussies— #RSP.

With as much stealth as possible, I try to escape Maxsim and Echo as soon as the sun starts to peek above the horizon and shine through the windows. I'm just going to take a moment to get my bearings, and then I'll make sure they know they are completely welcome in my family. I will have to ask them what they would like to do—join us back in the circus and keep their den in the lightning cat room, or create some space in my suite. It's perfect timing, because it's still being redesigned to accommodate the babies and making sure each of my mates has exactly what they need. The spare suite that Mark, Susie, and Aura's family had been staying in is being absorbed into mine to accommodate so many mates. My grandpas assured me it was no problem. If they needed to, they would relocate the captains and their own suite if I needed more room, but at the moment, I think just combining the two suites should be enough for the ten of us.

It's not until I'm standing, looking up at the high edges of the nest, that I realize I am once again stuck here... or am I? I try to think about whether or not I saw either of them leaping out of his nest in their bipedal form, and sure enough, I recall seeing them do it. Okay, I've got this. My new body should be able to make that leap, but before I can commit, a clawed hand wraps around my tail and tugs, unbalancing me, and I tumble into the bedding. They pounce and drag me back into the nest, putting a smile on my face as they assure me of their commitment to me despite our unusual start. Now that Maxsim's mating bite is on my shoulder and mine is on Echo's, he is a different pussy cat. He's cuddly and affectionate, and he purrs adorably when I stroke him the right way.

This morning, however, Echo won't meet my eyes. He's twitchy and restless, and despite all the exchanges of kisses, I feel distance between us. Is he regretting what we've done? I'm not the only one who notices, because Maxsim grabs his chin and makes Echo look at him.

"What is wrong, my omega? Please do not tell me this is not what you wanted. There is no going back for any of us." Maxsim is gruff and emotional, and I rub a soothing hand over his soft furry back, trying to calm him.

Tears well in Echo's eyes, and he bites his lip and looks at me. "I'm so sorry, Lila," he whispers, and my heart sinks.

I stand up and will myself back into my normal form. I feel the fur recede and my ears relocate to their normal position. It feels like pins and needles break out over my body, and it's painful, but it only lasts a few seconds before I'm back to normal. I reach down and grab a blanket to cover my nudity. It hadn't bothered me before, but it does now.

"What did I do? I thought this was what you wanted." My own voice sounds small and pathetic, but I'm so freaking hurt.

Echo shakes his head. "It's not what you did, it's what I did," he replies, and I watch as Maxsim suddenly becomes very alert. His nose twitches, and he leans in, inhaling a deep breath of air at the junction of Echo's neck. His eyes widen, and he starts to purr and rub his cheek against Echo's, a wide smile crossing his lips.

"You're pregnant! We're going to have a baby," he says with wonder in his voice, perfectly thrilled at the new situation. Goosebumps break out over my skin, and a wide smile spreads across my lips.

"That's wonderful. I know the two of you will make amazing parents, and the kids will love to have a cousin to play with." I'm not sure what the relationship will be between my kids and theirs, but that works for now. I drop back down, still grasping the blanket. "Why aren't you over the moon?" I ask the omega who I know was desperate for children.

His eyes are dim, and he nibbles on his bottom lip, looking between me and Maxsim before sighing regretfully. "Because they won't just be mine and Max's. I'm almost certain one of them is your baby as well."

His words have me freezing with shock. "I'm sorry, but could you maybe please explain that a little more?" I can hear the hysteria building in my voice, and tears well in his eyes as he reaches for my hand.

"I couldn't stop it," he murmurs, and I snatch my hand away, hearing something very similar to what Caspian told me so many weeks ago. "Female alphas are as rare as male omegas these days, and, well, I'd forgotten what can happen between a male omega and a female alpha. It wasn't until it was already happening that I remembered, and both of you had already locked and knotted me, and I couldn't stop it." His eyes plead with me to forgive him.

"Details, Echo, details," I say through gritted teeth. It's taking all my strength not to lose my shit, because despite everything, I still don't want to upset the pretty omega.

"When a male omega has sex with a female alpha, and it's his breeding heat, a long straw-like appendage comes out of their cock and sucks—for want of a better word—an egg up. It then coats it in the omega's cum as it slides along that tube and then deposits it in his womb where the male alpha can also fertilize it, thus creating a baby with all three's DNA." It's Maxsim who has taken over, because Echo is distraught, sobbing hysterically in Maxsim's arms.

"Are you saying that Echo is having my baby?" I can't believe I'm asking this question.

Maxsim nods. "Yes, and probably one or two more from his own eggs. Lightning cats tend to breed in multiples."

Holy fucking shit! I'm speechless, gobsmacked, dumbfounded. I blink a couple of times. Apart from the rise and fall of my chest, it's my only movement as I consider everything. Right, another baby. Shit, probably more than one.

After my first initial moment of fury, something settles inside me. The nudge from my inner kraken is kind and gentle and reassuring, as is the nudge from what I've come to know as my inner whisperer. Between the three of us, we're actually okay with this. I desperately love my babies, and I'm excited that we will be adding to my family. The reality of the possible danger we may be facing because of the orb worries me, but I have a plethora of mates who are powerful enough to protect them all, and let's face it, there are also enough to help with everything.

"Okay." I breathe out a big sigh, nodding like a lunatic. "Alright, more babies to love and snuggle." I crawl over to the two cats and wrap my arms around them. Their fur tickles my skin, and I can't help the giggle that escapes. It's slightly unhinged but happy nonetheless. "It's okay, Echo. I can't expect mating rituals to go exactly like a human marriage. Sure, I wasn't planning on having any more kids anytime soon, but I have to admit that the fact that I'm not carrying these ones is a huge blessing. Seriously, I wish all my mates could carry the babies." I place a kiss over his stomach, awed at the fact that this male is able to do the same things as a female from Earth. "But it does make reading up on all my mates a priority. I still have no clue how Vilaxians and warlocks breed, and to be honest, cyborgs are a little fuzzy also."

When I look up at the two of them, Maxsim looks as pleased as punch, his smile wide and his eyes grateful as he gives me a subtle nod, and Echo looks like he's been hit by a boulder.

"You're okay with this?" he asks hesitantly, sliding his hand down to cup his stomach in a familiar way.

"Of course I am, sweetie. How could I not be? I can't be angry at you when I wasn't angry at Caspian, but for any matings from here on out, I need to know the breeding side of things as well. As much as I love my little ones, and as much as I will adore these ones, that's six or so children in a short period of time, and that's a lot of work on top of the circus and needing to find the flower for John and everything else that is hanging over our heads." I need to read these guys into the orb situation, but that can wait until tomorrow. I lean forward and place a gentle kiss on Echo's lips, and he lunges, catching me by surprise as he smothers my face with little kisses, purring the entire time. Max just chuckles and watches as Echo mutters sweet words.

"How long is a lightning cat's gestation?" I ask Max, snuggling Echo into my side, and Max shrugs.

"I don't actually know for sure for male omegas. It's been so long since there was one. I was going to ask Echo's dad if it actually ever happened."

"Well, now there are a whole heap of male omegas we can ask." While I was under the sea, the location of the male omega prison was found, and there were over a hundred male omegas of all ages. Some of them had been sold off by their families, and some were thought to have been killed during challenges. Those families that sold them off had been terrified of Natalia's family and had seen no other option. Most of those omegas will need some form of counseling, and who knows if they will ever be the same again, but Echo's dad had been unharmed. They hadn't had time to talk before we arrived and that family lost the leadership challenge.

Echo nods. "I will call my dad shortly. Our families are going to be so happy, and I can find out everything I need to know. I hadn't wanted to hope that I would ever be able to have a litter, so I never asked too many questions in case I was ever disappointed."

Maxsim stands up, and I get a little distracted at

the sight of his naked body. You'd think I'd be weirded out because he's furry and has a tail and looks a little like Liono from *Thundercats*, but I am so freaking turned on. My alien kink is in full force, and I consider staying in the nest for a little longer.

"Sexy, isn't he?" Echo whispers in my ear.

"God yes," I sigh, and the two of us giggle like loons.

"Stop it now. I thought you wanted to go see the rest of our family," Maxsim scolds as he pulls on his loincloth, covering up that magnificent cock. I blow a raspberry and sigh.

"Fine, party pooper." I push Echo away and look around for the dress Oshan conjured for me. It will do for now despite the hole for a tail that no longer exists.

Maxsim frowns. "What is this party pooper you speak of? I assure you I am a very clean cat and use the facilities."

I snort, unable to stop the laughter from escaping. "Of course you are house trained. You wouldn't be allowed inside if you weren't." They both look very confused, and it's quite adorable. I turn to leave the nest, and once again, I've fucked up. "Ah, I don't suppose one of you can leap out of here with me in your arms?" I ask, and now it's their turn to laugh.

"Maxsim can do it," Echo assures me, and the big cat stalks toward me and scoops me up in his arms. He takes one step and leaps, propelling us up and out of the nest in one smooth jump. He lands softly on top.

"Thanks, big guy," I tell him, patting his cheek, and he snaps his teeth at my hand, causing me to yank it away. He then winks and gives me a cheeky grin before placing me gently on my feet.

Fuck! I'm a goner for these two. Hook, line, and sinker, or maybe fangs, fur, and claws. Echo follows quickly behind us.

"Come on. I can't wait to tell the others about our babies." He hurries ahead of us, and I have to run to catch up.

"Hang on, slow your roll. We should get Link to look you over to confirm everything. God, I hope the others, especially Xavier, aren't pissed about this. The poor warlock has been waiting so very patiently."

"I have no doubt that your warlock won't feel jealous. I know I would, but he is a reasonable man. He knows his time is coming, and he knows you are his intimate and that isn't going to change. How about Echo and I take a turn helping the others with the kids? It will be good practice for when our own arrive and give you some time alone with him and the Vilaxian. All three of you probably need to reconnect," Maxsim suggests.

Yup, fucking gone. I throw my arms around the big cat and press a searing kiss to his mouth. He startles but wraps his arms around me and returns the kiss with some scorching heat of his own. It's only Echo's whimper that has us pulling apart.

"Don't start that, we'll never get out of here," he complains, adjusting himself under his loincloth.

"Okay, but shower first. We reek, and we need to ask Xavier if he can use special cleaning magic to fix the nest or just get rid of everything and start again."

Echo shakes his head quickly. "No, please, I want to keep them."

"Cleaning it is, but us first, let's share a shower. It's more water efficient that way." I grab each of them by the hand and drag them back to my room. I really want to know what it's like to wash them, and if we can squeeze in a quickie, then all the better.

CHAPTER TEN

Lila

Showering with the cats was fun. Echo loved having his fur washed and soaked up all the attention lavished on him. Maxsim was the complete opposite. He looked at the water with the same disdain he used to look at me. It took all of my and Echo's coaxing to get him to step into it and a dual blow job to put a smile on his face. He grumbled playfully through the whole thing, but I think he secretly loved it.

There's a huge grin on my face as I go downstairs in search of the rest of my loved ones.

"Mama!" Jack cries the minute I enter the room. He gets up on unsteady legs and waddles over to me as fast as he can. My heart soars with love and joy at the sight. I was still a little worried that Mama wasn't as interesting as all their daddies.

Both Cordy and Cally follow closely behind, crawling on hands and knees. I scoop him up and swing him around, his delighted giggles music to my ears as he wraps his little chubby arms around my neck and gives me a sloppy kiss on the mouth. "We missed you. Did you have fun playing with the pussies?" Holy crap, his language skills are phenomenal. Caspian chokes on his drink, and Xavier sniggers quietly to himself as I flip them off behind Jack's back.

"Mama, I want kisses too," Cally demands, tugging on my skirt, so I drop down to my knees and scoop up the two girls. There are lots of giggles and childish cries as we all love on each other like it's been months instead of hours since we've seen one another. It heals my slightly wounded heart, and all is right with my world again. They do love me.

"Have you been good babies for your daddies and grandpas?" I ask, looking around the room and getting a better look at my loved ones. Grandpa Eric and William are both snoozing on the couch. Eric is snoring, but it's not overly obnoxious. My three husbands and fiancé all look like they've been put through the wringer.

"Why does everyone look like they've been

stomped on by Viggy?" I ask, and Xavier lifts a hand and points to my snuggly, adorable little cherubs.

"Your children are exhausting," he mutters, putting a hand over his face. Saxon is slumped next to him with his eyes closed, and his pale skin looks even paler and translucent. I'm not sure if he's even breathing.

"Your children conned Saxon and Xavier into giving them candy." Caspian is looking at our babies with so much love on his face, I'm not actually sure what's wrong with that. "Poor guys didn't realize that candy affects shifters similarly to human speed. It sent them into a hyperactive frenzy."

Link chuckles. Neither him nor Cas look quite as run-down as the other two. "The kids made their daddies entertain them for hours and refused to go to bed," Link explains with a slight grimace. "And both of them need to feed."

"But with all that emotional energy, why are you hungry?" I ask Xavier, surprised he didn't gorge on them.

He pulls his hands away from his face and looks at me with disgust.

"They are children. We never feed from children." He sounds aghast, and I hold my hands up.

"Whoops, okay, sorry. I haven't read that part of Warlock 101." Or any part really. "But what about when you are children?" I ask, and he rolls his eyes. His exhaustion is obviously making him a bigger asshole than he normally is.

"We feed from adults, of course." It has a silent, "Duh," on the end, and I narrow my eyes, but he's gone back to putting his hand over his eyes so he doesn't see it. The next free moment I have, I am doing all the research on my husbands' species.

Link must see me losing my patience, because he stands, pulls me up, and gives me a hug. The children grumble good-naturedly but wait patiently. "You're glowing. I take it your evening was a success?" He turns my head to the side to see my healed mating marks on either side of my neck.

I hear a rumble behind me and wave a hand to shush Maxsim. He's going to have to learn to play nice with everyone.

"Yeah, you could say that," I reply a little hesitantly, worried about how everyone is going to react, but I shouldn't have been concerned, because my other mates are wonderful men.

"Congratulations!" Caspian is beaming, and both my grandpas, who have woken with all the noise, come over and shake the cats' hands, welcoming them to the family.

"Well, at least we won't need to look for a new act," William mutters absently, and I frown at him.

"You want my husbands to continue to perform

for you?" I'm slightly pissed he would suggest such a thing, and he quickly backtracks.

"Oh no, of course not," he denies, but Maxsim steps up, putting his arm around me.

"It is fine, Lila. To be honest, I enjoy performing."

I look at him in shock, and Echo giggles.

"He really is a bit of a show pony. He makes me brush his mane until it shines before every show." My eyes widen at this information, and Maxsim's face fur pinkens slightly with embarrassment. Oh shit, that's kind of adorable.

"But don't you find it demeaning?" I press, and he just shrugs.

"Nope, it's fun. I love all the kids' expressions— their wide-eyed wonder and squeals of sheer terror when I roar. It's awesome," he gushes, and I just blink. Who is this man and what happened to the giant, gaping asshole he'd been?

"Aww, Max, I think you broke our new mate." Echo giggles again, giving me a hip bump, and I remember what we have to tell everyone.

"Ah, you guys are going to want to take a seat," I say, and all the smiles drop at my tone. Link's hands tighten on my shoulders, and when I look up at him, there's worry in his eyes. I try to smile reassuringly at him, but I'm not sure I pull it off.

"No, hey, it's okay, nothing bad, but Echo and Maxsim have something they want to share with you." The kids got distracted while we were talking and are back to playing with their toys on the floor, so I hurry over and squish myself between Xavier and Saxon, grabbing both of their hands. "Please don't be mad at me," I whisper to them, preempting their reactions to our news.

"What's going on?" Caspian asks, sitting up, all his attention on my two new mates.

Maxsim wraps his arm around Echo and pulls him over to show a united front. "As you all know, Echo was in heat."

"Wasn't that very fast? You have all only been gone a day. Doesn't a heat usually take longer to break?" Link asks, a wrinkle of concern between his eyes as his thirst for knowledge makes him question everything.

"Yes. We think having both a male and female alpha there sped up his heat time, but it also resulted in a pregnancy. We're going to have more babies." Max gestures to the whole group, and I love how he has jumped on board the harem train and is embracing it to the fullest. I expected complete resistance, but it seems mating me and breeding Echo has turned him into a different person—one who is relaxed, open, and accepting. I kind of miss the surly grump, but I don't hate it.

It's so quiet that you could hear a pin drop. "By we, do you mean you and Echo, or you and Echo and Lila?" Eric is the first to break the silence. I think everyone else is still in shock.

"Yes, the three of us. Much like when Caspian and Lila mated, Echo wasn't able to stop the harvesting of one of Lila's eggs, and one of Echo's kittens will have Lila's genetics," Maxsim explains while Echo bites his lip and waits for everyone's reaction. I can tell he's nervous with the way his tail is twitching behind him.

Caspian blows out a big breath. "Well, I'm the last person who can get upset about it. That's wonderful news. I know how that feels though. How are you doing?" He looks between me and Echo.

"We're actually okay," I assure him, and Echo nods his agreement. "I have decided to just roll with all the changes. Fighting it is just going to cause heartache for all of us. I love our babies." I look at three on the floor, who are babbling to one another in their own special language. "Adding a couple more isn't going to make a difference, and to be honest, I'm thrilled with the fact that I don't have to carry these ones. With all you very powerful men, including Xavier who is one of the most powerful men in the galaxy, I'm sure we will have no problem keeping them safe." I subtly stroke Xavier's ego at the same time I squeeze his and Saxon's hand. Saxon's eyes have popped open, and he's smiling, but he doesn't seem to be completely with us. Poor guy must be starving. I admire his self-control, considering he hasn't attacked any of the others yet, but Xavier is the one I'm worried about the most. All the others have a permanent tie to me, but he doesn't have that yet.

"Well, that's great. How about we go up to the ship and I run all the prenatal tests and scans. We can see exactly how many babies you'll be having." Link is grinning widely, and I blow a grateful kiss to my cyborg husband. All around me, my family is singing their joy and congratulations, but Xavier is quiet.

"Soon, I promise," I whisper in his ear, and he sighs.

"I'm fine. I'm happy for all of you, but I can't deny I'm a little jealous. I just want you to be able to feel our intimate bond." He looks sad, the saddest I've seen him since we've known each other. Xavier is usually so cocky and full of confidence, so seeing him like this makes me sad too and desperate to fix it.

"And I do too. How about we have a family lunch, and then I take you and Saxon upstairs and you two can have lunch as well?" I wink suggestively, and that perks him right up.

"The kids have run us ragged. Every time Saxon and I left the room to try and feed, they started crying, and Link and Caspian freaked out." Xavier drops my other two husbands in the shit, and I raise an eyebrow at the two men who have the grace to look guilty.

"Shit, Lila, it's hard work watching the three of them, especially when they are hyper," Cas whines, and Link nods his head in agreement.

"I have to agree. I thought I had this parenting thing down after Marcus, but three at a time is nothing like one. I now have complete sympathy for my poor parents." Eric grimaces, and I realize I know nothing about their parents. One day I will sit down with them and ask all about my family tree, but not today. Today, I need to worry about my own immediate tree that keeps sprouting extra branches.

"Well, suck it up, guys, because we're going to add a few more to the mix. We need to work out how long it will be until they arrive. So this is what's going to happen. We are going to have a nice, peaceful" —Xavier snorts— "family lunch, and then you are all going to take a nap." I point to my children, whose eyelids are starting to look heavy. "And you are going to call your families and give them the good news, and then let Link look you over," I tell the two cats and my cyborg. "While this is happening, I am going to make sure that Xavier and Saxon have all that they need to recover."

"And me?" Cas asks, raising his eyebrows, and I wave my hands around the room.

"You are going to tidy up. This place looks like a hurricane went through it."

"It did, hurricane Jack, Cally, and Cordy." William chuckles, standing up. "That sounds like a grand idea, and after that, we need to sit down and make plans. The spring equinox on Rilu is quickly approaching, and we need a game plan in place to get that flower."

"Okay, well, that's what we will do after dinner then," I agree, a wash of panic flowing over me. So much has happened in a short period of time, but he's right. Grandpa John's recovery needs to be our focus now that the kids have shifted.

But first things first—lunch.

"After the fourth time they shifted and busted out of their clothes, X lost his shit." Cas is regaling us with stories about their twelve hours without me. "He spelled their new clothes to be able to shift with them."

The babies are spaced out around the table. They are in little chairs that slide onto the side of the table, allowing them to join us for the meal. I've got Cordy next to me, and Jack is with Cas, but Cally threw a tantrum until she got to sit between Maxsim and Echo. The cats are lavishing her with attention and food. Our kittens? Babies? Whatever, they are going to be so well loved, but I can see the kids' eyelids are really starting to sag now.

The food is very similar to what's found on Earth, just different names and colors. I mean, I shouldn't be surprised, really, if the Skarrians were the original Earthlings. Everything tastes delicious, and Cordy is kind of partial to a vegetable that tastes like a sweet potato but is pink. We're having it mashed with some meat and other vegetables tonight, and all three of the babies are loving it, which is a huge relief. I thought they may want to stick to their raw fish diet in this form as well, and I'm not sure how long I could have coped with that.

"That's awesome. Mira was saying that there was nothing like that. I'm pretty sure she would like to join forces with you and create a line of children's clothing for Fluxx."

A shrewd look crosses Xavier's face, and it's the first time I've seen the arrogant warlock since we emerged from our nest. I can't say I'm not relieved, because I'm really worried about him, and as soon as we are done on Rilu and Grandpa John is up and about again, I'm going to insist on returning to Westalin.

"You know, that is a great idea, and not just for Fluxx. There are many species throughout the galaxy that can shift, and I'm almost certain none of their young have control when they are younger. Imagine the amount of money we could save parents. Other children's clothing companies would be gunning for us. They will lose so much money if everyone shifts to our product." He chuckles wickedly and nods his head. "I wonder if I can put a patent on it so no one else can do the same. It's a very complicated spell, and it took me a little while to get it right. There probably aren't many warlocks who could pull it off. Mom and Dad would, and maybe Zane, but he wouldn't compete with us. I'll give Mira a call and discuss it."

He goes to stand up, lost in his world domination plans, but I stand up too. "Wait. Both you and Saxon need to take care of yourselves first," I tell him, careful of my words around the children.

They are going to see and hear a lot of things in this family, but I'm hoping to keep them as innocent as I can as long as possible. Although sex seems to be more openly talked about across the galaxy, unlike Earth, so maybe I need to make sure their education is where it needs to be to protect them from making mistakes, especially if their inner beast is as pushy and irresponsible as mine is. She gives me a little nudge at the thought, and I can practically hear her grumbling, but there is a small sense of impatience suggesting she is looking forward to taking care of Sax and Xav.

Xavier's eyes narrow, and his scheming expression is replaced with one of hunger, hunger for me, and he changes direction and strides toward me as Saxon pushes his chair back.

"Right, you guys know what you need to do. Call your parents." I point at the cats and then turn to Link and Cas. "And you two get these munchkins to bed. Daddies are going to put you to bed now, and you will sleep. When you're good and rested, we might go for a drive later and see if we can find a park for you to play at." The weather is overcast, but there's no rain for the first time in days. The children have been cooped up inside since they were born, apart from swimming in the pool, and now that they've shifted, it will be good to get some fresh air and let them run around in a playground.

The children's eyes widen with excitement. "Oh yes, Mama," Jack says, speaking for all of them. "We sleep now." He closes his eyes and puts his head down on his tray, narrowly missing the pile of mashed sweet potato still on his plate. And just like that, he's asleep, his chubby little baby cheeks relaxed in slumber and so freaking adorable. The girls try to copy him, but we stop them before they can get themselves covered in food. I lift Cordy out of her chair as Echo carefully lifts Cally before depositing them both in Link's arms. Cas grabs the now sleeping Jack.

"Once I've done this and you finish your call to your parents, we'll teleport to the ship, and I can do a scan, so meet me back here," Link tells the cats, who quickly agree.

I wave goodbye to my grandpas and grab my warlock and Vilaxian by the hand, towing them to my bedroom. A rush of excitement flows through me at having both of them at the same time. It's something I've been wanting since I learned that they helped each other out from time to time.

CHAPTER ELEVEN

Xavier

I can feel Lila's excitement build the closer we get to the bedroom, and I greedily suck down the emotional energy, not afraid to feed on my intimate. She really is a feast for the senses. Her unguarded emotions float freely between us, and her excitement dulls the empty feeling I've had all day. Although Saxon and I discussed feeding one another, both of us were reluctant to do it without Lila present, not to mention the babies kept us busy. Who knew an innocent bit of candy would lead to us all not sleeping for the last twelve hours? All candy is henceforth banned from this house. We are not doing that again. Or maybe there is a candy that doesn't affect the children's metabolism like that. I will have to experiment with candy from different planets, though I will make sure they have something to counteract all that energy. I mean, I could have drained it from them, but that's not right. Feeding from children is a crime on our planet. They only have small amounts of energy, and it's easy to drain and kill one. You get the death penalty if you siphon energy off a child and damage it. That's not to say there aren't people who do it, but the punishment certainly does deter most people. Warlocks are not the most moral creatures, but that is one law that is sacred.

"Why didn't you two feed each other? I don't like seeing either of you like this." Lila stops at the top of the stairs, glaring at us.

"Because, my beautiful blood rose, we were too busy making sure the children didn't get into trouble, and it didn't feel right without you there," Saxon explains, slurring his words slightly and staggering to the side. I jump forward to catch him, and Lila gasps.

"Shit, he's really bad. Damn you. I order you to feed from each other if you have to, even if I'm not there."

I chuckle, steadying Saxon who holds onto me. I give him a little boost with my magic, and he is able to keep walking toward Lila's bedroom, but it drains my already depleted resources, and I start to feel a little lightheaded.

"You order us, do you? What else would you

like to order us to do?" My words sound slurred even to my own ears.

"I can think of many things I'd like the two of you to do to each other and me, but quite frankly, both of you can barely stand up, let alone do those things, so how about we get this show on the road?" She waves a hand at her bedroom door, and we continue our slow shuffle down the hallway with her muttering below her breath about irresponsible blood roses and intimates and something about kicking our asses when we are back to full health.

She opens the door, and I assist Saxon to the bed, where he drops like a sack of saluktat beans. He moans, and Lila closes and locks the door before hurrying over to the bed. "Never again, do you hear me, Saxon Whatever Your Last Name Is?"

"Vilaxians don't have last names, they have clan names, and I guess that means he's part of the Adams clan now," I tell her, going around to the other side of the bed, stripping my clothes off, and climbing onto the bed. Lila eyes my naked body hungrily, but she puts her hands on her hips.

"It's a bit presumptuous, getting naked right away, isn't it?" she asks, and I shrug.

"I'm a sure thing, love. No need for foreplay. Why don't you come over here and feed your Vilaxian before he becomes unconscious?" I say, coaxing the annoyed female to our bed. I know it's just because she's worried about us, but I can't help but needle her. It's in my nature.

Her gaze clouds, and she hurries over to the bed, climbing over me and settling herself between us.

"Naked might have been better, *phoeall.*" I roll onto my side and whisper in her ear, my rapidly hardening cock pushing into her skirt-clad ass.

"Can you take care of that for me? Sax too?" she asks as she pulls her long hair back from her neck, exposing it for Saxon to feed from.

I wave my hand and remove their clothes, my eyes roving over their now naked forms. Their coloring is such a contrast. Saxon is pale on the best of days, but today he's practically transparent. Lila has a beautiful, warm golden color to her skin, and she practically glows with vitality. She has the smallest silvery stretch marks on her stomach from the rapid growth of the babies, but she was diligent about applying a special cream Mira had given her before she left Fluxx. It's specially designed to prevent stretch marks from rapid growth, which occurs in some shifters during pregnancy, especially when it's a cross species mating. There are also the silvery, scarred tooth marks surrounding one of her nipples. Link told us all about it and that he suspects it's a mating bite from the bloody Aquilian, but he hasn't mentioned it to Lila because she already carries enough guilt about their interlude. She doesn't need to know just yet that there's a good possibility that her harem is indeed seven and not six like she thinks. It's a problem for future us.

None of those marks detract from her beauty. Instead, they enhance it. She was stunning when she was rounded and ripe with our young. I can't wait to plant my seed in her and see her grow round with my own child, but with Echo's pregnancy announcement, maybe I can wait a little longer. Our rapidly expanding family is a lot to take in, and for someone not used to such a fast pace, I don't want her to become overwhelmed and regret all of it. So far, she is handling it beautifully, but everyone has a breaking point, and I don't want to push Lila to hers. Her emotions are already all over the place, so I want to keep things as calm as possible for as long as possible. I'll just be happy when we can seal our bond. I'm getting impatient, and I must admit I was jealous when she came downstairs with the cats' mating marks on her neck, but I know my time is coming, and getting John back to full health is definitely a priority. Once that is done, though, wild mallac beasts will not be able to stop me from dragging her to my own planet and making her mine.

I stroke a finger over her side, mesmerized by the softness of her skin, as she tries to get Saxon to bite her, but he's so lethargic that she can't get him to respond. Instead, I watch as she bites down on her own wrist, her Vilaxian fangs having dropped into her mouth. When she pulls away, blood wells from the two holes. She holds it under Saxon's nose, trying to get a response from him, but when nothing happens, she looks at me with complete helplessness, and I feel my protective urges kick in. I feel affection for the big man, if not something a little stronger, and I don't like to see him like this either.

I push my finger between his lips and grab hold of her wrist, dragging it over to his mouth and mashing it against it. I see his tongue flick out and lap at her skin, and Lila and I breathe a sigh of relief at the same time.

His hands come up and hold her wrist, so I release it but don't move, staying where I am as he starts to take large swallows of her blood. "We need to be careful that he doesn't go into a blood frenzy and hurt you," I caution Lila, but she just grins at me.

"It's okay, Xavier." She blows a kiss at me, smiling with relief. "I'm a lot more resilient now, so I don't mind if he gets rough." She finishes her sentence with a wink and a smile, and I want to kiss her smart mouth.

I lean in to do so, but before I can, Saxon growls and yanks her toward him. I watch with rapidly building desire as he impales her on his cock at the same time as he penetrates her neck with his fangs. Her loud gasp, followed by a moan of pure pleasure, goes straight to my cock, and I reach down and stroke it as I soak up all the emotions filling the room. I watch as Lila lazily rides Saxon's cock, her pretty pink pussy sliding up and down as he drinks from her neck. I desperately want to get in and lap at her clit while she does it, but there's no room.

"Lila, are you hungry too? Did you take blood from the kitties?" I ask her, and she shakes her head.

"No, I didn't want to frighten them off. I wasn't sure how they felt about sharing blood. It's something we need to talk about," she mutters quietly, distracted by the pleasure that Saxon is wringing from her body. He's drinking deeply, and I think I'm going to have to intervene so he doesn't drain her dry, but Link assured us she can lose a lot more blood than most due to her Vilaxian transition.

"Please drink from me. We need to keep your strength up," I say, trying to keep my tone light so she doesn't know I'm worried.

"Yes please, your blood is yummy." She moans when Saxon thrusts harder as he releases her neck, his skin returning to its normal pale vibrancy. He continues to thrust into her but turns his head to look at me, his eyes glowing red with bloodlust.

"Get over here and feed my blood rose," he demands, and my eyes widen. I thought he would be more possessive, but he's not. I shuffle closer, my cock practically level with his lips as I hold my wrist out to Lila. She takes it absently, her eyes locked on my cock as Saxon leans forward and runs his tongue up the length of it. She groans and pulls my wrist closer, my body surging forward as Saxon takes my cock deep into his mouth. She bites down on my wrist and starts to drink heavily, her venom pulsing through my body at earth-shattering speeds.

I can't control the thrust of my hips, but Saxon knows how to take my dick deep and doesn't gag at all as I push into his throat. His fangs scrape against the thin skin on my cock, injecting his own venom into my body, and I can't control myself any longer. My orgasm bursts forth, and I spend my seed down Saxon's throat. I can feel Lila's and Saxon's combined pleasure, and I drink deeply of it as we all find our release.

Lila withdraws her fangs and releases my wrist just as I pull my cock out of Saxon's mouth. He gives it a lick to close the fang marks and winks at me. It's good to see him back to normal. I was worried about him.

"That was awesome." Lila sighs, leaning forward and kissing Saxon hard on the mouth. I watch with barely concealed awe as they exchange a passionate kiss, Lila not concerned in the least that Saxon just sucked me off. That makes my cock harden again.

"Yes, and it was just the beginning." I pull her off Saxon and flip her onto her back. "How about I fuck your brains out next?" I suggest, and she grins widely.

"Well, that's certainly an interesting offer, but what about Saxon?" she asks with wide-eyed innocence.

I play along with the act. "I don't know. I'm sure we can make use of that beautiful cock in some way."

Saxon growls and rolls over on top of me, pinning me between them. He puts his fangs against my neck, and I feel a shiver of excitement run down my spine, as well as an echo of the same thing from Lila.

"Does that excite you, *phoeall*? Seeing the beautiful vampire dominate me?" I ask as her hands roam over both our bodies, my cock probing at her wet warmth. Before I can thrust deep, however, Saxon's hand slips between us. I feel him shove his fingers deep into her pussy, and her eyes widen at the intrusion. He pumps in and out, coating his fingers in his and her combined release before removing them and probing my back entrance.

"I'm going to fuck the warlock, my beautiful blood rose, while he fucks you. What do you think of that?" Saxon growls as he preps me for his large cock. I feel my balls tighten at the intrusion, and I breathe deeply. Fucking hell, I was never this excited with my harem. Even the ones with the more interesting attributes never excited me as much as I am between these two. Real feelings must be what makes the difference.

"Oh yes, please," Lila begs, and she tries to look around me so she can see what's happening, but it's not possible, so I wave a hand and put a mirror on the ceiling before directing her gaze there.

"Is that better, *phoeall*?" I ask, and she just nods, lost in the view of Saxon feeding his cock into my ass. I grunt at the intrusion, but it's not anything I haven't done before, so I breathe through it until he's fully seated. He grabs my head and turns it so he can lean forward and kiss me. Lila watches it all with wide-eyed fascination.

"I'm going to wreck you, and you are going to feed on all our pleasure," he tells me.

I finally sink deep into Lila's depths, and she cries out with pleasure.

"Oh God, yes."

I lean in and kiss her. "Watch the mirror now. Watch us take our pleasure from each other. Know that this is what you have to look forward to for the rest of our lives," I command her, and she nods, locking her eyes on the mirror above us. Saxon grabs my hips and starts pounding in and out. I let his movements guide mine, and I lean down and nibble Lila's breasts just to increase the sensory overload. Her hands grip the sheets below us, and she struggles to keep her gaze focused on the mirror above us. Her eyes flick back and forth between her pretty green ones and her beast's black ones, but I'm not worried since the beast likes me. I think.

The suckers deep inside her pussy latch onto my cock, the pulsing sensation making the intense pleasure increase exponentially. Saxon's cock brushes across my prostate with every vicious thrust, and it's all I can do to hold out, but then he sinks his fangs into my neck, and I'm a goner. His venom pulses through my system as I desperately fuck into Lila, willing her orgasm to come. Her pussy tightens and ripples, and she throws her head back just when I can't hold out any longer.

I toss a burst of pleasure into the air, and all three of us orgasm as one. I feed hard and deep, the combined physical and metaphysical sensations sending me higher than I've ever been before. I gorge on the emotions until I'm as full as an Earth tick, their pleasure intoxicating. Saxon slumps down over me, breathing heavily and pushing me onto Lila, who just sighs and wraps her arms around us.

"That was incredible," she mutters as I brush her sweat-soaked hair back from her face and kiss her gently. "You two are beautiful together."

There is not an ounce of jealousy in her emotions at all, and I feel a sense of relief. I'm not sure that either of us could rely on just Lila for our feeding requirements, despite her Vilaxian changes and her being my intimate. We are going to need others, and the fact that she is comfortable and enjoys us using one another is a blessing.

"I need a nap, and then I want to see you both

suck each other's dicks," she says with a wicked glint in her eyes despite the yawn that breaks free.

"Sure, as long as I get a taste of your pretty pussy too," I counter, and she grins.

"I'm sure that can be arranged."

Saxon pulls out, allowing me to do the same, and I wave a hand, cleaning us all up magically before we gather our pretty mate between us and snuggle in.

"Just fifteen minutes is all I need," she says, her eyes blinking shut. Saxon and I grin at one another and settle down to wait. I'm not sure if I'll last fifteen minutes, but I'll try.

CHAPTER TWELVE

Lila

After a very delicious afternoon nap, we emerge downstairs and find the family in the living room, in chaos once more. Jack, Cordy, and Cally are all in tears, and wow, they have some lungs on them.

"Hey, hey, what's going on?" I ask as Xavier pushes past me and gathers up the two girls in his arms, cooing to them. Jack holds his arms out for Saxon, and Link and Caspian heave out sighs of relief. My grandpas, the smart men they are, are nowhere to be seen, and the two cats are in cat form with both of their front paws over their ears, trying to block out the sound. "Some help you two are," I grumble, and Maxsim shrugs elegantly.

"They were grumpy when they woke up,"

Caspian says wearily. "I don't think they've had enough sleep really." My poor kraken looks worn down. I really have dropped the ball on this parenting thing, but trying to balance it and having six mates is taking some getting used to.

"Okay, here is what's going to happen. Daddy Link and Daddy Cas are going to stay here and have a nap themselves, and Daddy Sax and Daddy X are going to come with us and find a park." The kids all stop crying and cheer, and I look around the room. "Where are Eric and William? I may need one of them to come with me, because all I've seen of Skarr is this house, so I have no idea if there is even a playground nearby. God, I hope there is," I mutter under my breath now that I've promised my kids an outing.

"They are trying to work out plans for Rilu, so they escaped to William's soundproof office," Link explains.

"Smart men," Saxon remarks, bouncing Jack in his arms. All of these guys have taken to parent-hood beautifully, even if they were nervous to start with.

"Okay, you guys find warmer clothes for these three while I find a grandpa to accompany us. Oh, what did you find out about Echo's pregnancy?" I ask, remembering what they were going to do while we took care of the other two's needs.

"Well, I did a scan, and Echo is carrying two

babies. I'm not sure how, but both of them contain the combined genetics of all three of you. I guess he must have sucked up two of your eggs, and he and Maxsim both fertilized them. I'm still doing research on lightning cat breeding specifics, and I don't have it all down yet."

A thrill of joy runs through me at hearing that both of Echo's babies are all of ours—not that I would have loved one of theirs any less, I've just discovered I'm greedy. "That's wonderful." I get down on my knees, and Echo and Maxsim crawl over to us. The girls squeal with delight and scream for Xavier to let them down. He does, and they pounce on the kitties. I stroke both of their heads, cooing to them about how pleased I am. They lick me with their rough tongues and purr with delight.

"And did Echo discover how long he will be pregnant for?" I'm dying to know how long it will be until our family grows again. He rolls onto his back, exposing his stomach, and I run my hand over it. There are no bumps yet. Do male omegas breastfeed? That's another question to ask, but maybe closer to the birth. I missed out on breast-feeding the other three because they were in kraken form, and now they don't need it.

"It works out to be roughly six Earth months. Days are shorter on Iceen, and it's approximately a year in their time, so I think I converted that right."

Link has been busy, and I love that he's so enthusiastic about it all.

"Okay, cool, so we've got some time. That will be nice. I wonder how old these three will be in six months. They may be able to help change diapers." I'm still having trouble trying to wrap my head around the accelerated growth of the children. I freeze when something occurs to me. "So if my eggs were fertilized, is that going to make them part shifter, part Vilaxian, and part Skarrian lightning cats?"

Link shrugs, and a frustrated look crosses his face. "I'm sorry, I don't know. Normally a Skarrian pregnancy will result in either a Skarrian or whatever the other parent is. There are no crosses, but because you changed your DNA by becoming a blood rose, there is a good chance that they will be at least part Vilaxian as well. I've started a log to keep track of all the children's traits. So far it looks like these three are straight shifters, which makes sense because you only just had your Skarrian and shifter genes activated when you got pregnant with them, but they did show a trace of Vilaxian DNA, and they were super fast when they were hyped up on candy. That may be the only trait they exhibit."

I secretly cross my fingers behind my back. "Okay, we will deal with everything as it happens, but keeping record of it is a great idea. You're so smart," I praise my cyborg, and he preens slightly. I have to keep reminding them they are equally loved.

"Alright, everyone knows what their jobs are. I'll find a grandparent and then meet back here in fifteen minutes." Everyone agrees and wanders off, except for Cas and the cats. The cats snuggle in a pile in front of the fire, and Maxsim uses his tongue to groom Echo. I feel a pang of longing and desperately want to shift and join them, but I want to lavish some attention on my kraken before finding my grandpas.

"Hey, how are you doing?" I ask, joining him on the sofa and wrapping my arms around his neck.

He closes his eyes and rests his forehead against my own. "Tired, and I need a swim. My tentacles feel dried out." Neither of us have been back in the ocean since the kids were born, and I knew he was jonesing for a long swim.

"I'm sorry I've let you down," I say, feeling incredibly guilty. His eyes pop open, and he vehemently shakes his head.

"No, honey, you haven't let me down at all. I knew going into this that it would be more than just you and me in this family, and I am okay with that. The kids run us ragged, and a nap and a swim will do wonders to make me feel better, I promise," he assures me.

"Okay, well, why don't you nap, and after dinner, you and I will read the kids a story and put them to bed and then go for a nighttime swim? I'm sure the whatthefuckasauras have lost interest since the babies are no longer around for a snack, and if they haven't, you and I are big enough in shifted form to take them all on."

A big grin crosses his lips, and his eyes flick back and forth from his beast to normal. "Sounds perfect." He presses a kiss to my lips, and my kraken perks up. I can feel her anticipation for our swim later, and my own excitement rises.

"Cool. Find Link and take him with you. I don't want to think about either of you ending up exhausted."

He agrees, and I hurry off to find my grandpas. The kids will be ready even before I am.

"This really is amazing." I am still astounded by the playground that both Eric and William directed us to. Thankfully the car was already set up for the three children, with futuristic car seats strapped onto one of the bench seats. We all piled in and drove for about twenty minutes, my face glued to the window as I took in my new home planet.

The area we're in is definitely for the rich, and the large mansions are spaced out so nobody can see their neighbor if they don't want to. The park is a wide open nature space, and in the middle of that space is a huge lake with a nice picnic area, and on one side of that lake is the mother of all playgrounds. There are slides and swings and monkey bars, and things I've never seen before. There are also children all over it, going crazy.

When we first arrived, we got some interested looks. My warlock and Vilaxian are quite obviously not Skarrian, and although there are still some furtive glances and whispers, most people have lost interest. Saxon and Xavier are over near the playground, pushing our children on a set of three swings, and I'm sitting on a picnic blanket that Eric produced with my two grandpas.

"Okay, so give me the 411 on Rilu," I say, making myself comfortable. Eric pulls a flask out of the backpack he brought and pours us all a cup of something before passing it out. I take a tentative sip and moan as the deliciousness crosses my taste buds.

"What is this?" I ask, needing more of it in my life. It's like a mocha—half coffee, half chocolate, and all awesome.

"It's saluktat. It's a Westalin version of coffee. It packs a hell of a punch, so don't drink too many cups," he warns me. "But we all definitely needed the pick-me-up today."

"I've made sure the staff knows not to keep any

candy in the house," William assures us, and I give him a thumbs-up.

"Poor Xavier. He loves spoiling the kids, and he was dying to get them Warlock candy. There's a special one that is like Earth's pop rocks that was a childhood favorite of his. He couldn't wait to let them try it."

"I promise he's totally over it." Eric laughs as we watch my children with my husband and fiancé.

"Okay, well, Rilu is a desert planet, hot and dry, so I'm afraid neither the cats nor Saxon will be of any use to you," William starts.

"Hang on, why not Saxon?" I ask, interrupting him.

"There is almost no cloud cover on Rilu, and I'm afraid the sun shines for way too long for him not to be constantly drinking blood to function normally."

Oh, they have limited hours of daylight on Vilax, so I should have known. "Okay, so it will be you two, Xavier, Link, and Cas."

"We talked with Link and Cas while you were otherwise occupied, and both of them would like to stay back and look after the children while you are gone." I smack my head. Of course, the children. Fuck, I still need to get used to keeping them in mind.

"Right, and the award for worst mother of the

year goes to Lila Adams," I mutter, and they chuckle.

"Give yourself a break, Lila. It takes some adjustment, and you have had a lot to deal with over the last couple of months." Eric tries to reassure me, but I still feel guilty.

"Eric and I won't be joining you on Rilu either. We want to return to Celestia and check on John. They've been giving us daily updates, but we feel like we've been gone too long. Now that you are all sorted and the babies have shifted, we feel comfortable returning."

I reach out and grab his hand. "Fuck, I've been selfish. I'm so sorry. Of course you want to return to your brother."

"Nonsense. We've loved every minute of it, but Will is right, I need to see John with my own two eyes to feel reassured, and we know you and whoever you take with you are going to be able to get the plant."

I scoff. "Hopefully Xavier and I will be able to convince whoever we need to, to allow us access. I'm pretty sure his power of persuasion is on point."

Eric and William exchange a glance. "I'm not sure how much use he will be to you. Rilu is a fairly isolated planet, and they don't take kindly to strangers."

"But don't we have a performer from Rilu in

the circus? Aren't the larnuks native to Rilu?" I'm confused.

Eric sighs. "Yes, Zala is the larnuk mistress, and we do have a good relationship with the tribes, but it took a long time for them to warm up to us, and they don't like strangers butting in. Not to mention their gem trade means they get a lot of dishonest people trying to home in on it."

"But aren't they only the gatekeepers of the plant? Isn't it a Celestian plant?" I argue, feeling a small spike of panic.

"Nobody owns the plant. They hold a reciprocal agreement to protect it. The Celestians have advised the elder who holds the knowledge of its whereabouts that they are allowing you to use it. The cavern it is in is reported to be haunted, and people avoid it like the plague." William looks worried, or even more worried than his normal worried.

"Also, the environment is harsh. It takes a special person to survive on Rilu. Zala has agreed to help, and Cas has arranged for Silac to accompany you."

"Silac?" I can't hide the surprise in my voice as I think about the naga shifter.

"Yes, his snake will be perfect in that harsh climate, as well as an asset to you underground. Allowing yourself to mimic both him and Zala should give you an advantage others don't have."

"How is his big snake ass going to get around underground?" I remember how large he was during the show, and I can't see him slithering easily through tunnels.

"He can change size, especially when he fully shifts. He will be fine, and Cas assures us he is more than capable of protecting you," William argues.

"Okay, but Xavier is just as capable."

Eric grimaces. "I'm afraid Xavier's arrogance may upset the Rilunese, but you never know, he may learn to rein it in." The three of us pause for a moment before bursting into laughter.

"Yeah, good thing you got me Silac, otherwise I may be doing this on my own." My heartbeat speeds up at the thought of what's to come, but so far I've survived five matings, being changed into a shifter, Vilaxian, and lightning cat, and endured a death match for a mate. I've got this shit.

"Also, we have been talking, and depending on how John recovers, we may need you to step up into your leadership role quicker than we planned." William becomes serious again. "So let's have a little chat about the future. Cas has elected to semi-retire from his act because of the children, but his brother will be joining us, and they will alternate shows."

"Yes, that's awesome. I can't wait to introduce Malik to Magenta."

Eric rolls his eyes playfully. "Matchmaker."

"Hey, I can't help it if I want my friend to experience the fun of a tentacled lover." He grimaces, and it's my turn to chuckle.

"Which means with the return of the lightning cats and hopefully the mer show, so nothing should change."

"Are we not sure about the Aquilians yet?" I ask, experiencing a mixture of feelings when I think about that stupid can of tuna.

"No, there has been radio silence from them. I know that apart from Nikos and Nixie, the others weren't returning. Their family pod was expecting, so they are choosing to stay home. Unless they find another couple of Aquilians to join the show, we will need to find a replacement act."

"How do we do that?" I ask, ignoring my own feelings of disappointment. It's because I really liked Nixie, no other reason.

"We have a list of applications a mile long, so it won't be too hard. It's just about finding the right fit. I'll forward all the information to your tablet, and you can screen them."

I swallow a lump of nerves in my throat. "Me?" I ask, and William nods.

"Yes, this will be part of your job as owner. You will need to make those decisions, and there is no time like the present."

"Okay, good, sure. I can do that," I stammer,

and they just smile warmly at me without a bit of doubt on their faces, which truly does help.

Suddenly, there are screams and shouts, and I jump to my feet, looking for my children. I can't see them anywhere, but I find three little baby krakens hanging from the monkey bars and roll my eyes. Of course we couldn't go anywhere without bringing any drama, though if you ask me, their children are weenies.

CHAPTER THIRTEEN

Lila

Caspian and I finally got a chance to reconnect when we went for a swim. It was the first time since we emerged from the deep with the babies in tow, and it was well and truly overdue. Judging by the smug feeling from my kraken, I'm pretty sure our beast enjoyed the little swim as well, and so I went off to Rilu with a smile on my face, and although I will miss them all dreadfully, I'm not worried about any of them. Our little family is working as a well-oiled machine, and apart from being completely indulged, the babies are in safe hands.

Rilu is a five-day trip from Skarr, and my grandpas insisted that I take their personal space-ship. I have no clue how to drive it despite my lesson from Bubby when we went to Fluxx, but between Xavier and Silac, they have me covered. Oh, and Tirrian. Yup, that's right, when we arrived at the spaceport above Skarr after a teary goodbye with the rest of my family, Silac was waiting for us with the surly dragon. He claims he had nothing better to do and dragons cope well with extreme heat. His father insisted on him accompanying us when he heard what happened to John and our plight to obtain the flamegem flower.

The two-bedroom ship has warp speed and is comfortable enough for us to make the journey to Rilu in style. We're taking turns in two-person shifts, while the other two take their rest. That way there is always someone manning the helm and looking out for space pirates.

"So how is motherhood treating you?" Silac asks as he and I take a turn to man the helm while Xavier and Tirrian each make use of the bedrooms. The dragon has been his usual, grumpy, passive aggressive self, and I wasn't sad to see him retire. I offered to accompany Xavier so he could feed, but he just laughed and claimed that he was still full from our time yesterday.

I look up from my tablet. I had been reading about the warlock race, especially the part about breeding. I need to be better informed so no more accidents happen. Thankfully there is a magical process that allows a warlock to breed, and it's not

something that can be forced, so that's one less acci-
dental pregnancy I need to worry about. "Really
good. I was actually terrified. I've made some
mistakes, and I know I will continue to make
mistakes, but between the six of us, I'm sure our
babies will make it to adulthood relatively unscarred
both physically and emotionally," I joke, but I'm
also serious.

"Ah, yes. Caspian told me you now have two
more mates. The lightning cats you stepped up for
during the mating challenge. That was very brave
of you, Lila." I see admiration in Silac's eyes, but
it's not creepy. In fact, it gives me a warm feeling
that I push very far down and ignore.

"Well, I could hardly let Natalia take Maxsim
from Echo, could I?" I reply, trying to play down
the incident, and Silac shakes his head.

"Many people would have. Lots of species don't
like to get involved in altercations like that." His
eyes turn a little cloudy, and I wonder if Silac is
having his own kind of trouble.

"Are you okay?" I ask, reaching over and
squeezing his leg. He's in his human form today,
since his half form wasn't practical for sitting at
the ship's console. He looks down at it for a
moment before plastering on a smile and shaking
his head.

"Ah, yeah, I'm fine. It's nothing you need to
worry about," he assures me, but I can't help

thinking something is wrong. I'll ask Cas if he knows next time I speak to him.

"Well, I'm not the kind of person who will let that kind of injustice happen. Thankfully it all turned out okay."

"I'm really happy for you, Lila, and Cas. He deserves someone who loves him with all their heart, and he looks like he hit the jackpot with you." He grabs the hand I had on his leg and gives it a squeeze of his own. I feel the telltale tingle on my shoulder as a new attraction mark forms.

Wow, okay. I can't help but feel excited. I thought he was being friendly strictly for Cas because they are former lovers, but it feels like maybe my interest in the snake is not so one-sided. Well, this is kind of awkward. I wonder if he's still carrying a torch for my kraken hubby.

His eyes widen in surprise, and one of his hands reaches up to his shoulder. A small hint of fear shows in his eyes, but before I can ask him what's wrong, a clearing throat has us both jumping back and letting go of each other's hand.

"Well, isn't this cozy?"

I heave out a big sigh and turn my back to the dragon who is seriously a pain in the ass. I should have said no to him joining us for this mission.

"Don't be an ass, Tirrian." Xavier pushes past him, and I realize that they've been gone six hours.

The time flew by, and Silac and I coexisted

comfortably the whole time. It was kind of awesome, with just the quietness of space and us not needing to talk, happy with our own company. I meant to ask him what he'd been reading, but I haven't had a chance to. I'll do it during the next shift.

"Hey, how are you?" Xavier asks, leaning down to give me a kiss. He smiles when he sees what I'm reading. "It makes me feel all warm and fuzzy that you are learning about warlocks."

"I don't want to fuck anything up. When we get a chance, can we practice some warlock powers? I want to get them down so it's locked into my mimic abilities."

Xavier nods. "Yes, of course. You'll probably be more powerful once we solidify our intimate bond, but we can work with what you've got now." He purses his lips and looks between the two shifters. "I think you should also mimic these two and add both of their forms to your repertoire. They are both powerful animals and will be a big asset if you ever get into trouble, not to mention helpful in the caverns of Rilu."

I bite my lip and look between the dragon and the snake. I'm not opposed to the idea, since I want every power available to give me, my family, and the orb every possible protection, but I don't know how they feel about it. It's almost kind of like stealing an identity. Sure, I'm me, but I'm also kind of going to be them, or a me version of them. It's confusing.

Silac and Tirrian exchange what could only be described as a loaded glance. Tirrian crosses his arms. "No," he grunts, and Xavier's eyebrows almost jump into his hairline.

Ouch. I mean, I know we're not besties, but I didn't think he hated me that much.

"Okay, and what about you?" He looks toward the naga shifter, who grimaces.

"It's not that I don't want Lila to have everything she needs, but…" He trails off, looking uncomfortable.

"Spit it out, snakelet," Xavier growls, and Silac's cheeks redden with embarrassment.

"I'm already attracted to her. My snake is practically frothing at the mouth to see her in the same form, and I'm afraid he will imprint on her."

"Silac has an arranged marriage. His parents and his fiancé have agreed to allow him to perform in the circus for one year, but after that he must return and marry his fiancée and assume the CEO role of his parents' business empire," Tirrian explains gruffly. "Him imprinting on Lila would be a disaster and make him miserable when he returns to Fluxx to marry her."

I stare at the man in question, my own confusion and hurt now prickling at my emotions. An arranged marriage? I guess that means neither of us can act on the attraction marks that just appeared on our skin. I refuse to be the other woman, and I have a feeling Silac is too honorable to step out on his fiancée. And what's the point if it can't lead anywhere?

"But I thought he had joined the circus to rekindle his relationship with Cas." I'm a little confused, and Silac shrugs, dropping his head and not looking at me.

"I would have liked to, even if it had been temporary. Cas knows I have an arranged marriage, and our relationship was fun, since neither of our animals wanted to create mate bonds with one another. I do love him, but I see how he loves you, and I can't compete with that. Also, my snake is very much interested in you. If I were to change and let you mimic me, I might not be able to stop him from imprinting, and that's not fair to anyone." Although I'm still confused, I am grateful that he is thinking ahead. I do not need to accidentally mate anyone else.

"Why didn't you say anything?" Xavier demands, anger evident in his tone. "You are less than useless on this mission if you can't change into your snake form." He turns to Tirrian. "And what about you? What's your excuse?"

Tirrian grunts and shrugs. "I don't want to."

Xavier starts to pulse, his power filling the control deck.

"Hey, hey." I stand up and put my hands on him, hoping to calm him. "It's okay. It's fine. I completely understand. They don't need to share their forms with me. I'm sure there are other dragons and nagas that I can ask. We don't need to force them, that's kind of like rape. I also don't get that uncontrollable urge to mimic everything anymore, so it has to be a conscious decision."

Xavier takes a deep breath and nods, his anger turning to calculation. "Fine. There is a space station on the way to Rilu. It's kind of a meeting place, part trading station, part pleasure palace for merchants to blow off some steam. I say we stop there and find you a few new forms to mimic. There are bound to be some other shifters or powerful beings that I can mesmerize."

"Ah, remember what I just said about rape?"

"Look, Lila, there is a reason there aren't many mimics around. It's because they were deemed too powerful and hunted. Oshan warned you to be careful and to make it known that you have little power and can only assume one or two forms. We have to do the rest in secret, which means me mesmerizing our victims." Xavier's tone is firm but kind. He understands my moral dilemma, but that kind of thing just doesn't bother him, and he has a point. I guess I do need to keep my abilities on the down low.

"Will we have time? How long until the spring

equinox? I'm not sure my grandpa will survive until the next one."

"It will be a quick stop. A couple of hours at the most. We are making good time and should arrive on Rilu with time to spare. Zala is greasing a few wheels for us to make the process quicker," Xavier assures me.

I heave out a reluctant sigh. "Fine, let's do it. Having a dragon or a naga would have been awesome, but I am happy to try to find other beings. I don't want to force my friends to help me if they don't want to." I'm referring to Silac, because Tirrian and I are most definitely not friends. Maybe frenemies at best.

Silac turns back to the control console and pushes a few buttons. "I've set a course for Station X69. We should be there in a few hours." He won't meet my eyes anymore, and I think maybe our comfortable silence is a thing of the past.

"Hey, it's fine. I totally get it, and I'm not upset," I assure him. "In fact, I really appreciate your honesty. I wouldn't want to trap another male into a mating that wasn't of their choice. I've over-filled my quota of those." It's my turn to feel guilty. All but Link weren't given a choice to be with me.

Xavier squats down in front of me and gives me a little shake. "Hey, don't be like that. We all love you, and I love that you're my intimate. Remember that mating bonds don't ever give the person an option. It was something we were expecting anyway. All of us are thrilled that we love the person we are bonded with."

His reassurance goes a long way to easing my guilty heart, and I stand up. I feel awkward as fuck now that both of these two have asked me not to mimic them. It's like the minute they said it, my mimic powers rose, and now I feel this energy running through my body, pushing me to mimic them despite my assurance to Xavier that I had it under control. Thankfully both are in human form, so the mimic powers can't take over and force a replication like it did when the powers first activated. I don't need the bracelet anymore, but it makes my skin itch. Even the grumpy dragon hasn't pushed the limits this trip.

"Right, I'm going to get some rest before we get to the station then." I don't wait for anyone's reply, I just hurry out of the room, the itchy feeling easing the farther I get away from the two shifters.

"It's fine with strangers, but if our friends say no, they mean no." I try to convince the mimic side of me that forcing it is not the answer, but I'm not sure it totally gets it. There's this weird sensation, like it's rolling its eyes at me, but it settles down again, the itchy feeling dissipating completely.

I breathe out a sigh of relief, and the tension I was holding in my shoulders drains away. Once I get to the room that Xavier and I are sharing, and the door closes behind me, the rest of the anxiety I had been carrying slips away. I don't know what it is about those two, but I don't feel comfortable around them, and it's probably going to be worse now that I know they don't want to share their forms. I mean, logically I get it, but personally, I feel a little hurt. Logical Lila understands Silac's point of view. His snake could take over like Cas's kraken did and force a bond, an imprint, I think Tirrian called it. That would be a disaster if he has an arranged marriage, which in itself seems unfair, but who am I to judge what other species do? His poor fiancée would always have the ghost of me in the marriage, and there wouldn't be an option for his snake to imprint on her. I wonder if she's a naga like him. I got the impression that cross matings between species is still slightly frowned upon despite Cas's family being so open and welcoming.

I wonder if they have the same coloring or, if like krakens, the coloring ranges from person to person. I kind of secretly hope she's pink, which will clash horribly with his beautiful green, orange, and black.

And Tirrian! What is that asshole's problem? I mean, I don't want to shift into a beautiful, black, oil slick dragon with gorgeous pink wings anyway. I don't want to risk ending up with his dragon going all googly-eyed for me, not that I think there's any chance of that. He has been hostile since the moment we met. Fuck him and his misplaced loyalty to his cousin. Sure, I can be a little sympathetic if his internal beast is causing problems, God knows mine does, but it doesn't make me a raging cunt, so he should just chill the fuck out.

I cross the room and drop down onto the bed, lying back on the super comfortable mattress, but there's no point in closing my eyes and trying to sleep. My mind is racing, so I pick up my tablet and flick to the information about Fluxx shifters. I've read everything about krakens, but my curiosity about my two travel companions is piqued, so I scroll to the page about nagas and settle down to learn everything snaky. Dragons will be next. Just for research purposes of course. If I find one of each on the station to mimic, well, I'm going to need all the information I can find regarding their species, and it would be super cool to be able to fly. My Vilaxian flying hasn't gotten very far or been very successful, so having a beast that can do it may be an option.

CHAPTER FOURTEEN

Lila

Station X69 is noisy, loud, and crowded, and my skin starts to itch out of control. I'm scratching at my arms like a junky in need of a fix as we make our way through the teeming mass of beings, all trying to find some sort of entertainment or make a deal. I feel like I've been dropped smack-dab into a *Star Wars* movie. The circus has a variety of creatures, but nothing like here.

"You can find any form of entertainment imaginable here, from gambling and fighting to food and fucking," Xavier explains, keeping a tight grip on my arm as we enter an arena that we need to traverse to get to the private accommodation rooms he temporarily booked for us. I think they are intended for other use, but it's a private place for him to bring creatures to for me to mimic, so we'll make use of it the best we can.

I feel like a child in a candy store, all wide-eyed with excitement as I take in the sights and dubious smells of the station. The arena seats are filled with cheering and jeering creatures as we try to make our way around to the other side through the aisle, but I can't help but stop and check out what is keeping them so entertained. My mouth drops open, and I step closer to get a better look, leaning on one of the rails that's there to prevent the crowd from falling into the pit.

"Holy fuck, what the hell is that?" I ask, mesmerized by what is happening down on ground level.

Xavier peers over my shoulder and starts to chuckle. "Well, this is entertaining. We managed to get to see the annual Flobberstum mating challenge." He slides in next to me as I watch in amazement. Silac and Tirrian crowd in behind us. Both of them still wear their human glamour out of respect for my mimic abilities and not wanting to share them. I suggested they should stay behind, but Xavier wanted them with us for the intimidation factor. Despite being in their human glamour, both are formidable-looking men.

The crowd jeers and cheers, and I see exchanges between people. "What are they doing?"

I ask, pointing to someone farther around in the crowd.

"Placing bets on the outcome," Tirrian replies gruffly. He's closer to me than I expected, his words brushing against my ear, and I almost jump in shock.

"On what outcome?" I'm actually not a hundred percent sure I want to know. Are these death matches like the Romans used to have to entertain the masses? But as I turn my attention to the arena, it becomes achingly clear that a death match is not what we are about to witness.

The creatures entertaining us have no human-like features whatsoever. If I could describe them, I would say they are similar to something in a David Attenborough documentary about sea creatures. They are a large, flat and wide worm-like creature, with brilliant colors and patterns covering the backs of their bodies while their fronts are a smooth black. There are no discernible features, but as one of them stands upright, something seems to grow out of its body.

"Please, Lord, tell me that is not what I think it is," I say to Xavier, who just chuckles again.

"Flobberstums are neither male nor female, but both, and they cock fight to see who will bear their young each year. What you see are their mating swords, I guess for want of a better term. The first one to pierce their opponent, implanting their seed into the other, is the winner, and the loser is responsible for carrying their clutch to term."

I'm sure I look like a slack-jawed fool as I watch with complete fascination as the two creatures grow not one, not two, but a three-pronged cock much like a trident, and then they go for it. Writhing and twirling, each tries to stop the other from trying to pierce their skin. It's actually a magical, hypnotizing dance, their spectacular colors making them look like two Latin dancers doing some sensual tango of love.

"Would you like to find one of them for you to mimic?" Xavier asks as we watch one of them finally overpowers the other, stabbing its trident deep into its opponent. There is no sound, I'm not sure if they even have vocal cords, but as it pulls free, a trail of clear slime flows out of its trident and, well, I'm done.

"Fuck no. I don't see that form as having any benefit to me whatsoever," I reply as we start on our way again, leaving behind the cheering crowd. Money exchanges hands as people who bet on the outcome collect their winnings.

"Okay, so I have a list in my mind of potential beings that would be a big asset. The naga and dragon of course, but I thought if we could find a Barcoa, and all four kinds of Elementi, then that would be a good start," Xavier says, though I have no clue what any of those are.

"That's a good range, but I think we should see if there is a necro on the station too," Silac suggests, and I see Xavier mulling it over in his head.

"Yes, their ability to move through solid objects is a good skill to have, and who knows when she will need to communicate with or control the dead."

My eyes just about cross at the thought of three more alien races I know nothing about, but I trust Xavier and, to some extent, Silac to know what is best for me. It's just more research I need to do, and this time I will be vigilant.

We've made it to the other side of the arena, and we enter a causeway that has different venues on either side of it, all with bright neon flashing signs. Xavier points out the different establishments. There are casinos and gambling halls, restaurants, bars, clubs, and even a suva drug den, which is the drug that Caspian's family are the sole suppliers of. I can see people gathered around tables, sharing big, multi-hosed hookahs with a thick, red smoke floating out of the door.

The next establishment has me stopping dead— not from amazement, but complete curiosity. The big sign reads, "Pleasure Bot Industries sex robots for hire and sale," and in the doorway are a couple of giggling girls in lingerie and a ripped dude wearing just a pair of boxer briefs. They aren't interacting with the crowd so much as performing the same movements over and over again. I watch with fascination as a large, skeletal-like being walks up to one of the girls, and another person appears out of the doorway. This one has the same metallic sheen that Link has, so I'm assuming this one is a cyborg as opposed to the robot sex dolls that are there to entice the crowd. The skeletal being has a conversation with the cyborg who taps a tablet in his hand before one of the girls peels away from the others and sashays up to the skeletal being, grabbing his hand and disappearing behind the door with him. Right, a sex robot brothel, and it seems like they are happy to service anyone or anything.

"Come on, stop dawdling, we are on a tight timeline," Tirrian growls and gives me a little nudge in the back. I glare at him but don't bother arguing since he's not wrong.

We keep walking, and a few doors down, there is another sign for a brothel, but this one says it has live girls and boys for sex. And what do you know? Standing in the doorway, trying to entice clients, are two of Xavier's former harem members.

"Fucking hell," he grumbles as they catch sight of him, the light in their eyes turning hopeful as they call to him.

"Xavier, have you forgiven us? Have you come to return our powers and status to us?" one of them calls. She's the voluptuous redhead, but I can't remember either of their names. They leave the doorway and hurry over, shoving me out of the way, each desperately grabbing hold of one of his arms. I can't be annoyed in the face of this much desperation. It's really kind of pathetic.

"Please, oh please, at least return our healing powers so we can service more customers," the dark-haired one begs, and I can't stand the absurdness anymore.

"Just do it, Xavier. Look at them, they are a mess." Both girls look disheveled, and there are bruises all over their bodies, which I can see a lot of because neither are wearing more than panties and a scrap of see-through material.

Xavier sighs. "No, Nambra, I haven't forgiven you nor am I likely to." Their hopeful expressions fall. "But my intimate is too kind and wishes for me to return your healing ability, Lexus, so it will be done. It is linked with your warlock powers, so I will return both, but you will both remain banished. If either of you show your face on Westalin again, it will be the death penalty."

They exchange a glance and fall to their knees. "Oh, thank you. You are so merciful," Lexus grovels, kissing Xavier's feet despite the fact that I was the one who facilitated the return of their power.

"We hope that one day you will find it in your heart to allow us to return." Nambra pushes her luck, but Xavier just snorts and mutters, "Unlikely," under his breath.

I feel his power activate and watch as a sort of

peacefulness settles over their faces. Both of them seem to age backwards slightly, as if having their power returned made them younger somehow.

They scramble to their feet again, thanking him profusely before returning to the doorway of the brothel. They seem more confident and cocky now, and I don't think that bodes well for them if the other girls glaring at them have anything to do with it, but that is their problem, not ours.

"Come on," Tirrian growls again, and this time he takes me by the arm and drags me along. I guess he doesn't trust me not to get distracted again—not that it was my fault this time.

Again, I find myself grinding to a halt a little farther down the breezeway. Off to one side in a rough-looking dive bar, I spot a Madovian. It's the same Madovian we killed on the ship, with her blue snake appendages coming out of her head and her blue skin on display, though thankfully the outfit she's wearing covers that horrible stomach. Her small, bat-like wings are tucked in behind her, and her fangs are hidden behind a thin pair of lips beneath those terrifying nose slits. My heart starts to race, and anxiety goosebumps break out across my skin. Tirrian growls and turns to see what I'm looking at and freezes.

"Didn't we kill her?" I hiss at him, not sure what to do and hoping she doesn't recognize us as I look around for somewhere to hide, not even ashamed of my terrified reaction.

"Easy, *tián xīn*," he coos, his voice the gentlest I've ever heard it, and his grip on my arm tightens. "That is not who you think it is. She was well and truly dead. I made sure of it before we stuck her out the rubbish hatch. The Madovians are all very similar. There will be a slight difference to her scale pattern when she's shifted, but their coloring is mostly the same. Breathe easy."

My heart rate begins to slow again with his calm and gentle reassurance as Silac and Xavier catch up to us, and I start to make calculated plans. My previous idea may be able to come to fruition eventually, so I may as well prepare for it.

"That one," I say to Xavier, who frowns at me with confusion.

"What one?" he asks, looking around, so I point discreetly in the direction of the bar and snake woman.

"I want you to bring me that one to mimic," I tell my warlock fiancé, who finally catches on to whom I mean.

He starts to shake his head violently. "Absolutely not. No way. I know what you are planning, Lila, and I will not have it."

I whirl and place my hand on my hips, glaring at my warlock. "Are you seriously trying to be the boss of me right now? Because I don't believe I gave you permission."

"I don't need permission. You are my intimate, and your safety is my utmost priority."

"Isn't that why we are here? To find me creatures to mimic to give me every possible trick in my arsenal?" I counter, and he continues to argue. I can't see him due to that blasted mist he insists on wearing in public for intimidation, which has worked wonders for crowd control but also means I can't see the expression on his face. I bet he's wearing that condescending, all-knowing, cocky prick smile that makes me want to kick him in the nuts.

"Yes, but that is one trick you don't need in your arsenal. They are nasty creatures, and your idea of going undercover is asinine."

I growl at my fiancé. "We still have that communicator from when her room was tossed after we disposed of her. All we need to do is wait until they try to contact her, and we have an in with the Syndicate." I am determined to find out who else is a part of this group making a play for the orb and how they know the circus has it. I think that's even more important, as well as disposing of everyone who has that knowledge. I will do whatever it takes to protect my family.

"You know the girl's idea is solid, though it would probably be better for you to use your ability to glamour to infiltrate the Syndicate as opposed to sending her. She'd probably mate someone by accident."

I turn my glare on the stupid dragon. "Fuck you, Tirrian. I've just about had it with your aggressive as fuck comments. We've explained about Dylan, and you know I had no control over any of my matings except for Link. Why did you even come on this mission? You don't like me, so why even spend any more time with me than you have to? You could have just let Silac come on his own, but instead, you're hanging around like a bad smell."

Smoke starts to drift out of Tirrian's nose, and his skin flickers back and forth from his glamour to his half form as scales ripple across his arms.

"Ah, that's enough. How about you take a walk and cool down?" Silac steps between us, but before either of us can respond, something in the dingy dive bar draws my attention.

"Holy shit, no fucking way," I mutter, and everyone turns to look at what I'm staring at. "Speak of the devil and he shall appear."

CHAPTER FIFTEEN

Lila

"Is that…" Xavier trails off as Tirrian pushes past us and strides to the bar, his anger now directed at another target. Taking a seat at the table with the Madovian woman is none other than Tirrian's cousin Dylan—the same shifter who caused so many troubles and was booted off the circus for trying to attack me. His uncle, who is Tirrian's father and the king, had also banished him from Fluxx due to the shame he brought on their family.

I start to follow them over, but Silac grabs my arm. "If you go in there, you may mimic Dylan. I'm pretty sure you wouldn't want that reminder every time you shifted into a dragon form."

I shudder at the thought but shake his hand off my arm. "It seems like my mimic abilities are actually pretty choosy. The itchiness left my body the moment I saw him."

Silac frowns but releases my arm, and we follow Tirrian into the dive bar to hear Dylan greet Tirrian rather caustically.

"Well, look who it is. If it isn't my dear old cousin, the prince of the dragon shifters, and the warlock, the snake man, and the whore. My day just got a tiny bit shiny seeing you all here."

His sarcasm is thick and obvious, and we stay quiet, my attention locking onto the woman next to him. Tirrian starts to talk, but I ignore what he's saying and take in all I can of the other creature. I wonder if I can mimic this form and if I'll get the snake form as well. Oshan didn't mention it, but I'm assuming I can. I only have to mimic a shifter in half form to get the full range of abilities. The itchiness returns to my skin, but I rein it in, not allowing it to take over, but I hope I have enough of her features locked into my mind that once I get a moment alone, I can assume her form.

A gasp of shock has my attention returning to the conversation between Tirrian and Dylan.

"What the fuck happened to you?" Tirrian demands, and my mouth drops open in disgust as I catch sight of the other side of Dylan's face. He had been sitting, so we could only see one side of him. The other side is a mess of jagged, puckered scars, and his eye is completely white.

"Well, when you get banished from your home and you have no other skills but performing in a fucking circus, then you have to take whatever opportunities you can. Being a mercenary is a dangerous business, and sometimes you get hurt." The angry sarcasm must be a constant state now, or maybe it's just for us.

"Mercenary? You're a killer for hire." Tirrian sounds disgusted, but Dylan just shrugs.

"It pays well. Now why don't you fuck off? You are interrupting a business transaction, and we have nothing else to say to one another." Dylan has been surreptitiously side-eyeing me the whole time, but he hasn't actually addressed me apart from the first insult, so I see no need to involve myself in the conversation. Xavier's mist pulses aggressively next to me, and that might be a suitable deterrent.

The Madovian has been quiet this whole time, but now she bares her fangs and hisses, and I take a step back.

"I'll be letting my father know about this," Tirrian threatens, and Dylan snorts with amusement.

"Of course you will. Now run along, and I'd watch whose company you are keeping, Tirrian. I'm not sure whore Skarrians are a suitable match for a crown prince."

Dylan's last dig actually hits its mark as we walk away from the angry dragon. His words trigger a concern that has been on my mind almost constantly since I realized that my mates are powerful men. Saxon is the Villaxian queen's nephew, Xavier is Westalin's crown prince, and Maxsim is the leading matriarch of Iceen's son. Then there is Link, the heir to one of the biggest conglomerates in the galaxy. I'm sure they were all expected to have prestigious pairings suited to their stations, and yet all they have is me, and not only that, but they are also stuck in a harem of six men. Hardly prestigious. I'm just grateful Mira and Murphy were so accepting, and I guess Maxsim's mom too, since she gifted them to me, but I'm terrified about meeting the parents of my other mates, especially Link's mother who seems like a raving lunatic, sending her son approved fiancés.

"Lila, stop it." Xavier's hand reaches out of the mist and gives me a little squeeze. "I know what you're thinking, and none of it is true. My parents are going to love you, I promise."

"Stop with the mind reading crap," I mutter and shake him off.

"No, *phoeall*. How many times do I have to tell you that you just have a very expressive face? I've also met the Queen of Vilax, and she adores her two nephews almost as much as she does her own daughters. She wouldn't have sent the blood rose cup for you if she hadn't been thrilled. She would have denied him use of it, which would have been messy."

"If she had denied him, he would have died, so I'm not sure it had anything to do with being thrilled," I say dryly. I hear Silac and Tirrian talking quietly behind us, but I don't have any energy left to snoop.

"Let's get this done. I'm suddenly very keen to see the back of this station," I say as we finally make it to the accommodation suites.

Xavier puts his hand against the panel of the one we rented, and it opens up. We enter a lavish yet slightly gaudy room with a humongous bed as its center point, but the stripper pole with small stage and the giant, bubbling hot tub are also big selling points. I flop down on the large plush sectional sofa and grimace.

"How are we going to do this? It's a big place. How are you going to find what you want without people running scared from 'the warlock' approaching them?" I ask Xavier as he lets his mist recede, and he grins.

"Well, firstly, I'm going to do this." His body shimmers as he assumes a glamour, and I sit bolt upright when I see exactly what he's done. Gone is the beautiful lavender male, and in his place is the spitting image of Magenta. "And when they realize I'm Skarrian and down to fuck, I'm pretty sure I can get them to come with me, but in case they won't, I will mesmerize them and bring them here like that."

"Hey, are you implying my magenta-haired bestie is a slut?" I scold him, and he shrugs.

"Yeah, kind of, but only in the best way. She makes it clear that it's one night and one night only."

I narrow my eyes at that little bit of information. "Do you have firsthand knowledge of that?" I growl, and Tirrian and Silac chuckle as Xavier/Magenta holds his/her hands up defensively. It's really bizarre.

"No, I promise I haven't gone there. I had my harem, and there was Saxon if I had needs," he reminds me, and I'm not sure I'm any happier about the harem reminder, but I relax back again.

"Okay, fine, let's do this. What about you two?" I ask the two shifters, hoping the two of them will leave the room as well so I can try mimicking the snake woman.

"We will help Xavier scout. Our presence may scare off other dragons and nagas. Both of us are the top of the food chain so to speak, and we wouldn't want to intimidate potentials," Silac explains, and Tirrian just crosses his arms and grunts, still out of sorts after seeing his cousin, but then it really is his default mode, so maybe he's not. Who the fuck knows?

My heart rate picks up with excitement as Silac

tells me that, and his head cocks to the side. He must hear it. "Is everything okay?

"Yeah, yup, sure, I just want to get this done," I explain, not admitting the truth, otherwise they will never leave me.

"Okay, well, sit tight, because we may be a while. Like you said, it's a big station, but I think I saw a couple of Elementi as we made our way here," Magenta/Xavier tells me.

"And I definitely saw a Barcoa in the stands of the arena. They are usually pretty standoffish, but if you offer to suck the inside of their elbow for them, I'm pretty sure they'll be a sure thing," Silac says matter-of-factly. Suck the inside of their elbow? What the fuck are they making me mimic? I must look as confused as I feel.

"Barcoa are a slightly primitive warrior race that is big and beefy. They kind of look like rocks, but the texture of their skin is more like leather. They are not all that intelligent, but they are good at following orders and almost indestructible. They are often used as security guards for high profile people. They are humanoid in shape, but they have a centralized mouth situated on their stomach and they eat moss. The thing that makes them good at security is they have several decentralized eyes—one on their hand, one on either side of their head, and one on the back of their knee. It gives them three hundred and sixty degrees of vision. But their sexual organs are in their elbows, and they are both male and female. They have a vagina-like slit on one arm and a penis, which is retractable, on the other."

I'm almost speechless after Tirrian finishes describing the creature they want me to mimic. One, because I think he just spoke the most words he's ever said to me in one go, two, because there wasn't a hint of aggression, and three, what the fuck?

"And we think it will be an asset for me to mimic this?" I ask, and the three of them nod enthusiastically.

I blow out a big sigh and shrug. "Fine, whatever. You guys are the experts. I'm going to take a little nap and maybe make use of the replicator while I wait. Don't get lost," I caution them, leaning my head back and closing my eyes.

I wait until I hear the door close behind them, counting to one thousand before I allow my eyes to pop open again. I need to be quick, because for all I know, they stepped through the door and found their first victim immediately. I search the room for a mirror, and sure enough, there is a mirror above the bed almost as big as it is. I rush over to it and try to get a good look, but it hurts my neck to look at it standing, so I resign myself to lying on the bed. I make myself comfortable and picture the Madovian woman in my mind. It's weird, because since I awoke from being electrocuted, my memory has sharpened, and I retain images in my mind, so I have no trouble recalling what she looked like sitting next to Dylan in the booth of the dingy bar. It's almost like water flowing over me as my skin starts to itch again, and that develops into full body pins and needles. When I look once more in the mirror, I screech in fright. Looking back at me is an exact replica of both the woman we killed and the one I'd just seen, down to the cross-shaped slit in my now very naked stomach.

I take stock of how I'm feeling. My vision has sharpened, so I can see everything in the mirror, down to the tiny little scales of the serpents that are writhing on my head. Their hissing is loud in my newly sensitive ears, and my sense of smell has definitely increased. I can smell whatever cleaning product the housekeeping used on this room after the last guests. At least that's reassuring.

I reach up and poke a finger at one of the hissing snakes. It nips me, but it doesn't hurt. It then proceeds to affectionately lick the spot it nipped. I smile at it and almost shriek again at my mouth full of vicious fangs. Holy fuck, I look nasty, but then a feeling of aggression starts to roll through my body. A searing need to fuck causes throbbing inside my stomach slit, and I leap off the bed and start to pace back and forth across the room.

My mind starts to blur, and Lila seems to check

out as something else slips into the driver's seat. "That naga would make a good breeding partner. A strong incubator for my eggs, and a tasty snack for our babies once they hatch. The dragon would too, and I bet his cock is huge. I wonder if it is barbed like dragons are rumored to be. I'd love to feel that thrusting in and out of my sexual slit." The words are sibilant and rumbly as I try to wrestle back control. Holy fuck, this being is strong, and I understand what Oshan was cautioning me about, but I manage to slip back into the driver's seat, and as soon as I do, I imagine my real form. The same pins and needles sensation overtakes my body, but I shimmer, and when I look back down, my body has returned to its former shape.

"Fuck, that was weird." I flop back onto the bed again, not caring one little bit that I'm naked, despite Silac and Tirrian possibly returning at any moment. I need a few seconds to get my head on straight again. I was me, but I wasn't. Or was I? I think if I dig deep down into my psyche, she… me… whatever was only saying exactly how I feel. Silac does intrigue me, especially in his half form. He has two cocks, and I want to know what that feels like. And the dragon? Yeah, I can't help but think he's sexy despite his fucked up attitude. I mean, who wouldn't? With all that gorgeous, shimmery skin and those sexy pink wings, he's hot as fuck. I think my mimic side has her eye firmly set on those two despite neither of them having any interest in me at all, which is going to make things awkward. All I can do is continue to pretend to be disinterested.

The doors to the room whooshes open, and I lift my head. Of course I didn't even have time to find a robe.

"Lila, we found your first victim," Silac calls cheerfully as he and Tirrian manhandle a huge, rock-like creature into the room. The Barcoa, I'm assuming. They get it situated, and it seems to be in a bit of a trance before turning to face me. That's when they both recognize that I'm naked.

"Holy shit," Silac squeaks endearingly, but Tirrian narrows his eyes even further.

"What did you do?" Tirrian hurries toward me and hauls me up off the bed, shaking my body. "What have you done?" he demands again, his eyes roaming over my naked figure before meeting mine to glare at me. "You better have not done what I think you did."

CHAPTER SIXTEEN

Tirrian

I can't help the way my eyes scan the beautiful naked girl in front of me. She's not mine, and she never will be, but my dragons want her with a passion of two suns. They push to shift and shove our cock deep inside her luscious body, but I grit my teeth and force them back down. I'm not even sure how my attraction mark hasn't appeared on her shoulder yet, letting her know exactly how I feel. It must be through sheer stubborn will, especially now that I'm seeing all that gorgeous, naked skin. Her body has proof of her fertility in the silver marks over her stomach and hips, but they do nothing to turn me off. If anything, it's a bigger draw, and it's all I can do to stop my claws from popping through my fingertips as I shake this irresponsible woman.

I know what she's done. I could see it in her eyes while I was talking to Dylan, I was only half listening to what he was saying because I was so focused on where Lila had her attention.

"Hey, Tirrian, what are you doing? Leave poor Lila alone," Silac demands, but I won't turn away from the infuriating woman in my hands. I shake her again, her bountiful breast jiggling with the movements, drawing my attention once more. The ring of scars around one of her nipples almost makes me want to bare my own fangs and sink them into the opposite one. I wonder which of her mates marked her there. Probably one of the cats, judging by the shape of the scars, and I don't think any of the others have a full set of sharp teeth.

I shake my head to rid myself of the image of me biting Lila's nipple and focus on the problem at hand.

Hey! A voice pierces my mind, making me wince. *Get your hands off the lady.* The voice is deep and gruff and almost childlike, and I know it has got to be the Barcoa. Damn it. Why didn't we find Xavier and have him subdue it? *I want to fuck and can't fuck if you hurt her.*

Lila's eyes widen in panic, and she starts to wriggle in my arms, but I hold her tightly. She must have heard him in her mind too.

"Don't worry, you won't have to fuck him. I'll knock him out if I have to, or you could try mimicking the warlock and use his mesmerizing powers," I suggest quietly, and she stops struggling. "Don't get too relaxed, I know what you did. There is no reason for you to be naked unless you mimicked something."

"You don't know that." My friend puts his hand on my shoulder, but I shrug him off.

"Like hell I don't. She's reckless and stupid, and of course the moment she was alone, she mimicked the Madovian. It's what she wanted from the start. You heard her and Xavier arguing about it. He's a love blind idiot for not considering it and leaving someone to supervise her." Smoke drifts out of my nose as my anger returns.

"Let me go you, ballsack," she cries and kicks out, her leg connecting with my balls.

I drop her as I sink to my knees and moan as blistering pain shoots through my body. There's nothing worse than being kicked in the cock except being kicked in an erect cock.

I'm unable to stop the tears that well in my eyes from the excruciating pain she just inflicted on my person, but my dragons chuff, happy that their mate can defend herself, even from us. They are fucking idiots.

"Keep your hands to yourself, otherwise you'll lose them next time." Her eyes briefly change to slits, like the Madovian's, and my mouth drops open in shock. She should not be able to do that. A mimic is only supposed to be able to change into a full form. She should not be able to be part Skarrian, part Madovian. I made sure to read up on everything I could about mimics. My father's library had extensive information on the various powers that Skarrians can exhibit, even those thought to be extinct. I know all I can about whisperers and mimics. You know what they say about keeping your enemies closer, or that's what I keep trying to tell myself. Even now, in the face of seeing my cousin and how far he has fallen and knowing it is all her fault, I should hate her. I do, but there is a fine line between hate and lust, and I am walking that line like a man on a two-day bender.

She turns and flounces off, her scent of petrichor and freshly baked bread hitting my nose. I can't stop the growl that rumbles up and out of my chest. Luckily she mistakes it for annoyance and flips me the bird before slamming the door to the bathroom closed behind her.

"Hell, Tirrian, what was that?" Silac asks as he tries to settle the Barcoa, whose eye in the middle of his head is clearly glaring at me.

"You didn't notice she was naked?" I shuffle to my feet, my balls still firmly cupped in my hands, the ache nowhere near gone yet.

Silac snorts. "Fuck, man, it's all I could do not to stare."

"Well, why do you think she was naked?" I ask

him, trying to get him to come to the same conclusion as me.

"I don't know, because she was preparing to mimic the beings we brought her?" he suggests, but then his eyes widen as all the pieces snap into place. "Or she already did. She wouldn't have, would she?" he asks, his eyes wide as he looks toward the bathroom door like he can see her on the other side.

"You bet your sweet snake tail she would." I go over and bang on the door.

"Get your cute ass out here, Lila. You can't avoid this forever," I call. The door opens as I go to raise my fist again, and out steps Lila, now covered by a robe. It's not much better than being naked, because it's almost translucent.

She puts one hand on her hip and starts jabbing my chest with one finger. "Now hear me. I will do what I think is best to protect my family and the—" She breaks off, her eyes wide before slamming her lips shut. "Circus," she finally says. "And if it means that I need to have a repulsive creature like that as one of my forms, then so be it. I bet she would do some damage if I unleashed her on our enemies, and if it allows me to go undercover to find out exactly who the Syndicate is and what they want, then I am going to take the chance. I am not going to spend the next few years looking over our shoulders, constantly worrying about who and what might be coming for us. Now, the sooner we can finish that, the better, and none of you were going to help, so I took matters into my own hands." She's breathing heavily, and her chest is flush with mine now, her eyes alight with anger. I can feel the rise and fall of her breasts against my shirt-covered chest, and it takes all of my strength not to sweep her up into my arms and kiss her hard. Fucking dragons, making me stupid.

"Just as I suspected, you're selfish and uncaring about what your mates and grandpas or children might think. They only just found you, and fuck, Xavier isn't even mated to you yet. Haven't you realized that if you die, Saxon will become a casualty too?" I lash out, my own fear influencing my reactions instead of cool-headed logic.

The anger in her eyes fades and is replaced with guilt and sadness, which then triggers my own guilt and sadness. Fuck. I whirl around and move over to the Barcoa. "Let's get this done, and we can talk about the other thing after we are on our way to Rilu. We are running out of time." My tone is gruff and annoyed, but Silac and his damn reptilian vision still catches sight of my guilt and nods knowingly. Asshole.

I take the Barcoa by the arm and lead it over to the annoying woman. Its stomach mouth pulses, looking like a pair of lips, or an asshole, puckering up. It puts its hands out, exposing its elbow creases. One has a shimmer of lubrication around the slit that's in it, and the other has a bulge that is starting to undulate. Fucking hell, this creature thinks it is here to fuck. That was not the right approach.

Lila ducks its grabby hands, and I watch in fascination as her body shimmers and her skin turns a pale lavender color just like the warlock's. She also has the same silvery markings he has in the same places on her body. Her robe actually stays in place this time, which, again, is another thing that is not supposed to happen. The change is supposed to destroy whatever she is wearing. Maybe she mimicked the spell Xavier put on their babies' clothes when he'd grown frustrated with them destroying them. My father is going to go into business with both him and Caspian's parents to provide this for all shifter children.

I observe as the two of them have a private, telepathic conversation, or I think they are. Her facial expressions are hilarious, but I will not indulge her by laughing. She doesn't deserve my humor. Finally, the big creature relaxes, dropping both arms, and sort of just stands there.

"Phew, that was tricky, but I managed to mesmerize it. Its mind was weird, almost childlike, but then it wanted to fuck. It was awful." She shudders and looks down at herself before looking back at both of us. "Okay. I'm going to mimic it. I thought I might lose the robe when I took on the warlock form, so I'm hoping it will stay for the next one too," she says hopefully, and Silac shakes his head.

"Lila, the size difference between the two of you is huge. The robe will not be big enough."

She rolls her eyes and huffs, "Fine," before stripping again, not concerned with her nudity one little bit.

A growl rumbles out of me, and smoke billows from my nostrils.

"Close your eyes if you're offended. I don't have time to deal with your prudish sensibilities." She waves me off, and I just about let go of the Barcoa in shock. I see Silac shake with barely controlled laughter, but Lila isn't paying attention.

"Shut up," I mouth at my asshole friend who just grabs his stomach and keeps chortling.

Lila's whole body is lavender with the silver warlock markings all over it, and her hair is a deeper shade of purple with pink highlights throughout it. There is no hair covering any other parts of her body, and her mound has a silver swirl that looks like a target on it. It's practically showing me exactly where I need to put my tongue to give her the most pleasure, at least in that form. I desperately want to see her in dragon form. Unlike Silac, there really isn't anything stopping me from letting her mimic me, but I know if that happens, my dragons will push forward and there will be no way I will stop them from sealing a mate bond. I can't let that happen. I am the future king of the dragons, and I need a purebred heir.

She can give you pure, one of my inner dragons snarls, but I shake my head and ignore him. *I will kill any dragon you put in front of her,* he warns me, but again, I ignore him as Lila's body starts to shimmer.

She grimaces in pain as a shimmery, metallic, sparkly mist shrouds her body from our sight, but within the mist, we see a shadow, and that shadow grows up and out. Her features lengthen or shrink as needed, and when the mist finally fades, standing in front of me is almost an exact replica of the Barcoa I'm holding—except the eye. The one eye I can see is the same green as Lila's.

Holy fuck, this is weird. Barcoa Lila holds out her hand with the eye on it, waving it around as both Silac and I clap our hands over our ears at the sound of her voice in our minds.

"Shit, turn the volume down," I say out loud, and the stomach mouth purses.

Sorry, she says quieter, but she also takes a step toward me, both hands coming out and turning grabby. *Me want to fuck. You suck my elbow dick?*

I stare at her in shock as she comes closer, her elbow penis pushing out of the crease, and unlike the rest of her stony, gray body, it's bright yellow. I'm so shocked I don't move in time as she offers her arm to my mouth.

"What the actual fuck?" Xavier's voice finally

knocks me out of my trance, and I whirl to see him staring at the four of us. Behind him are two creatures. I think they are Elementi, but he's obviously already mesmerized them, because there is no intelligence in either of their eyes.

Distracted by Xavier, I don't notice Lila has reached me until one of her arms wraps around me from behind, her elbow in line with my mouth, and her yellow dick pushes against my lips for entrance.

"Aggghhh!" I shout and go to push her away, but I opened my mouth when I screamed, and the Barcoa cock slips in. I reach up and grab her arm, but not before I catch a taste of the Barcoa cock. It's earthy and mossy and gross, and my stomach rolls with disgust. I'm not opposed to sucking cock, but only ones I choose to.

I wrestle Lila. She's strong in this form, and we go down hard, smashing the coffee table into splinters as we land on top of it. She continues to try and mouth rape me while the other two look on with a sick fascination and no fucking help whatsoever.

Just a little taste, Lila's Barcoa voice begs inside my head.

"Lila, stop it. Get a hold of yourself. Don't let your inner beast rule your actions." Silac has finally gotten control of himself and has decided to help. "I know it can be hard, but it needs to be you in the driver's seat, or a merged version of both of you.

What you are doing is rape, and you're no better than that Madovian from the ship." That finally has her freezing, and I can almost feel her inner struggle.

Oh my god, Tirrian, will you ever forgive me? Lila sounds mortified as she releases me from her arms and legs and scrambles backward. Her body shimmers, and once again, Lila, Earth Lila, is there, naked and shaking, her arms wrapped around her knees as tears drip down her face.

"Oh baby, it's okay." Xavier hurries over to her, waving his hand and covering her with a robe, this one completely opaque to give her a small modicum of modesty despite everything that has happened.

"What did I do? That was not okay. When I first mimic a creature, it's like I completely merge myself into their being. I wanted to fuck, and I didn't understand that he didn't want to."

Xavier glares at Silac and me as I pull myself up and out of the mess of furniture. "That might be our fault." I grimace and smooth down my clothes, brushing off the remnants of the destroyed coffee table, trying to avoid the death glare the warlock is aiming at us. "We told him that if he came with us, he would have sex."

"What the fuck for? Why didn't you have Silac mesmerize him? Isn't that a naga skill?" Xavier demands, and I gesture to my friend to explain.

"A Barcoa's mental capacity isn't great to start with, so there was a chance that if I did trance him that I wouldn't be able to release him from that. There's a fine line between my powers of mesmerizing and killing someone. If they aren't mentally strong, well, it's usually instant death, and I need to be in half form to do it."

Xavier huffs out an exasperated sigh. "Fine, I guess that sounds reasonable. I will bring them all here. You stay and make sure Lila is okay." He turns to the woman in his arms. "And baby, you need to be strong of mind. I can imagine it is overwhelming, but if you can get into the driver's seat, or at least quickly come to a shared arrangement with your inner creature, I'm sure using their powers will be much more harmonious."

"Shit, that's easy for you to say, you're not the one experiencing it. What is it with all these creatures that fucking is at the forefront of their minds?"

"Reproduction is as essential as breathing," Silac tells her, "and most creatures aren't afraid to indulge in pleasure when they feel like it. It's healthy, and as long as everyone is aware of limits before things kick off, then why not have fun?"

"It's so different from Earth. I mean, it can't be the only planet out there with more restricted views."

"No, of course not. There is one planet whose inhabitants think they are above bodily pleasure and reproduce using technology, though there is a roaring underground trade for pleasure of the flesh, so I'm not sure how successful that is. There is, however, a heavy penalty if you become pregnant outside of a lab, and the child will be taken and raised by a government facility," Xavier tells her, and she scrunches up her nose.

"I'm not sure that's something to strive for."

He helps her to his feet. "Okay, how about I watch as you assume these two forms." He points to the two beings that he brought with him. "And then I will return all three of them outside and keep searching."

Lila straightens out the robe Xavier conjured for her and blows out a large sigh.

"Yeah, okay, let's do this. I'm ready to go to Rilu and then go home. I miss everyone."

CHAPTER SEVENTEEN

Lila

My attention turns to the two beings Xavier found. "Okay, tell me about these two while I psych myself up again," I request, stalling for time. I need to know a little more before I just mimic them. I think that might help immensely.

Xavier has them step around the Barcoa, putting them front and center for us all to see. "These are two types of Elementi—earth and fire," he says, gesturing to each creature. The earth Elementi has antler style horns and a tail with the end fanning out like a leaf. On his back, I see wings that are also leaf-shaped and double-fanned. His skin tone is mottled shades of green. He is fine and almost fairy-like in stature, with long, lithe limbs despite his shorter build.

"Okay, and tell me about this guy first," I ask him, and he quickly explains.

"He is an Elementi who has control over elements related to the earth, which means you can manipulate, reshape, and control earth elements at will, including all crystals, metals, and minerals. You can make and command golems, which gives you access to an entire army of beings at your command. Another useful skill is that you can create tunnels in the ground to transport yourself. Something both of these creatures share is the ability to create, control, and manipulate volcanoes, lava, and magma, and in addition to this form, they also have another form that's like a bear, but green with antlers, wings, and a tail. They are also herbivores."

Xavier prattles off a list of eye-opening attributes and I'm kind of excited to assume this form but there is one question I need to ask.

"And how do they breed? Do they have fated mates?" Those are two things I want to know more than anything else.

Xavier grimaces. "They do have fated mates, but they are rare and only found within their own kind, so usually it will be a life partner pairing with no cosmic and divine intervention. However, although it isn't forbidden to have sex outside of their own kind, it is frowned upon to choose a life partner of a different element, and any children born from a nonmatched union will result in the child taking on only one element of its parents. Those kinds of pairings are often seen as outcasts in the community. In fact, on the planet Elemental, there is a whole city made up of odd pairings, as they are often shunned by their birth families."

"Okay, so I should be fairly safe in mimicking them. I'm not going to jump any of you after I do?" I want to double-check, and Xavier shakes his head.

"No, Elementi need to breed with Elementi. Children won't happen with another species."

"Okay, cool, I've got this then." I wipe my sweaty palms against the robe before pulling on the tie and dropping it again. There is no point in destroying it. I'll need something to cover up with later.

I step closer to the earth Elementi and try to capture all of his likeness inside my mind. The itch that signals my mimic abilities starts to activate, followed by the painful pins and needles. The now familiar mist covers my body as I feel myself start to shift. Antlers grow out of my head as my skin changes to pretty shades of pale green. My breasts start to shrink, and my body becomes smaller. A pain at the base of my spine signals the tail growth, and wings burst out of my back with a searing bite of pain. My mind whirls as I wrestle with the new being inside me. This being isn't as aggressive as the Madovian or as childlike as the Barcoa. It's intelligent and quick, and it settles down almost instantly, allowing us to act in harmony.

I open my eyes as the mist recedes and look around the room. My eyesight has stayed the same, as has my hearing and sense of smell, but there is an internal beacon that allows me to feel any earth elements around me. You would think that would be difficult on a metal space station in the middle of the galaxy, but I can feel each individual metal element that makes up the structure of this floating den of iniquity—elements that are not familiar to the earth side of me, but the Elementi is very familiar with. It's like I don't just assimilate their body but their knowledge as well, or lack thereof as the Barcoa proved. I could reach out right now and rip a hole in the hull of this vessel if I wanted to with my mind. There's also a small amount of nausea, which I also know comes from the fact that this Elementi has been in space for an extended amount of time, and that it needs to immerse itself in the ground to revitalize and renourish its body.

I run my hands over the antlers sticking out of my head, marveling at the velvety surface and the steel tough core. I thought they might be a little flexible, but they are as strong as steel. Next, my hands drift down my body, and I flick my tail out beside myself to get a good look. Unlike my fur-covered lightning cat tail, this one is covered in the same velvet as my antlers and has a fanned leaf at the end of it. Reaching back, I run my hands over my satin soft wings, sure that there is no way they are going to be able to let me fly. There are only thin, vein-like supports running through the middle like a real leaf.

I can't help but hope, though, so I take a step forward and think about flying. My wings spread open and start to flutter, and I feel myself rise from the ground as a huge smile crosses my lips. Unlike flying with Saxon, I feel graceful and light, and it is easy to maneuver up and down and back and forth. I drop back to my feet and smile at the guys. "This is awesome."

I see the three of them heave sighs of relief. They must have all been waiting for something to go wrong.

"Oshan said that once you mimicked a creature you should be able to assume male or female forms. Why don't you give it a go and change into a female?"

I frown and look down at my naked body, and sure enough, there's a fairly decent-sized cock hanging between my legs that I hadn't noticed with all the other added bits.

"Okay, hang on." I imagine the cock disappearing and my pussy returning at the same time as I think about my breasts growing.

This all happens rather quickly, almost instantly, and in the time it takes for the hair on my head to lengthen into a long, green mass of curls, I've gone from male to female. I hold my hands out and do a twirl, not self-conscious about my naked body. Silac stares for a moment before averting his eyes, but Tirrian just grunts. He's gone back to his usual self, but I know it's just a matter of time before he tells Xavier what I did. How the fuck he knew, I have no idea, but I will defend my decision to Xavier the same way I did with him.

I hold my arms out once I feel the change stop. "What do you think?" I look down my body. Unlike my normal figure, this one stayed slight and lean, and the breasts are small and bud-like, hardly enough to fill a large hand, but the stomach is flat and there is no hair on my mound.

Xavier has his mischievous smile on his face. "You're like a one-woman harem. It's going to be so much fun having you as a mate."

I roll my eyes playfully at him, smiling so he knows I'm not annoyed. I mean, he's not wrong. All the potential fun and games we can have in the bedroom with my different forms will ensure my love life is never going to get boring, even with six mates.

"Okay, now this one. We're on a deadline." Tirrian shoves the poor fire Elementi forward. He stumbles in his trance, and Silac lunges as Xavier growls at the stupid dragon.

"Hey, stop it. I want to return them in one piece please."

Tirrian rolls his eyes but steadies the fire Elementi. "Hurry up. We've run out of time. We need to get going if we want to make it to Rilu in time for the flower to bloom."

"Okay, I'll return that one and wipe its mind of any interaction or memory of us, while one of you tells her about this one, then I'll be back," Xavier instructs Silac and Tirrian, who quickly agree. He disappears with the Barcoa following woodenly behind him, still completely mesmerized.

"Alright, lay it on me. Tell me about this one." Unlike the body I'm still wearing, this one is

devil red in color, and its wings are more bat-like and have a smoky shimmer to them. The horns on this one's head kind of look like molten lava, and its tail has flames on the end of it.

"Fire Elementi are all solid colors. This one is red, obviously, but they come in amber, orange, and yellow as well, but the color is solid, unlike the mottled shades of the Earth Elementi. The wings will flame up when you use them, and your body can withstand any sort of flame or fire. They also have a second form, where the wings, horns, and tail stay the same, but they get a lot bigger and more gray in color and have cracks in the skin that look like lava. They are meat eaters. They can eat vegetation, but they prefer meat," Silac explains.

"And what can they do apart from flame on?" I ask, and both guys look confused. Okay, not Marvel movie fans then.

"Well, they can create, control, and manipulate anything fire and heat related, including plasma, as well as the volcano ability that Xavier told you the earth Elementi share with the fire ones. But what's really cool is that you can generate and control a magical fire that will do your bidding."

"Do my bidding?" I'm completely enthralled and fascinated now.

"Yeah. Say you wanted to burn down a building in a town far away. You would create a firestorm and command it, and it would move to that location and do as instructed."

"Like a sentient being?" I ask, awed, and Silac nods his head.

"Yeah, and then there's also control over fireworks and the ability to teleport through fire and, my personal favorite, self-detonation."

"What is that?"

"You can blow yourself up like a bomb and then your body reforms. It's phoenix-like powers, and it's awesome."

I smile at his enthusiasm, but Tirrian just grunts. Silac's eyes narrow, and his awe turns to mischief.

"Oh, and then there's Tirrian's favorite power. You can breathe fire."

Tirrian scowls at the snake man and flips him off when Silac starts to chuckle. He is a shit stirrer.

"These are awesome powers. Okay, let's do this."

Silac and Tirrian move backward.

"Try not to kill us," Tirrian says dryly.

I ignore him but angle my body more toward him rather than Silac. If anyone can survive out of control flames, it's going to be the fire-breathing dragon. I don't like the idea of roast snake. I saw it on TV once before, and it made me feel sad, not to mention I gagged when someone ate it.

I scan the fire Elementi, making sure I have all his features locked into my mind as the itch activates and I'm shrouded in mist. My body starts to change, but this one is not as dramatic as my change from human to Elementi. I guess only a few things had to change around this time. An inferno rages through my body, and unlike the calm, gentle emotions of the Earth Elementi, this one is angry and aggressive, and before I can stop myself, I raise my arms and feel my body engulf in flames. The sound is like a firestorm in my ears, loud and crackling. I can see through the flames, and I watch as Silac puts his hands up against the heat I'm producing and steps backward, grabbing hold of the two frozen Elementi and dragging them out of the line of fire.

Tirrian stands his ground, approval showing in

his normal expression of disdain. He steps forward, raising his hands like he's trying to calm a wild animal. "Come now, *tián xīn*. I know the fire feels good and makes you feel invincible, but you need to let the flames die. You don't want to hurt everyone in the room," he coos, and his words wrap around me, causing a shiver of something to spear down my spine. His own eyes are glowing now, and he drops his glamour, showing me his half form. His beautiful pink wings arch high above his body, shielding the people behind him.

"Can't," I grit out. "It wants to burn down the world and everyone in it." It's all I can do to hold myself immobile and not start splashing fire all around the room.

"Yes, it's no wonder with everything that has happened to you in such a short period of time. I'm not surprised there's a whole heap of hidden, angry emotions inside you, and that is what the fire Elementi is feeding on. Try thinking happy things." He's so close to me now, he almost has to be burning, but he just grimaces and grits his teeth and pushes through the flames, wrapping his arms around me and holding me tightly. "Think of your babies and your mates, and saving John Adams. They need to be your priorities. Think about how they all make you feel."

His embrace is tight and strong, and it allows me to feel a little more grounded, helping those happy thoughts and memories take root inside my mind. Bit by bit, the flames recede until they completely extinguish, leaving me panting and breathless from the struggle. I slump in Tirrian's arms, and he scoops me up and hurries over to the bed, placing me on it. He pushes my sweat-soaked red hair back from my face, his finger brushing one of my horns as he does. I almost moan at the exquisite pleasure his touch evokes, but I manage to swallow it down at the last moment.

"Good girl. That's it, just catch your breath, and I will get you something to drink." The look in his eyes is softer than anything I've seen from him before, but he turns away before I can work out what it is.

"Whoa, I think it's safe to say you are one powerful entity," Silac says from his safe place across the room.

"Maybe too powerful," Tirrian remarks as he programs the room's replicator to get me a drink. He returns holding out a bottle, and all signs of affection or softness have disappeared, replaced with the same look of disdain that is always in his eyes when he looks at me. "Here, this is a drink we give our young dragons when they are learning to control their fire breathing. It helps replace the nutrients and electrolytes you sweated out."

I take the offered bottle and, without even blinking, down the sweet but salty mixture. It's not pleasant but not horrible either.

"Thank you," I tell him, wiping my mouth with the back of my hand. "I will need to practice with each of these forms, but I think I've got them locked in."

"Good. I will take these two out and see if I can track down the warlock to wipe their memories. I will meet you two back at the ship. We need to be back on the mission." Tirrian turns and leaves, his half form dissolving behind his glamour again. I watch his back as he herds the two Elementi out of the room, the door closing silently behind them.

"Did you feel the urge to take his form?" Silac asks, grabbing my robe off the floor and hurrying over to me.

Oh right. I'm still butt naked. I gaze down at my body, getting a better look at this form now that I'm no longer shrouded in flames. Okay, so same kind of body type. Good to know. I let the form slide away, my original one taking front and center once more, and gratefully take the robe from Silac, wrapping it around my body. "Not really, I was too distracted by not wanting to burn everything down."

He heaves a sigh of relief. "Okay, good."

A pang of disappointment prickles at me, but I push it away. *I'm sure there are plenty of dragons who would be happy for you to mimic them, stop being so silly*, I tell myself, but I mean, none of them are really volunteering for the job, are they? Thankfully I don't actually steal their minds as well as their bodies and traits. I'm still mostly me, and the inner beast is a completely new entity. It would be horrible if the whole being transferred over. It would be like having a million different personalities, and it's hard enough with my kraken and whisperer. Shit, I wonder if I will end up with inner beasts if I mimic another shifter too.

That's a problem for future Lila. Current Lila needs a stiff drink and a nap. Some blood will probably be good too. There's a bag of Saxon's on the ship. He gave me plenty for Rilu, but told me I may need to assume one of my other forms because my DNA is part Vilaxian now. The almost unending daylight might be a problem for me also. Once we hit the caverns, I should be okay. Xavier and I were planning on snatching a Rilu native for me to mimic once we got there, or that was the plan, but I'm pretty sure the Barcoa or either one of the Elementi will be useful on the desert planet as well.

"Well, come on then. Let's not keep our surly dragon waiting. I wouldn't want him to shift and eat me before I can at least save Grandpa John," I joke to lighten the mood as I tighten the robe around me. I could shift to warlock form and conjure more clothes, but I'm incredibly tired all of a sudden. That's something to talk to the guys about. This mimic stuff is going to be useless if I can't actually use any of the forms because changing into them tires me out.

"Oh, I'm sure he wants to eat you, I just think he's at war with himself regarding which way," Silac jokes, following behind me.

"Yeah, and I'm pretty sure Rilu would need to turn into Iceen before that way was anything other than chewing on my bones."

CHAPTER EIGHTEEN

Lila

I've spent the last three days trying to master the abilities from each of the creatures I mimicked. My grandpas' personal ship has a well-equipped gym that Xavier moved all the equipment out of and then basically bombproofed everything so I could practice.

When I wasn't practicing physically, I was reading or watching videos of each different species. Tirrian made me admit to Xavier that I had also mimicked the Madovian, and after much ranting and raving from him, I also had to study them. Now that was nauseating. I think he found the grossest and ugliest stories or information he could find on them just to punish me, or maybe there isn't a single redeeming quality in the whole race. Who knows, but if they suddenly disappeared from the galaxy, I don't think anyone would be upset.

I am now pretty proficient on lightning cat, both Elementi, the Barcoa, and warlock abilities, as well as the Celestian I accidentally mimicked when it first happened. Their healing ability came in handy when I accidentally burnt Xavier when my fire Elementi became a tad angry again. It's the dragon's fault. He was there, deliberately trying to make me mad so I could learn to control it. I didn't practice my Aquilian abilities, though, because there was no pool for me to be able to change into that form, so that's a problem for another day. Xavier has become a drill sergeant, and not even my naked body between shifts could distract him from the task at hand. Apparently I had involuntarily shifted into a couple of others when I'd first been struck by lightning, but no matter how hard I tried, I couldn't recreate it. Silac suggested that maybe it was because I didn't actually see them and have not been able to lock their form into my mind. I mean, it makes sense.

I'm still short two Elementi, a dragon, a naga, and the mysterious necro they talked about, but there will be other opportunities to find willing or not so willing volunteers.

I pull the last bag of Saxon's blood out of the fridge and stick it in the replicator to heat. I've gone through a lot more than we anticipated, my mimic abilities needing even more than I normally would. I am going to have to feed from Xavier while we are here, but hopefully not so heavily that he becomes incapacitated. He muttered something about asking the dragon and snake to donate, but I haven't heard anything about it, so I'm assuming they declined. Maybe we can buy some bagged blood somewhere in Rilu.

The replicator beeps, signaling that it finished heating the blood, and I pull out the mug before taking a seat on the couch in the living/dining area of the ship. I watch in fascination as the ship approaches the landing pad in one of the only cities on Rilu. Bright orange sand stretches as far as the eye can see, and smack-dab in the middle is a futuristic-looking city with tall buildings all made from a glinting silver metal and glass.

Silac told me it's their main trading hub and is mostly for tourists and businesspeople. It's the heart of their gem trading business. The mines of Rilu are so prolific, they never expect to run out of the precious resources. Something about the desert sand keeps the gems perpetually growing. Once one mine has been exhausted, they move onto another. In a few years, they will be able to return to the previously exhausted mine and start all over again.

Most of the residents of Rilu are miners and larnuk traders, and they live in small nomadic villages much like the bedouin from Earth. We will be traveling from the city to the small oasis that sits above the gem mine that we need. Zala will be meeting us there, but she has a contact in the city meeting us to help us with the journey across the barren, ever changing sands.

I feel our ship set down and hear the now familiar sound of clamps securing us in place as I take a sip of the delicious, rich, spicy blood of my mate. A pang of yearning hits me as his flavor crosses my taste buds, and I feel a tear form in my eye. I've been separated from the rest of them for five days now, and the ache in my soul is fierce. The quicker we can get this job done, the better, but somehow, I doubt it's going to be straightforward and easy—when is it ever?

I drain the blood, and the familiar buzz it gives me starts to race through my body, making me ready to face what is to come. Putting down the glass, I stand up and run my hands over the outfit Xavier produced for me to wear on Rilu. I feel like a harem girl. It's one long piece of material that wraps around my body and ties around my neck, creating a loose dress that covers me from head to toe. There's also a separate piece that wraps around my head to protect my face and shoulders from the blowing sands. It has a pretty pattern on it in orange, reds, and yellows. Xavier said it's what most desert people wear to protect and camouflage them against the sand and the major predator that roams the desert, which is an honest to goodness sand-worm, just like from *Dune*. Well, kind of. This one apparently looks more like a hairy millipede with millions of legs, and it spits lightning and is mostly blind, which is why it's attracted to vibrations in the sand. I've been told that if we come across one to stand very still. With their terrible eyesight, they get blinded by the sun, so they rely on movement and a lucky strike of their lightning to hunt. We don't have time for sandworm encounters, though, so I'm praying I won't come across one, but the plan is to change into lightning cat form if we do and fight lightning with lightning.

Apparently there are certain paths through the desert that a knowledgeable guide will be able to lead us through. These paths follow a limestone ridge, and as such, there is no sand flowing under-neath them. If we were to venture off these paths, then we'd become fair game to the sandworms, who restlessly hunt the desert in search of meat to sustain them and their families.

"Are you ready?" Xavier asks as he enters the room. He's wearing a similar form of dress, but he has pants under his. I asked him why he didn't give me any, and he winked and told me he liked the teasing glances he got when I walked and my legs became exposed. I replied that I better not get sand rash anywhere important, and he provided a pair of

Lycra shorts for me, which I accepted as a compromise.

"Yes, let's do this. I miss our family, and I want to get Grandpa John sorted so we can get the circus back on the road."

"I wouldn't worry too much. I'm sure the performers are all enjoying the impromptu paid holiday, but I agree about the rest. I miss the devil spawn. Who would have thought that I would miss having them wake me so early in the morning?"

"It's because they wake you with love and kisses and hugs. Don't think I haven't heard the giggles coming from your room in the morning. You love it as much as they do."

He pretends he is unaffected by our children, but he adores them, and one day, I can't wait to give him one of his own. His grin is huge, and he doesn't argue about it. He just holds out his hand. It's then I notice a slight tremor in it.

"Are you okay? Do you need to feed?"

He shrugs. "The station was a riot of emotions, and I fed deeply, but it is starting to wear off."

"I would have thought that with Tirrian and me at each other's throats all the time, there would have been plenty for you to feed from," I say as we make our way to the exit of the ship.

"You know I don't like to feed from individuals without permission. The station was different, but

Tirrian hasn't given me permission to feed from him."

I raise my eyebrows in surprise. "You asked?"

"Yes. When we first left Skarr, I asked both of them if they would allow it. Neither of them were keen, much like they don't want you to mimic them." He sounds thoughtful.

"Why do you think that is?"

"You mean apart from the dragon being an asshole? I would guess it's because they don't want me to know how they are feeling."

"Can't you just feel that anyway?" I ask him. When we were practicing, I was bombarded with everything he was feeling, which was mostly frustration and a heavy dose of lust.

"No, I have enough control that I can lock that down. You will too eventually. It's an invasion of privacy when you think about it. It's like being able to read someone's thoughts."

"Yeah, I guess it would be. I know I try to hide what I'm feeling at times so I don't upset or influence anyone. I hadn't thought about it that way. Is that why you wouldn't let them in the room while I was mimicking a warlock? You know I got nothing off them the other day at the station when I did."

"I'm guessing you were pretty distracted by everything else that was going on that you didn't even pay attention. Had you, you would have picked up a lot more," he explains as we arrive at the now open boarding door. Silac and Tirrian are already waiting down at the bottom of the stairs, and I can feel a hot, dry blast of air coming through the open doorway.

"Whoa, that is hot." I put my hand up against the blowing breeze. "Very different from the weather on Skarr at the moment. What are you going to do? Would you like a quickie before we get going so you can top up?" I ask him, putting my hand out to stop him from leaving the ship. "I'm sure the guys can occupy themselves while we knock out a fast one."

Xavier chuckles. "I'll be okay. We are meeting our contact in the local gem and trading market, so there will be plenty for me to feed from there. I'm hoping we can find a moment to mimic one of the natives here too, so you can make use of their tolerance to the heat while we are here."

"Okay, but let me know if you have needs. Even a quick blow job will at least be a snack." I mean, it's no hardship to take one for the team. Xavier is delicious, and I would happily suck his dick any day of the week.

"Of course, my *phoeall*, and let me know if you need blood. I know you just drank the last bag. While we are at the markets, I will make inquiries about getting us some more. I will not be able to sustain you and stay healthy with the amount you are drinking now."

"I will. When I called home last night to speak to everyone, I asked Saxon and Link to continue bagging his for me. He has an overabundance without me there to feed from him, and like you said, I'm drinking more than normal with my new abilities. It's not going to hurt to have extra bags at home."

Xavier presses a kiss to my forehead. "Good thinking. Come on, methinks the dragon grows impatient."

I snort. "When is he not?"

We make our way down the stairs, and Tirrian turns and leads us forward. The spaceport isn't all that crowded. To be honest, apart from us and a few staff, there aren't many people around. One person came over and checked our landing permission when we first arrived, but Silac and Tirrian dealt with that. They say that you need special permission to land on Rilu, and it is hard to obtain.

"Have you been to Rilu before?" I call to him since he seems to know where he is going. "William and Eric thought that maybe Xavier wouldn't be allowed in the market, and that they are wary of strangers."

"Yes, the dragons trade with the Rilunese regularly," he says gruffly without turning around, and Silac turns and smiles.

"Dragons have hoards, and shiny pretty gems are a prized possession. The trade between them is abundant. Prince Tirrian is a favorite here on Rilu, and anyone with him will be welcomed with open arms."

"Ah, I'm finally seeing the logic behind bringing the asshole now," Xavier mutters in my ear as Tirrian waves down a futuristic-looking vehicle.

"Are they going to recognize him in his glamour?" I ask, and Silac nods. "Yes, he assumes this glamour when he attends the market. Although they welcome him with open arms, his half form is a little intimidating, and they negotiate better when they are not terrified," Silac says with a smile on his face, and I look at the dragon with new eyes.

"I would have thought them being terrified would be an advantage." My curiosity is well and truly piqued.

"Dragons are honorable. There is nothing honorable in scaring someone to get a better outcome unless they are the enemy. These people are our friends, and keeping them happy is a priority."

A shiny car pulls up along the sidewalk we are walking down. Out jumps a dark-skinned man, who hurries around and bows to the dragon prince. He's wearing an outfit very similar to all three guys, with loose, billowy pants and a tunic. His eyes are quite shocking. They are the palest blue, with only a very small black iris. His hair is black with stripes of different gem-like colors. I remember one of the guys telling me that's what happens when you bond with a larnuk. He must have a huge herd of them with the amount of stripes he has. There's hardly any black left, and it's the same with his short, neatly trimmed beard.

"Prince Tirrian. I was just alerted that you arrived unannounced and hurried over here to transport you wherever you need to go." His accent is thick but easily understandable. If I had to compare it to something, I would say he sounds Middle Eastern. My translator is the best thing I could have ever been given, otherwise I would be screwed. It must be a galaxy wide thing, because no one has had any trouble understanding me yet.

Tirrian bows back, a huge smile breaking out across his face, before the men exchange one of those manly back slapping hugs, and I just stare in shock. Holy fuck, he's hot when he smiles. I mean, the surly aggressive man is sexy too, but wow. Xavier chuckles quietly beside me, obviously feeling my shock, and I nudge him with my elbow to shut him up. "Chief Zana, it is wonderful to see you. This is Lila Adams, the Adams brothers' granddaughter and heir to the Galaxy Circus. She is here with the blessings of the Celestians to harvest the flamegem when it blooms. This is Prince Xavier Colest and Silac, the nagajara." He calls Silac something I don't know the meaning of, which makes me desperate to know.

Xavier gives me a shove forward, and I glare at him but smile for the man. "Lila, this is Chief Zana, he is the head chief of all of Rilu. I guess you could compare him to the president. His clan has been guarding the flamegem for all these years for the Celestians. Only him and a select few know of its whereabouts and what it can actually do."

Tirrian and Silac were both read into the mission when they were asked to escort me. I was confused about why we shared the information with Tirrian's father, since I think the more people who know means it's no longer a secret, but apparently he already knew about the flower, which made him an ally. I guess this is why. There is obviously a close relationship between the dragon clan and the leadership of Rilu, and I would be stupid to reject that kind of assistance due to not liking my escort.

"Sir, it is lovely to meet you. My grandpas sung your praises before we left and send their regards. They apologize that they can't be here themselves, but their worry for their brother kept them by his side." See? I can be polite and gracious and all formal as well.

He reaches for my hands and looks me up and down. "You are the spitting image of your gorgeous mother. I am sorry to hear about John, and I am thankful we can help in this small way. Come, I will take you to the market where your escort has agreed to meet you. I would have taken you myself, but unfortunately the spring equinox is also the time of the annual gem fair in Galliethain, and we have buyers coming in from all over the country in the next few days." He gestures for us to hop into his shiny silver vehicle. Tirrian offers me the passenger seat, but I shake my head.

"No, you take it. You're a lot bigger than I am, and I'm not sure all three of you would fit in the back. Xavier won't mind if I drape myself over him." His eyebrows jump in surprise, and he nods his thanks before opening the back door for me. I return the nod of gratitude and slide in. Silac, having gone around to the other side, sits to my right, and Xavier is on my left. Once we are all seated, Chief Zana begins to drive.

CHAPTER NINETEEN

Lila

"I would do the whole tour guide thing, but I think you are probably in a hurry. Just promise you will return one day and take in all that is Galli-ethain and the outer colonies." He looks at me through the rearview mirror, his heavy accent imploring.

"I would love to," I assure him as we ease into traffic, the streets relatively quiet compared to major cities on Earth. "I'm sure a holiday here with my family would be wonderful."

"Yeah, maybe not all your family," Xavier reminds me, and I grimace. Shit, that will be a problem.

"Oh, why is that?" The chief sounds curious but not angry.

"Some of my mates are not compatible with your climate, I'm afraid," I answer, and he nods his understanding.

"Yes, Rilu is not for everyone. Luckily for us, we have thicker skin and a higher tolerance for daylight and heat, as do the larnuks."

"Do you grow crops here? It doesn't really seem conducive to it." I watch the city go by, fascinated by all the little patches of greenery between the large buildings.

"Rilu is actually extremely fertile, but it is all below ground. The caverns that we harvest our gems from also make perfect growing grounds for many of our crops," the chief explains. "Our water is rich in nutrients and things grow quickly, making it easy for us to plant five or six crops each year."

"But what about light? If everything is underground, how do they get light to grow?" Rilu has two suns close together, which is what makes daylight almost never-ending and creates extreme heat. Even now in the climate-controlled car, I can feel sweat on my brow and upper lip. I use my head scarf to wipe it away.

"We use a technique called solar tunnels. A tunnel is made to the surface, and a clear plastic dome is used to cover it, allowing sunlight to shine down the tunnel. We then use mirrors to bounce that light around the caverns."

"Oh yeah, I know what you're talking about.

Ancient Egyptians on Earth used that technique as well." Once again, my movie knowledge comes in handy. Who would have thought?

"Apart from this city and two more large ones, the majority of our population either lives underground or are nomadic with their larnuk herds."

"What about the sandworms? Aren't they a problem for the larnuk herds?" I ask. The guys have been quiet, letting me quiz the chief on everything Rilu, and I appreciate it.

"The larnuks are poisonous to the sandworms, and they avoid them whenever possible. Their main food sources are desert rodents and one or two hardier species that live amongst the rocky outcrops. They like to hunt around oases because that's where these animals go for water, but if a nomadic village moves into the oasis for a while, the sandworm will avoid that particular one until they move on. The larnuks actually protect our people. Occasionally, a worm will get desperate and attack, but it usually has a bad outcome for the worm."

"Wow, I can't wait to get out there and see it all. It's amazing and so very different from where I am from."

The chief's car slows and pulls into a parking space in front of a large warehouse. It's one right in front, and I'm assuming it's reserved for him, because the rest of the parking bays seem to be full.

"Come now, your escort is going to meet you by the larnuk sale yards."

I scramble out of the car behind Xavier, hurrying after the chief who is moving toward the entrance at quite a pace. "Sale yards? You sell the larnuks to other races? I thought they needed to bond with their handler."

"We do, and they do. You'll see," he says with a mysterious little smirk. Okay, well now I'm even more excited, but I come to a halt as we enter the warehouse.

It must be soundproof, because there was no sign of this outside except for all the cars. The place is teeming with beings. A good majority of them have the same swarthy coloring and streaked hair as the chief, but there are also other races here. The sights and sounds and smells are mesmerizing, but I don't have time to stand and gawk, because the chief is on a mission, and there's no stopping him. I follow behind Silac and Xavier, with Tirrian bringing up the rear. He keeps having to nudge me to keep me moving because I keep getting side-tracked. I guess he learned from X69 that I'm easily distracted, and he's making it his mission to keep us on track.

Cloth, earthenware, wood carvings and exotic jewelry are in every store, sparkling and shining and drawing the buyer in. Here and there, people shout, hawking their wares, trying to attract buyers to their little piece of the market. A produce store has me stopping and picking up an interesting... fruit maybe. It has a sweet smell. "What's this?" I ask Tirrian who has stopped with me, the others getting lost in the crowd ahead of us. It's leather-like in appearance and shaped like a straight banana, and despite the sweet smell, it is rock-hard. I'd break my teeth if I bit into it.

Tirrian fishes into his pocket and pulls out a couple of coins and hands it to the woman who is watching us with an easy smile. "We will take this. She has never been to Rilu before," he explains with a smile, and the woman bows her head and takes his coins with both hands.

"Blessing to you both, Prince Tirrian."

A claw pops out of his pointer finger on his right hand, and he draws a line down the fruit. It splits in half, exposing bright red flesh, but I can feel heat wafting off it as I bend to get a better look.

"This is lollecado. Rilu has two types of cavern systems. One is thermal and hot, and the other one is cooler and damp. They grow different produce in each system. This fruit forms in the lava pools of the thermal system. It stays hot even once it's left the lava. It takes special gloves to harvest this, and people have to be careful not to fall in when they do harvest it, because they will die instantly. Rilunese are hardy, but not quite that hardy. They allow dragons to come and work during harvest season because they can withstand the heat in half form. It's a delicacy on Fluxx and prized by dragons." He scoops some out and blows on it before offering his finger to me.

"Will it burn me?" I ask, and he shrugs.

"It shouldn't. Once the fruit is split open, it tends to cool quickly. That's why you should eat it as soon as possible."

I lean in and suck the offered fruit off of his finger, my eyes locked on his as I do. The texture is a little bit gritty, like a dragon fruit with hundreds of tiny seeds, but the taste is incredible. It's like a slightly spicy pineapple with a creamy finish to soften the bite. "Oh my god, that is so good." I moan as I take the fruit from his hand and scoop out more with my own finger.

"Yes, good for dragon loving. Make tasty," the lady watching us says, nodding enthusiastically.

"Huh?" I ask, and Tirrian breaks out of his daze and glares at the woman before grabbing my arm and dragging me in the direction the others went. "Hey, what was she saying?" I ask, allowing him to guide me through the crowd despite the slightly harsh grip he has on me—it's allowing me to finish my delicious fruit. "Can the replicator replicate these?" I ask absently.

"No," he grunts. "And she was saying nothing. Just the ramblings of an old woman."

I offer him the other half of the fruit, but he

shakes his head. "You finish it. I've had them before." His dragon flicks into his eyes and startles me. The elongated pupil seems to wink before Tirrian gets control again. That was weird.

I finish up the fruit just as we arrive at a large open area, and from the smell of it, it must be the sale yards. Tirrian takes the now empty skin from me and tosses it in a nearby bin before we reach the other three who are standing next to a tall, dark-haired woman with purple streaks in her hair.

"Ah, there you are. I wondered where you had gotten to, but I knew you were in good hands with Tirrian," Chief Zana exclaims as we join them. "This is my eldest daughter, Zilla. She will escort you out to the settlement at the right mine. She insisted when she heard that Prince Tirrian was with the group."

"It is nice to meet you," she says rather woodenly to me, but when she turns to Tirrian, that melts away and she smiles. "T, I didn't know you were coming. Why didn't you send me a message? I would have met you at the landing pad." She throws her arms around him, hugging him hard, but it seems to me like he stiffened ever so slightly before returning the embrace. Hmm, I wonder what that was about.

"It was a last-minute thing, but Dad wanted to make sure Lila was safe." He steps out of her embrace and puts his arm around me, dragging me to his side, and then he looks down at me with actual affection. My brain screeches to a halt. What the actual fuck? My mouth drops open in shock, but Silac steps into the conversation before I can ask if Tirrian hit his head somewhere between the fruit stall and here.

"Lila is a favorite of the dragon king, and he sent his son along to make sure she was safe in the mines. We wouldn't want anything to happen to her." Now hold up, what the fuck has Silac been smoking? One of the stalls was a coffee shop style setup with hookahs with multiple pipes. There was purple smoke drifting off one of them, and I'm pretty sure it was the same stuff that Xavier used with me to relax my mind. Did they make a pit stop while we were distracted?

Zilla's eyes narrow as she takes a step back. "Of course not." There is some underlying tension that the chief is oblivious to.

"My sister, Zala, will guide you to the flower. She is the one the Celestians entrusted with the path. It's why she lives with the circus. It is much harder to gain access to her while she is traveling with her herd. She only returns home occasionally," Zilla tells me with an underlying tone of envy.

"Oh, Zala is your daughter? I didn't know that."

The chief beams and nods enthusiastically.

"Yes, Zala is the special chosen one. Larnuks of

every color have blessed her with their bond, much like our father. It signals that she will be the next chief. Most of us only get blessed by one gem horse." She points to the purple streak in her hair.

"Oh?" I need to know more, so the chief takes over the explanation.

"The larnuks eat gems, so they can sniff out where they are in the mine. Each colored larnuk has a specific diet of gems. Being blessed by more than one larnuk means you have the ability to find all the gems. Does this make sense? Zilla has a purple larnuk as her bond mate, which means she is adept at finding purple gems—amethyst, purple sapphires and diamonds, and khooni neelam, as well as a couple you are probably not familiar with."

"Oh, I think I understand now. Because Zala has bonded with multiple colored animals, she can find many different kinds."

He looks pleased and nods eagerly. "Yes, exactly. Zala is only missing an opalescent larnuk, and that is because they are nearly extinct. The one herd that still exists refuses to bond with anyone despite having thousands of people try."

"How does one bond with a larnuk?" I ask, and Zilla snorts with derision.

"Nothing you would be brave enough to attempt."

"Zilla," Chief Zana scolds. "It involves standing still and allowing the larnuk to approach you. If they believe you are worthy, then they will put their mouth on you somewhere. Next, you need to make the decision on whether or not you are going to allow them to bite you. If you hold still and they bite down into your skin, you form a bond, but not everyone is brave enough to hold still."

"Why not?" The sound of hooves rushing toward us have me looking up and watching in awe as a dozen larnuks of all colors are herded into the arena. Their wings are spread out, and they are trotting, snorting, and throwing their heads around. Plumes of steam come out of their noses much like Tirrian's when he becomes annoyed. One of them tosses their head back and growls like a bear. It's weird. I expected a high-pitched whinny, so hearing that makes me step back a little. That, and the sight of razor-sharp teeth glistening in their mouths.

"Because they have teeth sharp enough to cut through precious gems. If they decide to, they can kill or heavily maim the person they are bonding with. Many larnuk masters have lost hands or needed major surgery after a bonding attempt," Zana explains.

"And that is the only way to travel out to the colonies?" I ask hesitantly. "Are we going to have to bond with one of those?" I watch the brightly colored animals settle as a handler walks in and pours a bucket into one of the feed troughs. It sounds like pebbles on a tin roof, and when I see what he's pouring, I'm mesmerized. Tiny little gems in all different colors fill the trough, and the larnuks just dig in, crunching and snapping with larnuk joy.

"You are hardly worthy of a larnuk bonding, so no. We will use ones that are bonded to a master, and he will allow them to be used for transport between here and the settlements. It is a very lucrative business." Zilla waves at a set of stables down from where we are standing.

Well, isn't she a ray of political goodwill sunshine? Everyone is glaring at her now, including Tirrian and her father after that aggressive slight toward me.

"Zilla, that is enough. Lila is the heir to the Galaxy Circus and deserves as much respect as the warlock, Prince Tirrian, and the serpent king."

Wait, what? "The serpent king?" It's my turn to gape at Silac, who frowns and shakes his head.

"No, Lila, I am no more a king than Link is," he quickly assures me, obviously seeing some of the hurt I was trying to hide.

"While there are many types of snake shifters, cobras and pythons and others, his family is the only family of nagas, and as such, they have the nickname the serpent kings," Tirrian quickly adds.

"What about your fiancée?" I ask, incredibly curious now even though I shouldn't be.

"Kinga is a basilisk. Any children we have will

be basilisks. Naga can only breed true with other nagas, and my mother was the last one."

"Oh, I get it, so you didn't want me to mimic you because I would have been a female naga capable of continuing the line. That's why you thought your snake would imprint, thus ruining your arranged marriage. I'm so sorry, Silac."

"It's okay. We've come to accept that now. Maybe somewhere in the galaxy there is a female naga for one of my younger brothers when it is their time to mate. I can only hope."

"So you weren't actually looking for a naga shifter for me to mimic then?" I ask the three of them.

"No, even if we had run into one of his brothers, there's still a chance Silac's snake or any of their snakes would imprint on you. I wanted to find a basilisk. They are still pretty good options," Xavier explains, and I feel a sense of sadness, but I quickly push it down so nobody sees.

"Okay, fine, but now we need to find one of the locals for me to mimic so we can get this show on the road." I change the subject, not wanting to dwell on the fact that I'm attracted to the pretty snake, and he is well and truly off-limits.

CHAPTER TWENTY

Silac

I hate seeing the hurt in Lila's eyes as she changes the subject. I also hate the fact that I can't volunteer to help her. My snake is urging me to, pleading for me to allow her to shift and become our mate, but I have a marriage contract —one that will upset my father if I break it. He still has desperate hope that mating with a basilisk might make a naga youngster. His desperation to not see the end of the naga line has caused him to make some poor decisions. Kinga's basilisk family is involved in some shady deals and are ruthless when crossed. I don't dare tell him about Lila's mimic ability, or he would break that contract faster than I can blink and shove me at her instead. That will not bode well for my family if we end up on the bad side of the Bravalana basilisks.

I desperately want to tell her all this, but I don't want to get either of our hopes up, so I stay quiet, and my inner naga sulks violently.

"I would be honored if you would mimic me," Chief Zana volunteers, but Zilla gasps and shakes her head.

"No way. What if she steals your identity?"

"It doesn't really work like that," Lila says patiently.

"No, it really doesn't. Lila mimicked my warlock form, and I am still me and she is her own being. She just has all the powers and looks of a warlock now. She is essentially a brand-new warlock. Same with the other beings she mimicked. Queen Corethea of the Celestian royal family was another being she mimicked when her abilities first emerged and she had no control. She is still herself, and Lila has her own version of a Celestian," Xavier explains gently but firmly, looking between the two Rilunese while trying to reassure them both that she will not be stealing anything from Zana.

"Hush now, Zilla. I trust them, and it would be a great honor to assist the only Skarrian mimic in the world."

"Thank you, Chief Zana, you honor me with your trust." Lila bows her head at the chief.

"Shall we move somewhere more private? Lila

tends to lose her clothes when she mimics some-one," I suggest, looking around for a place to use.

"Back there a little ways is a cafe with private dining rooms. We can use one of those." Zana whirls and leads us back the way we came. The cafe is filled with people eating and drinking before the larnuk bonding auctions start. The Rilunese allow people to bid and then try to bond with a larnuk. If they fail, their money is returned to them minus a fee and hopefully not minus a limb. It is a bloody event that has locals coming from all around to view. That is why the markets are so packed.

The chief requests a back room, and we follow a server who cheerfully escorts us to one. Tirrian stops before entering the room. I know his dragon is pushing him as hard as my snake is to bond with Lila, and seeing her naked is not helping either of us one little bit. "I saw a Necro in the crowd earlier. Silac and I will go see if we can convince him to have a drink with us, then Xavier can mesmerize him."

Zilla's eyes widen, and she looks from Tirrian to Zana, obviously torn between staying and making sure her father isn't body snatched and trailing helplessly after the dragon she's had a crush on for a long time. There was talk about an arranged marriage between Zilla and Tirrian to cement rela-tions between the two planets, but Tirrian's dragon will have nothing to do with it. If a marriage is forced, he may kill her, and that would be disastrous. She refuses to accept reality though and pines for something that will never come to be. Tirrian doesn't discourage her as much as he should because he feels sorry for her.

"Here, use this on the necro so he doesn't give you a hard time." Xavier's hand reaches through the mist, and Zilla takes a step backward. In his palm is a spelled charm, so I take it from him, glad we are not going to have a repeat of the Barcoa. I'm sure Tirrian is too. "Maybe it would be best if you accompanied them. The less people around, the easier it is for Lila, and she still needs a couple of shifters to mimic. Maybe you would know if there are any on Rilu for the sale."

"Yes, alright, but make sure my father is okay." She bravely points a finger at the mist-covered warlock whom I can practically feel roll his eyes.

She's quiet as we leave the café, but the minute we're out of earshot, she's all chatter. "Aren't you worried about that mimic? I read somewhere that they become power hungry and try to take over the world. All those different powers and abilities must be too much for one person to handle."

"Don't tell anyone this," Tirrian begins, which guarantees that it will spread through the universe at light speed, "but Lila isn't very powerful. We aren't sure if she will even be able to mimic your dad. Xavier has a contingency plan to keep himself and Silac safe while we travel across the desert, and Lila will just be included in that."

"So why are we looking for more races for her to mimic if she's not very powerful?" Zilla seems incredibly pleased with Tirrian's secret. Almost smug.

"Because the warlock will use illusion to make it seem like she has mimicked them so that nobody will know she's not powerful," I tell her, passing on what we all agreed to share with others who aren't within the circle of trust. "They like the idea that no one will challenge her if they believe she is a mighty mimic." I only hope it doesn't backfire on us.

"Is that why she needs more shifters? I would have thought you two would be powerful enough for her to pretend to mimic."

"We don't want her to," Tirrian says gruffly, and I can tell by his tone that he doesn't want to talk about it, so before Zilla pushes, I change the subject.

"Let's just grab that necro, and then we can get going. We need that flower, and if we don't hurry, we will be cutting it close."

Lila's face is radiant, and her grin is a mile wide as we soar over the desert sands on the backs of our rented larnuks. Her hands tightly grip the mane of the bright red animal, but I can hear her whoops of glee from my own. Zilla is in the lead on her own personal purple one she called Jonti. I'm sharing one with Xavier, and he has a protection spell wrapped around us to protect us from the harsh suns. He has dropped his mist and assumed a Rolunese glamour, but it doesn't come with sun protection. Without it, we would be seriously burnt within minutes of being out here. Tirrian shifted into his dragon form and is flying on Lila's left flank. Larnuks are used to dragons, so none of them had been particularly concerned when he shifted.

Lila mimicked both Chief Zana and the necro without any problems, but her eyes were a little troubled when she resumed her own form after mimicking the necro. She refused to talk about it though. She just reassumed her Rilunese form and insisted we needed to get moving.

She has the same pale, watery blue eyes, and Chief Zana gave her a pair of goggles to wear to protect them from the sun. Her skin has the same dark tone, and her hair is long and straight down her back. She, of course, doesn't have any of the colored streaks, as she is not bonded to a larnuk, and that is not something that carries over in the mimic. I think both Chief Zana and Zilla were relieved to see it.

"Well, snakelet, this is fun," Xavier says behind me, and I roll my eyes. His arms are wrapped around my waist, his grip tight, and I can feel how stiff he is despite the relaxed drawl. He really isn't comfortable on the back of this animal, but he won't admit it anytime soon. "You know I did a little digging and discovered you are engaged to the princess of the Bravalana basilisk family. They are a nasty family. They have their fingers in all sorts of illegal pies all over the galaxy. You know they are being heavily watched by the Galaxy Council Task-force. Is that the reason you haven't told your father about Lila being a mimic who is able to give you pure naga babies? You know he's going to hear eventually."

I feel myself stiffen, and a wave of annoyance washes over me. "You should mind your own business."

"Uh, uh, uh, don't be like that. I could make all of your problems go away, you know. It just so happens that the Bravalana basilisks have made a few wrong steps on Westalin. They pissed off some influential warlocks who have appealed to my parents to have them dealt with. If anyone can take care of them, we can, but I guess I need to know if that is something you want, or do you happen to like your little Bravalana princess? I hear she is a sweet thing and way too good for the family she was born into."

My heart skips a beat as I think of Kinga. She was my best friend growing up. Raised away from the family drama, she and I went to school together and were close until her family realized what an asset she could be and tried to marry her off to the first influential family they could find. That's why I stepped in and asked my father to offer her a marriage contract. Although neither of us feel that way about one another, it would keep her safe and out of the hands of men trying to get ahead in life, ones who didn't have her well-being in mind. If I broke it now, all our lives would be in danger. But what if the warlock is telling the truth? What if he could help all of us?

"Ah, I can practically taste your desperation on the air," he mutters as the larnuk swoops down to land. My stomach rolls with the movement, and he grips my shirt tighter. "Think about it. Let me know once we return to the ship. It would seem that maybe it would solve at least one of the issues." Our larnuk touches down just outside of the village settlement. He and I slide off as Lila's and Zilla's larnuks follow suit, landing gently in the sand. Tirrian, on the other hand, practically dive-bombs into the desert, kicking up a wave of orange sand. We watch on with varying reactions. I just shake my head, and Zilla smiles indulgently as he rolls around, taking a giant sand bath, using the coarse sand to rub his scales shiny, but Lila's mouth is open in horror.

"Shouldn't we stop him from doing that? Isn't he going to attract a sandworm?"

"Yes, that's the whole point," Zilla says, unable to hide her amusement.

"What? Why?" Lila screeches, and Zilla rolls her eyes.

"Just watch," I tell her.

Sure enough, in the distance, there's a disturbance in the sand like something is tunneling underneath, burrowing its way toward us. It's fast and zigzags its way across the expanse, hunting for whatever is making the vibrations on the sand. Tirrian just continues flopping around like he has no cares in the world.

"Tirrian!" Lila shouts and starts to step forward, but she stops and screams as the sandworm launches itself out of the ground at a rapid speed a few feet from Tirrian. It howls a most ferocious sound and clacks its many teeth, its nearly blind eyes searching for its intended prey. Lightning spears out from the two antennas on its head as a horrific smell wafts toward us.

"Ugh, I forgot how bad they smell," Xavier mutters as Tirrian launches his body into the air, narrowly missing getting chomped on by the worm.

"Tirrian!" Lila screams again as she shimmers

and her body changes to a lightning cat, her worry for the dragon eclipsing any animosity the two of them have. She obviously wasn't thinking about the type of climate her form is used to as she takes one step forward and instantly collapses. I leap forward and catch her falling body as Tirrian roars his own challenge and banks around, beelining toward the sandworm, a stream of flames bursting from his gaping maw.

"Easy now, Lila, he's okay, I promise. Now switch back. Your lightning cat can't stand the heat." Her body shimmers in my arms as she returns to her now naked Rilunese form. Her intoxicating scent of freshly baked bread and petrichor hits my nose, and I feel my tongue dart out to lick the scent from the air, my snake trying to burst out of my skin, but I grit my teeth and hold him in.

"What is he doing?" she mutters, her eyes wide as he flaps his wings, holding his ground. His stream of fire kills the unsuspecting sandworm within minutes.

"He's feeding this village for months to come." The sandworm goes down with a ground shaking thump, and a roar of approval goes up behind us before the villagers start chanting, "Prince Tirrian, Prince Tirrian," over and over again.

Lila just grimaces. "No wonder he's insufferable. Of course they are going to think he's wonderful if he feeds them for months," she mutters, and I just chuckle as Xavier conjures her the same outfit for her to cover herself up with again. "What does it taste like?" she asks, not moving from my arms, and I find myself leaning in and sniffing her hair, my tongue darting in and out quickly, tasting her skin, but she's so distracted by what the dragon is doing she doesn't notice.

The warlock narrows his eyes and smirks at me. "Chicken," Xavier says.

"When you're all finished rolling around in the sand, I'll be in my house waiting for you," a dry, husky voice says, and when we turn, we find Zala standing there with one of her own larnuks peering over her shoulder.

The villagers stream past us now that the sand-worm is down, each of them carrying swords and knives to start rending the now dead creature into more maneuverable bits as Tirrian's dragon sets down again. He roars triumphantly and slinks over to us, his big nose nuzzling into Lila's stomach. She giggles and pushes it away.

"Such a clever dragon," she coos, and it chuffs at her as she rubs a hand between its heavy eyebrow ridges. "Such a pretty dragon."

"Hey, Zala," Xavier calls, and she narrows her eyes at him, frowning.

"Xavier?" she asks, and he nods. She shakes her head ruefully and waves a hand before turning and heading back in the direction of the village, which Lila finally notices.

She drops her hand away from the dragon, which has him snorting with disappointment, and pushes my arm away. I reluctantly let it drop as she walks over to one of the buildings and runs her hand over it.

"This was not what I thought it would look like. I was expecting tents. How do they get these out here?"

The dwellings are dome-like buildings with round windows in them, and they are covered by foliage. They are the same purple green color as the water and palm trees of the oasis. There are probably twenty or so dwellings with larnuks of all colors wandering in and out. On the other side of the water is the opening to the mine, where a large, looming cave exists.

"It's a special technology. You just press a button, and everything folds down into a box small enough to slip into your pocket." Tirrian has changed forms, and Lila goes to turn to look at him, but I stop her.

"He's naked," I warn her, knowing he was going for the shock factor, and he scowls at me. Xavier rolls his eyes and waves a hand, producing the clothes he'd given him before he shifted and tossing them at him.

"Come on. Maybe Zala will show you how it

works." The warlock takes Lila by the hand, and they start following after the girl. Zilla is staring hungrily at the naked dragon as he starts to pull his clothes on.

"Spoilsport," he grumbles, and I shrug.

"For someone who hates the girl, you do like to stir trouble to gain her attention," I mutter quietly so only he hears it.

"Stupid dragon is head over heels for her," he mutters back, and I feel my eyes widen in shock as he admits it out loud.

"What are you going to do?" I ask him, and he shakes his head.

"Nothing."

"Yeah, okay, sure. I'm pretty sure that's not going to work, but you do you, bro." I slap him on the shoulder and follow the other two. I have my own beast problems to worry about, and he's a big boy, but I can't see that ending well for anyone.

CHAPTER TWENTY-ONE

Lila

The houses are these adorable, foliage-covered, dome-like buildings that have cute little round windows in them. If they can fold down into one pocket-sized thing, then maybe we can get one to put at home on Skarr as a cubby for the kids to play in—though I'm not even sure they are going to stay kids long enough to make use of it. Maybe they need to be granny units for the teenagers they will be in a few, short years.

The door is wide open as we approach the one Zala entered. Her golden larnuk's body is half in and half out of the doorway, making it so neither Xavier nor I can enter.

"Hey, Zala, do you want to move your horse's ass?" Xavier calls.

"Dhahabi, back," she calls, and the larnuk backs out of the doorway, snorts at us, and shows its teeth, which has me shrinking backward. It gives us a horsey grin and ambles off.

"Come on." Xavier tugs my hand and enters the dwelling. The interior is more like what I expected, with soft furnishings covering all the walls and an abundance of cushions on the floor. Zala is sitting at a small coffee table on the floor, a steaming mug of something in front of her. In the corner, I can see a bed area surrounded by more gauzy curtains. There's another, more solid wall blocking off another area of the dwelling, which I'm going to assume is the bathroom. The room is cool compared to the outside, and a shiver runs down my spine. Zala is eyeing me with interest, her watery blue eyes not hostile but not exactly warm with welcome.

"You look like one of us," she comments offhandedly as Xavier leans down, giving her a kiss on the cheek. She waves a hand absently at the cushions before turning her attention to the warlock. "How did Zilla end up as your guide? She doesn't leave the city unless Father makes her. I'm surprised her larnuk could make it all the way out here."

I move over and take a seat. Xavier joins me, his descent so much more elegant than mine. He leans over and pours a mug of the steaming beverage into a cup for both of us and hands it to me.

"Thank you, but I'm still a bit warm," I tell him, flapping a hand at my face in the hope to cool down somewhat.

"*Barid,*" Zala calls out, and the room is instantly flooded with a cool breeze.

"Oh, thank you. It really is rather warm. I'm not sure how you and Silac can cope," I say to my fiancé who grins.

"Cooling protection spell." He waves a hand at his body, and I frown.

"But don't you need to be with Silac to protect him too? Is he out there becoming roast snake?" I go to scramble to my feet so I can check on him, but Xavier stops me.

"No, the spell is still on him."

I narrow my eyes on the warlock. "So why did you need to ride with him?"

A mischievous grin crosses his face. "Because I could." I huff out an amused laugh at his ridiculousness. "Zala, I don't think you've been properly introduced to Lila."

"It's lovely to finally meet you," I say to the girl who just studies me for a moment before grinning.

"You too, Lila. I can tell that there is never going to be a dull moment when you're around. Although the drink steams, it's cool," Zala says, waving a hand at the beverage Xavier placed in front of me. "Try it, it is good."

I lift the steaming mug to my mouth and blow on it, but when I place my lips on the cup and take a sip, it's not hot at all. It's cool and refreshing and sweet, kind of like a sweetish peppermint tea.

"Zilla graciously offered to be our guide out here," Xavier says, answering the question from before, and it's hard to miss the sarcasm in his voice.

Zala rolls her eyes. "I bet it was only after she heard that Tirrian was with your party." Speaking of the dragon, both him and the snake enter the little dwelling, followed by the aforementioned sister who wrinkles her nose.

"God, it's so small in here," she grumbles, and I gaze around the room in amazement. It really isn't. There's plenty of room for all of us to lounge around Zala's table, and apart from the curtained off bed and bathroom area, there are a couple more mounds of pillows for relaxing.

"Zilla, it's been a while. Dad expected you to come and have dinner with the family when I first returned home, but you didn't show up," Zala says blandly, and Zilla wrinkles her nose.

"And listen to everyone fawn all over you all evening? No thanks. I hear enough about how wonderful you are and how you are going to be such a great leader one day." A sly look emerges on her face. "How is the opalescent bonding going?

Don't think I don't know what you are doing out here. This is where their herd was last seen."

Zala's eyebrows jump in surprise. "It is? Nobody told me that. Last time I was home, they were living on the other side of the planet."

"Yes, they moved here about six months ago. Don't tell me this wasn't all a well-coordinated attempt to finish the collection and surpass Father."

"No, it really isn't, Zilla. I'm here for the flower and the flower only. I've only been out here a few days. I was at home with Mom and Dad, visiting with Grandma. She says you haven't been to visit in a while."

"That woman gives me the creeps." Zilla shudders, and Zala's mouth purses in annoyance as she sits upright, her spine stiff as a board.

"Well, she is still our grandmother and deserves your respect. Everyone else would kill to have her wisdom and advice, but you just shun it. You can't avoid it because she is here."

Zilla's face pales, and she looks around the room like her grandmother is going to pounce on her at any second. She fidgets, her gaze going between Tirrian and the doorway, and then she starts stepping toward the latter.

"I better get back to the city. The larnuks that brought you here will be able to see you safely back when you are done."

Zala jumps to her feet. "No you won't. Your

larnuk must rest for at least a couple of hours before you attempt that return flight. It would be dangerous for him to return straightaway. Stay here while I take Lila into the cavern. You can't avoid her forever."

"Watch me."

"Sit down, Zilla." A voice in the doorway has us all turning, and I watch Zilla's complexion pale considerably.

This woman looks old. She is short and slightly hunched in stature, and her dark skin is wrinkly and looks paper-thin. The expected watery blue eyes are completely white, but I have a feeling this woman sees more than most. She gives off an air of wisdom and grace as she moves into the room easily despite her lack of sight. Finally, someone who ages somewhat normally. Her silver hair is also streaked with many different colors, almost the same amount as Zala. Tirrian, Silac, and Xavier all jump to their feet and bow to the woman with reverence.

"Zamala, it is lovely to see you again," Tirrian says politely, reaching for her hand and bowing over it.

"Ah, young dragon, it is I who am pleased to see you." Her lips part, and she laughs at her joke as she pats his hand before turning her body to the other men. "And the serpent king and the warlock prince. Well, this is a treat. Sit down, you don't need to stand for me." She stops, and her focus turns to me, her unseeing eyes widening with surprise.

"A mimic. It has been a long time since the Skarrians had a mimic present itself. Trouble must be coming." Her words are said carefully, like they hold weight and she knows what's coming.

A shiver runs down my spine at her words, and Zilla pales even more. As Zamala's attention turns to her.

"Ah, child. You need to stop pining for what is not yours and find peace with it. Otherwise, your life is going to be so very sad."

"Ugh. I am out of here. I'll be in the communal tent until it is time to leave." Zilla leaves in a huff. I can't believe how rude she is to her grandmother.

"Ah, that girl is going to be nothing but trouble for this family. It is inevitable. I try to steer her back onto the right path, but she believes my words are the ramblings of an old woman. Her end will not be pleasant, but all I can do is comfort my son when he grieves." Zamala turns her attention back to us. "You need to go now. The flower will start blooming in the next hour, and it will only last for a few hours after that. To preserve its magic, you need to wrap it in this." She pulls a fabric bag from the pocket of her long tunic and passes it to me. "No one but you should touch it, Lila. Make sure of it, and make sure you are in your Celestian form when you do."

I stare in shock at the old woman, and she waves the bag at me, so I reach out and take it. How did she know I have a Celestian form? Or that I'm even a mimic in the first place?

As I reach for the bag, my hand brushes across hers, and she strikes like a snake. Her hand latches onto my wrist and won't let it go. Everything fades away, and a crooning, keening cry echoes inside my mind.

"Your grandmother is still alive. Until recently, she was being held in this very cavern by an unsavory faction, but she was recently moved to another location when they learned you were coming for the flower."

I frown at the old woman and snatch my hand away. "Why didn't you tell my grandfathers this?" I demand as excitement and annoyance war inside of me at the information the old woman just revealed.

She sighs. "That is not how my visions work, unfortunately. It was only seeing you just now that caused the knowledge to come to me."

"Did your vision show you where they took her?" Xavier asks gently, and Zamala shudders.

"Yes, they have her in stasis, and they have placed the box in the middle of the death forest on Husadavia."

Everyone in the room gasps, and I frown. I've heard the name of that planet before, but I can't remember where or what the big deal is.

"How did they even get her there?" Silac asks, and Zamala furrows her eyebrows in a deep frown.

"The people who were tasked with placing her there did not make it out."

"That is a suicide mission," Zala argues. "There's no way anyone will survive to retrieve her."

"That's not actually true. There are the halla fruit harvesters. They come and go from the planet with relative ease," Tirrian points out thoughtfully.

"Focus on today's task and worry about the future task later. You will need one petal of the flamegem flower to be saved to revive your grandma, and you will need a carevasta bear to break that stasis box they have placed her in."

"Why didn't anyone know about this before? She has been missing longer than I've been alive. How come none of your people have found her before this?" I'm so confused.

"This cavern is a no-go zone for Rilunese. It is sacred and guarded by this village. No one has been inside it since the last time the flower was needed, which was back during the time of the Una's and Aaz'axian war," Zala explains much more patiently than I would, that's for sure.

"So you've never actually been where we need to go?" Xavier says dryly, and she shrugs.

"The knowledge of the path is in my mind. Apparently we will be guided there by the cavern itself if the one seeking the flower has pure intentions." Her gaze slides to mine, and I flinch.

"You mean we may not get it at all? That Grandpa John may end up succumbing to the unknown virus?"

"I hope for your sake it doesn't happen, but that is in the hands of the gods now," Zamala says as she and Zala bow their heads.

"Do not worry, *phoeall*. You will get the flower, and all will be right again. I have no doubt." Xavier reaches out and gives my hand a squeeze.

"Well, I guess there's no point in hanging around and waiting. Let's get this done. We will either die in the process or come out triumphant, but neither is going to happen if we sit around here." Tirrian stands up and bows his head to the old woman. "It was a pleasure seeing you again, ma'am."

"You too, young dragon, and take care to listen to your inner beasts. They know what they are talking about. Stubbornness is not going to get you anything but pain and sadness."

Tirrian frowns at her message, and smoke wafts out of his nose as she turns her unseeing gaze to Silac, who has been relatively quiet.

"Serpent king, take the warlock's offer, if not for anything but freeing the galaxy of the influence of that terrible family. Many times they come here searching for gems. Many Rilunese, good men and women, have lost their lives to the greed that infests that family. It is time to put an end to it." She looks back and forth between Xavier and Silac, and both of them nod their heads reverently.

"It will be as you say," Xavier promises her, and she smiles broadly.

"Zala, have care. What you seek is not for you but for another, but be at ease with this knowledge, for you will be very happy with your lot in life, I promise."

Zala looks a little confused and somewhat stunned at Zamala's revelation, but unlike Zilla, she takes it to heart.

"Thank you, *Jadati.*"

Finally, she turns to me. "Love hard and love well, Lila. Your time will be filled with challenges, but I see you meeting them with grace and dignity, even as trouble lashes at you from all sides. Stay true to yourself and your mates, and you will triumph. Oh, and forgive the can of tuna, he is a product of his upbringing, but you will be able to put him on the right path."

With that, she bows her head to us and takes her leave, shuffling out of the dwelling as quickly as she shuffled in.

CHAPTER TWENTY-TWO

Lila

The opening to the cave system looms high above us like a gaping maw, and piercing, jagged rocks line both the top and bottom, making it look much like a sandworm breaking up out of the sand to swallow us whole as we approach it.

"Before we go any farther, you need to know that we may not return. Many people have entered this system and not come back out. The villagers have many tales to tell of the poor lost souls who never return. Some are greedy off-worlders looking for easy gems to score, and some are misguided locals all looking to get ahead in life, but all have the same outcome—they never return."

"So there's something inside the cave that is

killing them?" Tirrian asks, peering into the darkness, and Zala shrugs.

"Maybe, or maybe it is the cave itself. We won't know until we go in."

"What about your ancestors? The ones who have traveled it before? And how did this 'faction' get my grandmother down there? If you, your father, and his mother are the only people with knowledge of the path, then doesn't it make one of them responsible?" I can't help the accusing tone that comes out when I ask the question, but Zala doesn't seem upset.

"You're right. I have no idea how they got in there. I doubt that it was either Father or *Jadati* who helped them, and if she knew how, she would have said so. Her vision obviously didn't show her that much."

"A warlock could bypass the path if they had a firm picture of where they needed to go in their mind, and that could have been pulled from either your father's or grandmother's minds if they were prompted to think about it, but there are not many of them powerful enough to do it," Xavier muses.

"Think back over twenty years, when you were just a child. Was there someone back then who could have achieved it? Because that is the time frame we are looking at," Silac suggests, and Xavier purses his lips. While he thinks, I take a seat on a nearby outcrop, suddenly feeling slightly woozy, my body shimmering between my Rilunese and my original forms.

"Lila?" Zala notices, and I wave her off, breathing heavily as I try to get my form stable.

"Shit, what is happening?" Silac looks between me and Xavier, his concern warming something inside my chest. Xavier steps up and runs a hand over my arm, pouring some of his strength into me.

"Lila is going through a lot more blood than we planned for. Oshan said the key to her energy would be sex with her mates, but none of them are here, so we have been substituting it with blood, but it just isn't helping like it needs to. She needs more and more, and she drank the last of it when we landed. I wasn't able to secure a supply in the city as I had hoped."

"But you're her mate, can't you just bend her over one of the rocks and help her out?" Tirrian is sarcastic as fuck, but he makes a good point.

"I am not officially her mate until we cement our intimate bond, which can't be done until she has her memories unlocked by my parents. Although I would take great pleasure in, as you said, bending her over a rock, and it will only help temporarily, it won't be the fix a fully sealed mate would give her."

"What about the blood from the sandworm? I could drink that." I almost want to gag at my suggestion, because that thing smelled horrid, but desperate times call for desperate measures.

"That's actually not a bad idea," Xavier says, but Zala shakes her head.

"The villagers bleed the worm once it's killed because its blood taints the taste of the meat. I'm afraid it's soaked into the sand on the outskirts of the village. It also helps ward off any other sand-worms that become bold."

"Shit. Well, I can feed her, but I can't give too much to be able to use my powers effectively. Can we ask any of the villagers to donate?"

"Of course, I'm sure they would be happy to," Zala says and turns to leave.

"But that is not going to help us if Lila needs to change while we are in the caverns. She can drink from me," Tirrian announces gruffly. "I will take dragon form. He has more than enough for Lila while we are beneath the surface." My mouth drops open in shock, and the grumpy dragon crosses his arms defensively. "Of course I knew one of us would have to come to her rescue during this mission, I just didn't think it would be before we started," he growls, wearing a sneer on his lips, but I just ignore that because he is being incredibly selfless.

"Will your dragon allow her to feed? He will see her as another predator, so won't he fight back?"

Silac sounds curious, and there's a funny light in his eyes.

"No, he insists he is happy to do it," Tirrian bites out reluctantly, and his eyes flick back and forth, his beast clearly making himself known much like my horny kraken does.

She pokes her exhausted head up. *Good, strong, big dick*, are her words before she sinks back down again. Well, it's comforting to get her approval.

"Look, hurry up and decide, because if we don't get started, we won't be there in time, and it won't bloom again until next year." Zala taps her foot impatiently.

"Thank you, Tirrian, I appreciate your sacrifice. If there is anything I can do to thank your dragon, please let me know." His beast flicks back into his eyes again, and his whole body vibrates much like mine does when my kraken tries to push her way through, but Tirrian clenches his fists and holds on.

"Here, drink from me, and let's save the dragon for inside the cave." Xavier is side-eying the dragon prince now, wearing one of those annoying smirks on his generous mouth. He holds out his wrist as Silac starts walking into the cave.

"We will just give you a moment." He waves for Tirrian and Zala to follow. Both of them do, but not without a backward glance from the smoke blowing dragon.

"That is going to be fun," Xavier mutters as he

holds out his wrist for me. "Would you like to shove me up against the wall like we did on Earth?" He turns back to wink at me, and I feel myself relax for the first time in forever. My entire body aches from all the tension inside it.

"As fun as that sounds, I would never forgive myself if we missed the blooming of the flower because I was getting my pussy pounded," I tell him wryly, and he grins.

"No, I guess not. Okay, messy pants for me, and luckily I can change them."

Oh yes, my venom is going to make him come hard. "Pity Saxon isn't here to help us out," I joke, and he smiles gently.

"Bite me, baby, and let's save your grandpa."

My fangs drop down with just that little bit of encouragement from my warlock. I lean closer and run my nose over the thick vein in his wrist, his familiar scent making my mouth water. It's all I can do to stop myself from draining him completely. I'm so freaking thirsty.

I pierce his skin easily, and when I draw away, his blood starts to run freely. I seal my lips around the holes and drink deeply. Xavier moans and pulls me against him, grinding into me as my venom pulses through his veins. His whole body stiffens as he comes, and his small sigh of pleasure as he relaxes against me has me smiling. His blood, fizzy and delicious and sparking with power, rolls through my body, pushing away all the exhaustion and revitalizing me. It's exactly what I needed. I swipe my tongue across the holes and pull away.

"Thank you," I tell my fiancé, who just shakes his head and smiles.

"No, thank you." He winks and changes his clothes. This new outfit is in darker colors, making it easier to blend in with the environment. "Okay, let's go. I can feel Zala's impatience."

Holding my hand, he leads me deeper into the cave, my eyes adjusting to the low light quite easily, but Xavier throws a ball of light into the air that leads the way, illuminating so much more. This cave is humongous, and large enough that the village we just left could set up camp inside it and still easily have room for all their larnuks. It's also dryer than I expected. I thought it would be cold and damp, but it's not. It's quite cozy, and shiny gems glitter in the walls, reflecting the glow of Xavier's light. I'd love to stop and get a closer look, but we are on a time crunch.

As we move farther into the wide cavern, we find the other three have come to a stop at a large rock wall which has three separate tunnels in its face.

"Which way?" I ask, peering through the darkness at the others. Xavier's light is not the only one now. There's a slight phosphorescent glow all around us, almost like the walls of the cavern are covered in something that makes it light up. It's also a lot cooler back here, like there's a breeze racing through the tunnels, and I feel a shiver run down my spine.

"See that large rock there?" Zala points to a dais sitting just in front of the three tunnels. "You need to put your hand on it."

Frowning, I walk over to where she points, and as I step in front of it, it lights up. Okay, not a rock, but some form of technology. There is an illuminated palm mark, so I'm assuming it's asking for someone to put it on there.

"Why me?" I ask.

"Because you are the one who is seeking something from this tunnel. It needs to read your intentions."

"How does a hunk of rock read your intentions?" I ask, completely unsure about all of this, but a sinking feeling is telling me I have no choice if I want to save John.

"Come on, Lila, you're wasting time. Just get on with it," Tirrian snarls, back to his default asshole mode, but he's not wrong.

I lean in and place my hand against the palm reader. It's cold, but as I push down, I feel something click and pierce the tip of my little finger. "Ouch!" I snatch my hand back, sticking my finger in my mouth to stop the bleeding, but within moments, the tunnel on the left lights up, acting like a beacon. "I'm assuming that's the one. Let's hope it leads to the castle at the center of the labyrinth and not certain death," I joke, and of course they don't get my movie reference, but I'm comforted by it.

"Castle? There is no castle, just the flower," Zala says, sounding confused, and I wave her off.

"Never mind. Maybe I should have a weekly movie night once we get back to the ship," I murmur as we walk the path that is lit up.

"We have those," Xavier says, taking the place next to me and grabbing my hand to offer me comfort, his ball of light trailing above us.

"Earth movies?" I ask him, and he shrugs.

"Sometimes. Where do you think we learned about that rugged and handsome captain of the sea, Captain Jack?"

Ah yes. How could I forget they named our son after a rum swilling pirate?

My free hand trails along the wall of this tunnel, trying to figure out where the light is coming from.

"It's the gems," Zala calls from behind us. "This cavern is one of only two on the whole of Rilu that has these opalescent gems." I stop and lean in to get a closer look. Xavier's ball of light dips down, and I can see the wall is practically riddled with gorgeous white opalescent gems, and it's their glow that illuminates the tunnel.

"They are gorgeous," I say, reaching out and

running the pad of my finger over one of the super shiny smooth stones.

"They really are, and they are prized for jewelry all over the galaxy. Many crown jewels and wealthy individuals are always begging for access to the next harvest. Occasionally the cavern allows me to venture into one of the tunnels, but never far from the entrance, and I can only gather a few before it firmly tells me to leave," Zala explains.

"Tells you to leave?" Silac asks, looking around skeptically. "How does a solid rock structure like this tell you to get out?"

"An invisible wall appears, and you cannot go any farther."

"You're basically implying that this structure is sentient." Xavier sounds curious, not skeptical, as his own hand caresses the wall.

"Yes, I am," she replies.

"I've seen stranger things happen in the galaxy. Come on, we're wasting time," Tirrian snarls.

We continue on our way, the tunnel sloping downward and around, leading us deeper into the center of the planet. The journey itself is slightly boring, to be honest. I had revved myself up for drama, excitement, and terror when they told me most people don't come back out, but so far, this has been a cake walk.

I turn around to face the others and walk backward. "I'm not sure what you all were worried about. This has been easy."

Of course I had to go and speak too soon. I stumble, not looking where I'm going, and as Xavier jumps forward to steady me, he smashes into an invisible wall that has appeared between me and the others.

Xavier's expression goes from relaxed to terrified in an instant, and he bangs on the invisible wall, shouting, but it's completely soundproof. I hurry back, trying to find some gap or something. I check either wall to see if there is a hidden latch, but nothing. I watch as they all do the same on the other side. Xavier's body shimmers like he's trying to teleport, but I can tell by his look of frustration and his silent shout that he's not going anywhere. Tirrian makes them all back away, and we watch as his form shimmers, and he assumes his half form. He sucks in a deep breath and blows a stream of fire directly at the invisible wall. It just hits it and disperses, and my heart races as my anxiety increases. I guess the cave has spoken. I need to do the rest of this journey on my own.

Suddenly, I watch on in horror as four trapdoors open below them, and one by one, they drop away, disappearing from sight and leaving me all by myself.

CHAPTER TWENTY-THREE

Lila

"Xavier!" I scream, pounding my fists against the invisible wall between me and the now empty space, but of course it's futile. They don't suddenly reappear, and I slide down the clear surface, slumping at the bottom as a tear trickles down my face. Why does everything have to be so hard? Why is everything a test? I'm exhausted, and I'm on my own again, but I guess that's nothing new. All my life, I've been alone apart from Susie.

Luckily for me, Xavier's little ball of light was on my side of the wall when it went up.

A sob of frustration leaves my mouth, but I give myself a moment to feel pity before wiping my tears and standing back up. I can't go back, so forward is the only way, and everyone is depending on me.

Shit, John's life literally depends on it. How could I go back and tell them I failed because I was left on my own? How will they ever entrust me with the running of the whole circus if I can't even get this one thing right? I've got this.

Sucking in a deep breath, I blow it out and continue on my way, Xavier's ball of light keeping pace with me. At least that's something. It could have remained in place. As I move farther along, the walls become more and more crowded with the beautiful, opalescent gems. I feel my sandals kick something, and it tinkles as it rolls ahead of me in the tunnel. I crouch down, trying to see what I kicked. So far there hasn't been any debris or rocks littering the completely smooth tunnel. It's almost like it is regularly swept.

Xavier's light comes with me, and I find what I disturbed. It's a perfectly round, perfectly formed opalescent gem. It's gorgeous, and I pick it up and shove it into the top of my dress, hoping that it will stay safely nestled against my boob.

As I stand back up, I notice there is now a light at the end of the tunnel acting like a beacon, drawing me forward, when before it had only been darkness. I hurry, eager to see if my friends have been spat out farther up, but when I get there, I look around the cavern in disappointment. There's no one. It's empty except for a perfectly still, shimmery glassy pool of water. I'm tempted to crouch down and have a drink, but I'm not sure if it's suitable for drinking or not, not to mention that's clearly a stupid horror movie cliché, where I would bend down to drink and something would launch itself out of the water at me. Yup, no, I'm choosing to live today.

I scoot around the underground lake, trying to peer inside, but I'm not close enough, and I don't plan on getting any closer. Just as I get to the other side, there's a scream and a shout, and out of the top of the cavern falls two bodies, splashing hard into the lake. Holy crap, was that Silac and Tirrian? I hurry over, forgetting about the possible lake monster now that one of my friends has fallen in there. Can they even swim? Did they hit their heads on a rock as they fell in? I don't even know how deep it is. For all I know, he was crushed on rocks just below the surface. Do I dive in and try to rescue him?

While all of this is running through my mind, I toe off my sandals and reach up to untie my dress straps behind my neck. The cave floor is actually warm underfoot, which surprises me, but before I can remove my dress, a giant splash has me stepping back from the edge just as Silac lands on the side of the lake, like he had been tossed there by another creature. Peering into the looming darkness, I see a ripple on the water as something moves just below the surface. Something with long, green spines is swimming leisurely around the pool. It flicks its tail and disappears below the water.

"Holy crap, what was that?" I exclaim, hurrying forward to make sure Silac isn't missing any chunks, but he's all in one piece. Water drips from his emerald green hair, the same color as his hood when he's in half form. It's flopped down over one eye, and he looks thoroughly bedraggled as he flips it back out of his face. Before I can say anything, Tirrian comes flying out of the water. He's in his half form, his wings propelling him into the air so that he's hovering above the pool.

"Shit, don't stay there. Didn't you see the beast in the water?" I hiss at him, gesturing for him to move his ass.

He casually flies over, landing gently beside me, water running in rivulets down his body, but it starts to steam, and the steam wafts up and away from him. I guess central heating comes in handy when you want to dry off quickly.

"What beast? Are you sure? I didn't see anything down there." He peers out over the water as Silac starts to shiver, his teeth chattering.

"Oh, you poor thing." I hurry over and use my hands to try and warm him, briskly rubbing them up and down his arms. "We need to get you warmed up." I look up at the surly dragon. "Can you help him?" I ask, and he sighs heavily like it's a big inconvenience but crouches down and holds out his hands.

"You know, with your Elementi powers, you could start a fire and we could all warm up a bit."

I blink at him in confusion. "But there is nothing to start a fire with." I look around the big room and notice that there are plants in the rock face all around the cavern. "Oh, hang on, I guess I could use those." I go to stand, but Silac grabs me and shakes his head, droplets of water falling off of him as his teeth chatter.

"No, they are rilax berries. The Rilu people harvest those, even if they don't in this area, but let's not upset the sentient cavern any further."

I bite my lip and nod. "That's actually a good idea."

"And you don't actually need anything. You can create fire. Just put it on one of those rocks." Tirrian carries a boulder over to us and places it in front of Silac. "If you had the water ability, you could just draw all the water out, but because you don't, this will have to do. Try not to go apocalyptic on us."

"Okay, but I might need blood sooner rather than later," I warn the surly dragon, who crosses his arms and nods.

"I said we would feed you, and with the warlock nowhere to be seen, that remains the case."

Worry washes through me as I wonder what

happened to Xavier and Zala. Why didn't they drop into the lake as well?

"Alright then. I need to take my dress off so I don't lose it in the change."

Silac averts his eyes, and Tirrian turns his back, much to my surprise, but I appreciate it. I drop the dress, careful not to lose my little gem. I allow the picture of my fire Elementi to fill my mind and feel the change wash over me. Accessing its powers is as easy as breathing now that I've practiced with Xavier. I point my hands at the rock, willing flames to form around it. Within moments, it's crackling with warmth, the red and blue flames flickering gently in the wind free cavern. I change back and put my dress on as Silac holds his hands out and rubs them together.

"Oh, that's much better, thank you. It won't take me too long to warm up, and then I'll move quicker. I'm always so sluggish when I'm cold. It comes from being cold-blooded."

"What happened to you guys? Where did you all go? Where are the other two?" I fire the questions at Tirrian, since he seems to be coping better than Silac. He stalks around the room, pacing back and forth with nervous energy.

"I don't know what happened to Zala and Xavier. I was sliding along a tunnel until I slammed into Silac, and then we both fell into the lake. It doesn't seem possible to end up here from where we started, but we did. This cavern is freaky. No wonder people stay away from it." The usually surly, unruffled dragon is agitated. His wings keep shuddering behind him, and he can't seem to stand still.

"How are you doing?" I ask the snake, who smiles at me.

"Much better now, thank you."

"Did you see what threw you out of the lake? Thank goodness it didn't take a bite out of you." I move a little closer to make sure there definitely aren't any injuries, my eyes roaming over his body. I can't see any blood, but his clothes are molded to him, and I can see some very interesting muscles under those tight clothes.

"Ah, um. No, I didn't," he stumbles over his words, looking at Tirrian. "Maybe you did?" he asks, his eyes seeming to drill into the dragon.

"Nope. Not me," the dragon says without even turning to look at us. He's poking at something on the wall.

"What are you doing?" I get up and wander over to him. I thought he might be trying to pry a gem out of the wall—you know how dragons are about their hoards—but instead he's pushing a big, fat slug away from one of the rilax berry bushes. It seems to become annoyed at him and shoots some thick, pink liquid out of its back end.

"Ew, what is that?" I ask, grossed out but also interested.

"This is a silax worm. They eat the rilax berries, and their secretion" —he points at the slimy stuff— "kills the plants, but they also use it to make achom."

I feel my stomach roll as I remember drinking the stuff he's talking about. "Gross, I'm never drinking that again."

He chuckles, and his smile makes his whole face shine. I'm kind of gobsmacked for a moment while I take in his beauty. "It's like that with a lot of things in the galaxy. Better not to

know the how or why."

I'm still staring at him in wonder when Silac clears his throat. "We should probably figure out where to go next," he suggests, breaking the moment between the dragon and me.

Tirrian steps away and runs his finger covetously over a large opalescent gem in the wall. "You know, I don't have any of these in my hoard. I was hoping to maybe find a loose one while we were walking, but I've had no luck," he mutters absently, and I pat the one inside my dress to make sure it's still there. "Okay, so what's the plan, Lila?" he asks, still not looking at me.

"Well, I was heading in that direction when you two dropped out of the ceiling." I point to the only exit I can see in the whole cavern.

"Well, okay then. Come on, Silac. We need to get moving. Time is winding down, and I don't know how much of it we lost getting swallowed up. We will have to keep an eye out for Zala and Xavier on the way. Hopefully the cave just sent them back to the start or they are farther on."

Tirrian is all business now, and he holds out his hand to help Silac to his feet. He's relatively dry, since the fire was hot and did a good job, though he does grimace at his feet, which still seem to be wet. He takes off one and empties it over the fire, which hisses and steams, followed by the other, which puts the rest of the fire out.

"That was good thinking," I say to him, and he grins.

"Two birds, one stone, so to speak. Now my feet won't slosh as I walk."

"Okay, let's do this." I lead the way, Xavier's ball of light keeping pace with me as the two shifters bring up the rear.

I'm not sure how long we walk, but it feels like the tunnel system is endless. We don't find any more big caverns, but the tunnel widens and shrinks, and at one stage, all three of us were crawling on hands and knees because the tunnel was so small. Thank goodness we could all do that.

CHAPTER TWENTY-FOUR

Lila

Finally, after what seems like forever, we emerge back into a large cavernous space, one much larger than we'd been through up until now. It's probably the size of two football fields. I stop dead when I see what is in this cavern, and Tirrian and Silac run into me as I do.

"What the hell, Lila?" Tirrian grumbles, grabbing hold of me to steady himself. My skin burns under his touch, but it's a pleasant feeling, like being wrapped in a warm hug or sliding into a steaming hot bath, and I almost sink into his embrace, but I quickly get my shit together before I do something stupid.

"Wow." Silac's voice is soft and sounds as amazed as I feel.

Not only is this cavern large, but it's brightly lit by sunlight shining through holes in the ceiling. Down in the bottom of the cavern, probably twenty feet below where we are, is a herd of larnuks unlike any I've seen to date. Much like the gem shoved down the front of my dress, these shine like multi-colored opals, all oranges, pinks, and blues. They actually remind me a little of the beautiful but deadly Aaz'axian Brannock. He wouldn't look out of place walking amongst them.

I watch as one stretches its wings out, the bright colors reflecting beautifully as the sunlight hits them at just the right angle.

Off to one side, some small—I'm assuming younger—larnuks, are running and playing and kicking up sparks from their hooves on the cavern floors. One of them trips and tumbles, its wings akimbo as it rolls across the ground, but it shakes itself off and gets back up, running after its friends who didn't even stop.

The sound of animals crunching on gems echoes through the cabins, but despite the loud noise, one of them has noticed our arrival. It throws its head back and growls that deep, unexpected sound, causing the rest to stop what they are doing and look up.

"We are fucked," Silac mutters. "Without Zala to possibly control the larnuks, we have no chance of getting the flower." He points to a small grassy grove that is smack-dab in the middle of the cavern, surrounded on all sides by these beautiful animals. Probably no bigger than six feet across, the round garden bed contains five plants, all of which have a beautiful, flaming red flower in the middle of it. The colored petals literally look like flames bursting out of the stem, and I know this is what I need to save Grandpa John as well as my newly revealed grandma.

"I could shift form and fly across," I suggest, but Tirrian quickly shakes his head.

"The larnuks can fly too."

"Okay, what about shifting into the earth Elementi and using its powers to tunnel through the rock and come up over there?" I point to the grassy patch, and the infuriating dragon raises one questioning eyebrow.

"Do you think you have the kind of control you need to not come up and destroy the flowers?"

My heart sinks, because damn it, he's right. I can't guarantee I won't destroy them.

"Look, I think you should just try to approach the larnuks. They obviously have some symbiotic relationship with the cavern, and if it's allowed you to get this far, then what's to say that you won't be allowed to continue? We can shift into our animals and escort you in case they get any ideas. The two of us are pretty scary if we need to be," Silac suggests, offering some actual help instead of shooting everything I propose down like the dragon.

A huge sigh whooshes out of me. "Okay, well, I guess that plan sounds the most sensible so far, but if I end up as lunch to a crystal-eating winged horse, then I will come back to haunt you," I tell the naga, who chuckles.

He and Tirrian shift. Tirrian launches himself into the air, his beautiful pink and black dragon flapping lazily to keep him suspended just in front of me. I've seen his dragon form before, and it flicks out a long, forked tongue that slobbers on my cheek before returning to his mouth.

"Ugh, dude, that's gross," I tell him, and the dragon chuckles, smoke huffing out of his nostrils.

I shrink back when I turn to look at Silac. I've never seen him in shifted form, and it's scary as fuck. Gone is anything resembling a human man, and in front of me is a large, green hooded, orange and black scaled cobra-like snake. He's fifteen feet high, and his fangs look as long as my hand.

His head comes down to my level, and I can't help the little squeal that escapes my mouth, but instead of lashing out and biting me, he just butts my head with his affectionately before twining his body around mine. As he wraps me up in his coils, I get lifted into the air. I'm terrified, but I finally realize we are actually moving. Silac is slithering down the path that winds down the rock face to the bottom of the cavern. Tirrian keeps pace the whole way, his wings kicking up a breeze with every downward thrust. Eventually, I settle into the journey, Silac's coils warm against my skin. I'm no more nervous now than I was the first time we met. I know he won't hurt me no matter what form he is in, and this one is kind of awesome, much like Tirrian's dragon. His attraction mark on my shoulder throbs reassuringly, which is also comforting. I now know that I can't help but add more mates to my harem until my mimic powers are satisfied, and I'm not going to feel guilty about it—or not too guilty. Let's face it, Silac is sexy, but despite our mutual attraction, that's as far as it can go with his arranged marriage, and I am incredibly sad about it. Hopefully once we get some distance, the marks will fade.

The larnuks follow our path, not returning to grazing, intent on watching our every movement, but they don't seem scared to have two huge, apex predators entering their home. That in itself tells me everything I need to know. These creatures are just as badass as the two that accompany me.

When we get to the bottom, Silac releases me, waiting until I have my bearings before backing away. Tirrian also sets down, and they take up guard behind me. I take a step forward, but the larnuks suddenly move. Before I can blink, they create a barrier between me and the flower. If I want it, I'm going to have to go through them.

A lump develops in my throat, and I turn back to look at the shifters behind me. Silac stares at me, his unblinking eyes slightly unnerving, but Tirrian's dragon pushes his head forward and runs his tongue up my cheek again before nudging me forward.

"I guess you think I should try and get through them?" I ask him, wiping away the slobber again, not bothering to scold him because I think that's exactly what he wants.

He nods his giant head. Heaving a sigh, I turn back to face the animals. As I go to step forward again, one of the gangly teenagers comes barreling over, his steps awkward and hurried. He practically slides on his ass like a rodeo rider's horse when he comes to a stop, but he puts himself between me and the lead horse that is somewhat in front of the rest of the group.

I pause again and consider taking the form of my fire Elementi, but the thought of burning any of these beautiful animals is abhorrent to me, so instead, I stay in my Rilunese form and pray that they will move to the side and let me through. Bracing myself, I step forward again, one foot after the other. Behind me, I feel Tirrian and Silac follow,

Tirrian's lumbering footsteps shaking the ground slightly, but they don't crowd me.

I expect the larnuks to move out of the way, but instead, the teenager holds his ground next to his much larger herd leader right up until I go to move past them, then he strikes. Before I can even react, his teeth sink into my forearm, sending searing pain through my body.

I scream, the sound echoing through the entire cavern, but within seconds of the pain hitting me, it dissipates, and I feel another sense inside my mind. It's the larnuk, and he's so fucking happy with himself. He releases my arm, and his chest puffs up, and his awkward, gangly wings poke out as he turns and pushes his way past the herd leader, making a path through his fellow animals. I can tell he expects me to follow.

I look down at my arm that is now bleeding quite freely. I remove the head scarf that had been holding my hair back and wrap it around the wound, and as I do, my hair falls free around my shoulders, and I blink in surprise. Gone are the chestnut locks, which are now the same colors as this herd's coat. My hair is now completely opalescent, and at the sight of it, every single animal in front of me goes down on one knee and bows their heads in respect. It only lasts a moment, and then the larger lead animal stands up and throws his head back with a growl. The rest of the herd follows suit until the cavern echoes with the sounds. Goosebumps race across my skin as I consider what just happened. I'm assuming I bonded with the larnuk, but why is my entire hair this color and not just a streak? And what the fuck am I going to do with a larnuk?

A sense of impatience interrupts my thoughts, and I quickly follow after my new friend. He is standing in front of the flamegem flower, looking pleased. He nudges his horn at it before nudging me with the same thing. I brace for it to pierce my chest, but he just bumps it gently against me, and I can tell the little bugger is laughing at me.

Remembering that I need to change to my Celestian form, I allow my dress to fall away and let the mimic change take over, but I watch in utter amazement as my larnuk also shivers, and his wings change to match the ones that now grace my back.

"Holy fuck, did you see that?" I ask the two behind me, but they are not even looking at the animal. Both of them are staring at my naked form, with heat and so much more in their animalistic gazes.

"Whoops, sorry, guys. I guess you've seen me naked entirely too much on this trip. I'm sorry." I remove the bag Zamala gave me from the pocket in my dress and bend down to pluck the flower.

It's so hot I feel the skin on my hand sizzle as I tear it from its stem and carefully place it in the bag so as not to destroy the petals. I can smell my skin burning, but I grit my teeth and bear the pain. If this is what it takes to save my grandparents, then it's the least I can do for them.

Finally, I close the bag, keeping the precious flower protected. I'm pleased to see it's not burning like my hand did. I look down at the blackened flesh and feel sick when I see the extent of the burn. It no longer hurts because I have burnt through the nerve layer. Thankfully I have access to Celestian healing powers, and my hand starts to glow. I watch with amazement as the skin knits itself back together until it doesn't even look like anything happened.

I allow the Celestian form to fall away, but I can't return to the Rilunese one. I'm exhausted, and it's all I can do to keep myself on my feet as I bend down and wrap the dress around my body.

I can feel the worry from my new friend, and he nudges me a couple of times. When I look up, I notice all of the rest of the animals have returned to their grazing, paying no more attention to me and my companions.

Silac and Tirrian watch me silently before Tirrian gets down on his belly and crawls forward like a cat or a dog. His large head nudges against my stomach, and I absently scratch between the heavy ridge above his eyes. They roll back in enjoyment before he shakes his head and nudges me again before exposing his neck to me.

"Oh, you want me to feed from you?" I ask, and he quickly nods. I wrinkle my nose. "Are you sure, dude? Your human self doesn't like me very much." He just rolls his eyes and nudges me again.

"Well, okay then. I bet you're going to taste all funky and blugh." He frowns like he's insulted by this, but beggars can't be choosers, and there is no way we are getting back to the surface with me like this. Shit, I don't even know how we're going to get back to the surface.

At this, I feel an insistent tugging in my mind. I know it's my new friend, so hopefully he's going to be able to guide us out.

"Okay, let's just hope my fangs can pierce your hide. It's not like they are all that big to start with." He lifts a front claw and points to a spot tucked behind a large flared ridge.

When I run my finger over it, his whole body shivers, and I discover it's soft and fleshy.

"Okay, yeah, that will work. God, I hope my venom doesn't cause your dragon to orgasm, because that could make things kind of awkward, not to mention messy," I mutter, and I feel him chuckle.

When my eyes meet his again, he's rolling them playfully. Hopefully that means it won't. I lean over his huge head as he angles his chin up and away from me, giving me as much room as possible to get to the small space. Just like human skin, my fangs puncture it like it's a marshmallow. Pulling back, I look down to make sure his blood is flowing freely and squeak in surprise when I discover it's the same pink as his scales. It's flowing very fast, so I quickly seal my mouth around it and start to swallow, and I just about orgasm on the spot. It's hot, delicious, and spicy, kind of like queso, salsa, and chips. I guzzle it down, making noises of pleasure as it makes my taste buds sing. Eventually, I pull back, aware that I've taken a decent amount of blood, but I'm feeling fuller than I have since we left Skarr. Before I can thank Tirrian and seal the holes up, his big ass paw shoves my head back down.

"Drink more, Lila. He can take it," Silac says from behind me. I glance up and see he's in his half form, and I devour him with my eyes as I lean in and drink more. There's something kind of erotic about the way Silac is watching me feed from Tirrian. Beneath his scales, I can see his two cocks writhing like they are trying to push out of his skin. Jesus, I want to know what they can do, but it's not to be, so I turn my head back to the dragon and continue to drink.

Despite his surly asshole attitude, he's done everything possible to keep me safe, and I feel my feelings toward him changing. Thinking back over the last few days, I realize his actions have actually been the opposite of his words. He's looked after me, taken care of my needs, and made sure that I am safe. That doesn't seem to be the actions of someone who's indifferent. I can't help but allow myself to start to feel. I'm so incredibly attracted to him physically, but that is growing now, and feelings are starting to worm their way in. I try to rein them in and bury them down deep, but I know the minute his dragon flinches and stiffens that my attraction mark has appeared on his big body somewhere. Damn it. I pull away and seal the holes so they don't continue to bleed. Nobody likes rejection, and I know the minute he changes back, something nasty will come out of his mouth. I almost kind of wish that he will be stuck in dragon form for the near future.

I push his head away and look around the cavern. "Okay, I guess we need to get out of here. I'm sure Xavier is frantic with worry, and if we don't get moving, I don't doubt he will tear it down to get to me, and that will not be good for interplanetary relations."

"Lila," Silac calls out, but I ignore him. I can practically feel his question, and I don't want to face the fact that my attraction marks are now on two men who will never be mine, and worse, my mimic wants them. She's wanted them since the moment we set foot on the ship, and there's been this low-key nagging inside me, but I have enough control now to not take their choice away from them, and they both made their feelings clear on the subject. Time and distance will make the marks fade, but how can I get that when both of them are constantly in my face and will be as we go forward? Silac will be near me at least for the next year, and all I can do is hope that Tirrian finds a mate his dragon is happy with and returns to Fluxx to rule the dragons.

"Okay, new friend. How about you show us how to get out of here?" I ask him.

He does this weird growl and prances off across the cavern, pushing past the rest of his herd. Without turning back to see if they are following, I hurry after him. My fragile emotions are all over the place—embarrassment, disappointment, and seething jealousy—and to make it even worse, seeing Silac's writhing cocks beneath his scales has lit a fuse in my body, which had actually been well sated the whole trip. All of it floods my body, making me feel restless, angry, and desperate for a hug from my warlock. Actually, truth be told, I need a puppy pile with all my mates. I don't think I'm going to be happy until I have them all with me again, and I desperately miss my babies. It's like an ache where my heart is, and I know that I never want to be apart from them for so long again.

I also want to heal my grandpa. I'm ready to put this all behind us, and I can't wait to tell the three of them that their wife is alive. I have a feeling that they will want to head straight to the planet and break her out, but it's going to take careful planning, and I promised Xavier we would go to his home planet first. I will not put off having my memories returned any longer, and having the extra powers our intimate bond will give me will surely be an asset when we go to the inhospitable planet where both the plants and animals will eat you.

CHAPTER TWENTY-FIVE

Lila

The trip back through the cavern is silent and awkward. Tirrian had to shift from his dragon form to fit into the tunnel that my new friend led us down. Unlike Silac, who is covered by his scales, he's strolling through the tunnels butt ass naked without a care in the world. My kraken finally woke up and keeps trying to get me to turn around so we can see him in all his naked glory, but I refuse to give in to the urge. It's only going to lead to disappointment, because despite my attraction mark appearing on him, his hasn't emerged on my body. No one can accuse me of being dense. I know exactly what that means.

We've only been walking for half the amount of time as the previous journey when I see bright light shining at the end of the tunnel. My new friend breaks into a jaunty little trot, and I start to run, keeping pace with him.

"Lila," Silac calls, but I don't turn. "Lila," he shouts more insistently, and I slow my pace but still refuse to turn around.

"What, Silac?" I huff out my annoyance at being stopped.

"Switch forms, or you will burn very quickly," he says softly, and I want to punch myself in the head. Of course my normal form will not cope with Rilu's suns. I allow my form to shift, but then I remember he'd had protection from Xavier before. I wonder if he still has it now that he's shifted.

"Thank you," I say politely, still not turning around. "What about you? Do I need to send Xavier back in to help you?"

"No, Xavier's protection stayed on me and moved with my shifts. I should be alright."

Nodding my head, I continue my hurried pace, not waiting for either of them. I don't even bother asking the dragon, because I know he will be fine, and to be honest, a part of me wouldn't even care if he went up in a blazing ball of fire.

I emerge from the tunnel to find us in the entrance cavern where the journey first started. Sitting on some of the scattered rock formations are Xavier, Zala, and Zilla. I think we give them a fright, because the three of them stare at me and my new companion in open-mouthed silence.

"Holy fuck, what happened to you?" Xavier leaps to his feet and hurries over, but my new friend growls and puts himself protectively between me and the warlock.

"Xavier, stop moving," Zala commands, and something urgent in her tone has him stopping on the spot.

"Easy now," she whispers to the larnuk who is baring his teeth while a low rumble comes out of his throat. There's no mistaking the warning.

"How the fuck did an opalescent bond with a pathetic creature like you?" Zilla screeches. "And why the fuck is Tirrian naked?" she demands, and I guess Silac and Tirrian have exited the tunnel behind me.

Xavier looks from me to the two shifters, and I see amusement sparkle in his eyes. "Lila, you've got some explaining to do," he says, but I can tell he's joking. I roll my eyes at him.

"She sure as fuck does. The opalescent haven't bonded with a person in years. What kind of fucking witchcraft did she use on it to make it bond with her." Zilla and Zala have both approached. The latter is calm and accepting of my newfound friend, but Zilla is livid. Zala stops in line with Xavier, but Zilla pushes her luck and lunges forward, throwing herself in front of my new friend and bowing her head to it.

Zala clicks her tongue. "Zilla, look at Lila. She is well and truly bonded. This little one must be the future herd leader and he has chosen Lila to be their protector. There hasn't been a full herd bonding in years, but there is no changing what has happened."

"Is that why Lila's hair has changed color?" Xavier asks as we watch Zilla try to convince my new friend to bite her. Zilla holds out her hand, and my new friend sniffs it. "Can the bond be shifted?"

Zala shrugs. "If the person the larnuk bonds to dies, then the larnuk can establish a new bond if they wish."

Zilla's head comes up, and she turns slowly to look at me. Her eyes narrow, and I know she's considering what her sister just said.

"Surely she wouldn't be so stupid?" I hear Silac mutter behind me. "The Rilu people have no special powers, and Lila has hundreds. There is no way she could expect to defeat her, is there?"

I can tell just when Zilla decides to try. Obviously being bound to an opalescent means more to her than any goodwill between my family and hers. She reaches into the pocket of her pants and pulls out a futuristic-looking pistol. Before I can even blink, she pulls the trigger. I don't have time to change forms before I'm being yanked off my feet, and Tirrian wraps his body around mine, cocooning us within his wings. I scream with fright as I expect the gun to penetrate his wings and burn a hole straight through them, but nothing happens. I can smell burnt flesh and hear the others shouting, but I'm safe. My heart is pounding in my ears, but Tirrian's arms are tight around my body, and his naked skin is hot against mine, making me feel warm and safe and cozy. Our eyes meet, and his beast flashes in and out as I feel his cock start to harden against my body. I lean up to press a tentative kiss to his lips.

"Thank you," I whisper as I pull away. He looks like I smacked him with a two by four. There's a familiar burning sensation in my shoulder as the new attraction mark forms. I want to shout with joy, but I finally realize someone is calling my name.

"Lila! Tirrian, you can let go now." Silac tries to coax the dragon to release me, but his arms don't move a bit.

"Ah, buddy, if you don't, Lila's new friend is eyeing your ass with interest, and I don't think you want his teeth in those meaty globes." That's my warlock, and I laugh. Of course he's checking out Tirrian's naked ass. He's such an opportunist.

"Stop perving on the dragon. Please clothe him, then I think he will release me," I call out, looking down at the hard, thick, mouthwatering cock between us. I don't want Zilla or Zala seeing what he has to offer, despite it being off-limits to me as well, because I know that even though the attraction marks have appeared on our bodies, we're not going to be instantly in love. His asshole ways are not suddenly going to change. In fact, I have a feeling that they are only going to get worse.

I reluctantly release him, sad but resigned in the knowledge that I may never be wrapped in his arms and wings again.

Clothes appear on him—black leather pants that do nothing to hide his obvious attraction to me, and a tight shirt with a sushi dragon on it. I smother my smile, because I don't want him to realize what Xavier has done.

"Such a shame to cover all of that, but are you happy?" My warlock is smirking as we break apart, his eyebrow cocked in amusement. Above him, Zilla is floating in a bubble cage. I can see her banging on it, and she's shouting, but no noise makes it through. There's a pool of blood below her, and she's holding the stump of her arm against her body. I look at my larnuk, and he seems to be munching quite happily on the remains of Zilla's hand. Holy crap. Xavier and Tirrian have nothing on the protective instincts of my new friend.

"Are you okay?" Silac hurries over, checking both of us for injuries, his eyes flicking back and forth between his and his beast's. His forked tongue flicks out a couple of times in agitation as he runs his hands over my body. I don't even think he's aware that he's doing it, but you won't hear me complaining.

Xavier chuckles harder, because I know he's feeling everything I am projecting. I won't ever hide my feelings from him, and he doesn't seem the least bit upset that I once again have more men with my attraction marks on their shoulders. He's just a kinky perv.

"Prince Tirrian, please, I beg you, don't hold the actions of a deluded woman against the rest of her race." Zala is on her knees with her head bowed, pleading for him not to declare war or something on Rilu for Zilla attacking him.

His fiery gaze finally leaves mine, leaving words between us that still haven't been exchanged, but I really don't expect them to be.

"Zilla will need to pay for her crimes," he says. "Attacking Lila in an attempt to bond the opalescent herd was unconscionable. The larnuk bond cannot be forced and is considered sacred to the financial success of Rilu. Without it, your people would suffer. I will allow your father to punish her, but if I do not agree with his ruling, I will take her home to Fluxx and present her to my father and have her charged with trying to kill the crown prince's mate."

Excuse me, what? You could hear a pin drop at his announcement. Did he just say what I think he said? Xavier chuckles harder, grabbing his stomach, and I feel like kicking him.

"This is the best entertainment since the warlock council accidentally got served suva tea instead of their mind enlightening tea during a council session."

"Your mate?" Zala looks between the dragon and me, and her eyes widen with realization.

"Yes," he grinds out, sounding furious. "My dragons have made it clear that they will not accept anyone but Lila as their mate, and if I keep trying to find others, they will eat them on sight. That does not mean the mating will ever be sealed. I hate having my life dictated to me by creatures I share my body with, and it would be a deep betrayal to my cousin."

"Your cousin is a douche and deserved being banished. Shit, he kills people for a living now. It wouldn't surprise me if he ends up gunning for Lila, especially if he hears that she's your mate as well." Silac waves his hand in the air, his voice turning particularly sibilant with his agitation, and I feel an instant wave of gratitude for the snake man. Nobody likes having their choice taken away from them—shit, I am the reigning fucking princess of having my choices taken away, but I've suffered with grace and dignity all while learning about a completely new world that I had no idea existed.

"Fucking get over yourself, asshole. Just because

I'd like to take a spin on that half decent looking cock doesn't mean I want to tie myself to you for life. Get up, Zala. We're not going to hold a whole race responsible for one person's actions." I give Tirrian the side-eye. "If we did that, then I would hold the whole dragon race responsible for Dylan's actions when he tried to kill me."

"Oh snap." Xavier's chuckles fade away. "Lila is most gracious. I could very easily hold a race responsible for one person's actions, considering she is also my intimate. Zilla has made some very powerful enemies now, and if she sees the light of day again, it would be a mistake. Better to throw her to Lila's herd of opalescent and be done with it."

Zala sighs. "Yes, I don't disagree, but my father has always hoped that Zilla's ambitions would settle as she got older. She's been bitter since she discovered I would take over Father's position of chief when I was able to bond with more than one type of gem horse and she didn't."

"Jealousy is a terrible emotion, especially within families. One should be happy for the achievements of their loved ones. But I agree, it is fair to want your father to be involved. We need to hurry though. I don't want to wait any longer than I have to. John has suffered long enough, not to mention Eric and William, as they have been so very worried. It is time to put an end to this," I tell her, and she nods.

"Of course, Lila, and if you don't want me to return to the circus, I would understand. You have your own larnuk now, and you could have a couple more from the herd join you and perform that act yourself." Zala is still at our feet, and I stare down at her in horror.

"Ah, resignation denied. For fuck's sake, I barely have time to breathe, let alone add something like that to my schedule. No, Zala, I most definitely want you to return and keep showing your larnuks. My grandpas want me to start taking over their duties, which means I have the lightning cat show to work out, and I still need to find out if the Aquilians are returning or if we need to replace them, and I recently gave birth to three adorable but precocious children who are exhausting." I drop down on my own knees and grab her hands. "Please come back," I beg her, and she finally lifts her head, some of the anguish in her eyes fading away.

"You honor me with your friendship. I will not let you down again."

"Pfft, you never let me down, your skank sister did, but tell me what I am going to do with that." I point to my new friend, who has finished munching on Zilla's hand and is curiously sniffing at the three men who are listening with interest. Silac and Xavier both step back a little, but Tirrian just grabs him and wraps his arm around his neck, keeping him in place. My new friend closes his eyes and leans his head against the dragon's chest, looking happy and content.

"Well, he's yours now, so if you don't take him with us, he will get sick. He can join my herd on the ship, and you can visit him every day. Once he gets big enough and his muscles are developed enough to fly, I will teach you to ride him."

"Sounds like a good deal to me, but what about food? He's supposed to have opalescent gems, isn't he? How are we going to harvest them?" I look back the way we came, and Zala frowns.

"The cavern should let someone in to harvest them for him now. I think you will probably have to nominate one of the villagers to do it for you, and they will send us bags of them." My larnuk opens his eyes and gives a small nod of his head.

Holy shit, he is intelligent, but I guess I shouldn't have expected anything less. "They are just larnuks, aren't they? He's not going to shift and suddenly there will be another naked man looking at me like he'd like to devour me and not in the same way he just devoured Zilla, right?"

Zala snorts with amusement and shakes her head. "No, they are not shifters."

"Thank fuck for that," I mutter as I get to my feet and offer a hand to Zala to help her up. "Come on. I want to go home. Let's organize my proxy gem collector and head back to the city." Then I think about something. "How are we going to get him back to the city if he can't fly?"

"We have a sling system that we use to move younger horses. One of the other larnuks can carry him. Oh, and you will have to name him."

"Okay, I'll have to think about it."

CHAPTER TWENTY-SIX

Lila

When we return to the village, I tell Xavier to let Zilla down, and then I change to my Celestian form. I heal the torn flesh at the end of Zilla's arm. I probably could have regrown it with my power, but she tried to kill me, so making sure she doesn't bleed out before she can be punished is as kind as I can get.

I speak to a villager about harvesting opalescent gems for my new friend Shiny, and we return to the cavern to make sure he can get in and out. He can, and I heave a sigh of relief. One less problem. Xavier gives him some coins, and I will arrange for regular payments to go to him through Chief Zana.

Zala gets Shiny kitted out with a sling under his belly, and she was going to attach the ropes to one of her horses, but Tirrian insists on carrying the straps with his dragon.

Eventually, we are on our way. Xavier and Silac share a larnuk again, and I'm on the one I rode out to the settlement. Zilla is strapped onto one of Zala's, and the one she rode is flying with the rest of Zala's herd.

We are quite the procession back to the city, but I'm exhausted both emotionally and physically by the time we touch down at Zala's family compound. I've been replaying all of Tirrian's words of rejection, not to mention Silac's marriage arrangement. I can't seem to let go of the fact that neither of these men will be mine. My mimic powers start to press me to change, insisting if I take their forms, they will not be able to stop themselves from becoming mine, but I resist with everything I have. I will not take away anyone's will.

When we land, Chief Zana hurries out to greet us and frowns when he sees Zilla.

"What happened?" he demands, looking between us, but we let Zala answer.

She proceeds to give Chief Zana the whole story, and the way his eyes widen are comical when I remove my scarf from my head, showing him my hair. Apparently this is my hair now. It's permanently colored the same as my larnuk in my Rilunese, Skarrian, and Celestian forms. Who knows if it will carry over into other forms? Only time will tell.

Zilla was returned to her bubble of silence when she wouldn't stop yelling profanities, and her father looks at her with disdain and disappointment.

"What would you like to happen to her? You are the wounded party," he asks, sadness etched in his eyes.

"It's not in my nature to condemn someone to death for their actions, though I know that is quite normal in the galaxy. If she had come after one of my mates or my children, I may feel differently, but to be honest, I'm more vindictive than that. Death is too quick of an ending. I'd like to see her suffer. Jail her, and each week, we will send videos and updates on how amazing our lives are. I would like someone to read out these stories to Zilla. I'd also like her to be jailed in view of the bonding ceremonies. I want her to watch people bond with larnuks every day, knowing she is never going to be able to."

"Whoa, that is a whole new level of viciousness. I love it." Xavier adjusts himself when I say this. Obviously, I'm turning him on. I roll my eyes and shake my head at him.

"Thank you, Lila, you are most gracious, and I am forever in your debt." Chief Zana bows to me, his hands pressed together in front of him.

"But what about her larnuk? Will it suffer?" I

look at Zilla's poor creature, who is still with all of Zala's animals.

"No, we will return him to his original herd. As long as he is on the planet, he is close enough to Zilla to survive. We can't sever the bond, but I have a feeling it will fade on its own. Larnuks are honorable creatures, and Zilla's behavior was most definitely not honorable, so I doubt the bond will survive her betrayal. He will be fine."

"Good, now if you don't mind, we will take our leave. I want to head straight to Celestia and heal my grandpa. Zala, will you return with us?" I'm not sure how we will fit her and all of her animals on our ship though.

"I will follow in my own ship. I assume the circus will resume once John has healed?"

"Not immediately. We have a side trip to Westalin planned first, and then we will need to rescue my grandmother. I will send you a message when we are to start performing again."

"Sounds like a plan. I will keep Shiny here with me. He should be alright for a few weeks without you. If it changes, we will find you," she assures me.

We say our farewells, and Zala drives us to the spaceport where we quickly board our ship and set course for Celestia.

Saxon

"Saxon?" Lila's voice has me sitting upright in bed, looking at the tablet on the other side of the bed. Nestled in the blankets between me and the device are three exhausted little cherubs who were a little hard to put to sleep this evening. They miss their mom, and they made sure we knew all about it today. After lots of tears and pacing back and forth, they finally fell asleep. We put them together in my bed, and I said I'd take first watch while the others got some much-needed sleep. They haven't been asleep all that long, so I climb off the bed, using my advanced speed, and within a couple of steps, I'm snatching up my tablet and hurrying into the bathroom so it doesn't disturb any of the babies.

"Lila?" My beautiful wife is on the screen. She looks exhausted, she has tear stains on her face, and her beautiful dark hair is now a shiny, eye-catching, multicolored mass. "Oh my beauty, I have missed you," I say quietly, and she hiccups and wipes the back of her hand across her nose. "Lila, what's wrong?" My hearts starts to race with concern, and I feel my fangs drop and my body prepare for battle. Something has upset my blood rose, and I will burn down the earth to make it all better.

"I miss you so much, all of you," she sobs. "I can't wait until we heal Grandpa. I can't be apart from you all anymore, and I can't let Xavier wait any longer. I have information about Grandma. We need to rescue her, and I will need all the help I can get. All of that will mean I'm apart from you all longer, and I don't want that."

Her words come out in a rush of information that I have trouble keeping straight, but the one thing I do understand is that she needs us.

Her tears flow freely, and she grabs a tissue from somewhere and blows her nose violently. "My emotions are all over the place, and I can't seem to shake off Tirrian's and Silac's rejections."

I feel my eyes widen with surprise, but thankfully she doesn't see it in her sadness. The snake and the dragon? When did that happen? Add in the merman and that brings her mates to nine. Wow, okay, this is fine. Great, even more powerful men to protect our family.

"Oh, baby. They will come around. I'm sure they have their reasons why they are fighting the attraction marks, but they are being stupid and stubborn. I have no doubt that they will come to their senses eventually and realize that being married to you is the most wonderful thing in the world," I assure my blood rose, but I don't think she hears it in her sadness. "And if they don't, I will kill them."

This gets her attention, and the tears stop flowing as a tentative smile stretches across her lips. "You would?" she asks.

"Of course. If you can't have them, no one can."

"Aww, Saxon, you are my favorite husband right now." She's beaming, and I feel my chest puff up in pride because I helped make her less sad.

"Now how about I pack our family up, we recall Broderick, and we all meet you at Celestia? That way we can all be together when John wakes up and we can go to Westalin together. I'm sure Xavier's parents would love to meet their grandchildren, and our kids would love to wrap their new grandparents around their tiny little tentacles." I peer through the bathroom door to make sure our gorgeous little terrors are still fast asleep, and sure enough, they are. I breathe a little sigh of relief as the last of Lila's sadness drifts away.

"Yes, a million times yes. That would be amazing. We should have done that to start with. I never should have left any of you at home. We could have just left you on the ship, orbiting the planet. Will we need to recall the rest of the flight crew or is Bubby enough?"

She worries her lip with her teeth, and I growl,

the urge to replace them with mine hitting me hard. I'll need to grab a bag of her blood when we are done with this call. "No, the guys and I can handle anything that Broderick can't do on his own. Both Xavier and I have experience manning helms of big ships. Maxsim, Echo, and Cas probably not so much, but they will be kept busy making sure the kids don't get lost on the big ship, and Link will read a manual and be up to speed almost instantly. We've got this."

"Are my rooms finished being redesigned? Is it going to be a problem if we take it now? I don't want to put anyone out."

"We got word today that the redesign is completed. It will be fine," I assure her and see her heave a sigh of relief. "Now go find our warlock and have him distract you from all of your worries. We will be reunited before you know it," I promise her, and she waves goodbye and disappears from the screen. I quickly send Xavier a message, explaining what just happened and that we will meet them in Celestia. I ask him to fill me in on the Silac and Tirrian situation in case I need to make sure my swords are sharpened and ask why Lila's hair is the color it is. Hopefully he will reply as soon as he's taken care of our mate.

I leave my tablet in the bathroom so that any messages don't wake the children and sneak out of the room in search of the rest of Lila's mates. I have the baby monitor and will know if the children start to wake.

I head to Echo's nest first. If he and Maxsim aren't with us and the children, then that's usually where we will find them. Sure enough, the two of them are snuggled up together in cat form, but Maxsim raises a lazy head and blinks at me when I approach. He is no longer the snappy, snarly predator he used to be. Bonding with Lila, and Echo having been bred, seems to have mellowed him completely. He's just a huge pussy cat at heart, and he adores our children. He suffers the hair pulling and cat rides with grace and dignity.

"I just spoke to Lila, she wants us to bring the ship and meet them at Celestia. She is really distraught about being apart from all of us, and things on Rilu might not have gone as well as she hoped." I'm guessing they got the flower because why else would we be meeting them at Celestia, but it's everything else I want to know about.

This gets his attention, and his ears prick up and his tail starts to twitch with agitation. Echo opens his eyes and stretches, yawning widely as he does. He shifts, turning from cat to man cat, and then he jumps to his feet and puts his hands on his hips.

"Well, what are we waiting for? We can't let our Lila be upset. Max and I will get all of the children's stuff ready to transport to the ship while you wake the others."

"Thank you, that would be great. Most of our stuff remained on the ship so it won't take us long to pack our own gear. Once I'm done, I will come and swap so you and Maxsim can retrieve anything you want to bring with you."

Max shifts into man cat form and stretches his arms high above him. I can't help but look at the length of his muscular body, admiring it for its strength.

"Are your babies still sleeping?" Max asks, reaching for his loincloth and pulling it on before tossing Echo's at him. Neither of them has concern for nudity, and I'm not complaining.

"Yes, on my bed. Here's the monitor. Can you keep an ear out and grab them if they wake? I will wake Cas and Link, and then place a call to Celestia to let them know we are on our way." I toss him the piece of equipment, which he easily snatches out of the air. He then kisses Echo on the cheek and leaps up out of the nest to land next to me. Echo quickly follows.

"Find out why Lila is upset and get a name if we need to kill anyone," Max instructs me casually before grabbing his omega by the hand and leading him off to complete their tasks.

I follow them out, chuckling. How is it that we both had the same kind of idea? I won't tell them that it's Silac and Tirrian yet. I don't want to cause conflict in case things change on their way to Celestia. It's two days for us, which makes it about seven for Lila's group. Lots can change in seven days.

I turn in the opposite direction of the cats and knock on Link's door. When he calls, "Come in," I'm surprised to find him sitting up in bed with a book in hand and Caspian lying next to him, fast asleep, with his tentacles wrapped around Link's legs. Link motions for me to be quiet then gestures for me to come over to his side of the bed.

"Cas is missing Lila fiercely and didn't want to be alone," he explains as I sit down on the edge of the bed. "He gradually wrapped his tentacles around me in his sleep." Link doesn't seem concerned, he just smiles affectionately down at the sleeping shifter.

"You don't need much sleep either, do you?" I ask him, and he shakes his head.

"No, I don't. I can keep going for days without sleep, and I thought it was more important that he get some."

"Okay, but Lila called, and she wants us to pack everything up and meet them at Celestia. She misses us all dreadfully, and it seemed to me like her emotions are all over the place again."

Link frowns and puts his book down. "Yes, Oshan said they would be until she had a full harem, but when she left, she seemed a lot better."

"It might not hurt for you to do regular checkups with her just to stay on top of it all, and I think maybe the trip didn't go to plan. She mentioned something about Silac and Tirrian."

"I bet that dragon has done something to upset her. He's like the proverbial bully, pulling her hair to get the pretty girl's attention. Does the dragon king have other sons in case his oldest suddenly went missing?"

I snort a chuckle of amusement. Looks like the cyborg is as bloodthirsty as the rest of Lila's mates.

"Let's leave that as a last resort. I'm going to call Celestia and let them know we are coming. Can you get Cas and yourselves organized? The cats have the kids for now."

Caspian groans and rolls over. Instead of unwrapping his tentacles, he just wraps his arms around Link's waist and buries his face into his stomach. "I need to call my brother and let him know what is happening. He can redirect his transport to Celestia and meet us there too, and someone needs to let Broderick and Magenta know we are leaving."

"Magenta can join us once the circus resumes. There are things we need to do before that happens. Lila mentioned her grandmother." That finally has Caspian turning his head from Link's stomach and opening his eyes.

"Her grandmother? Whoa, okay, but tell

Magenta anyway. We do not want to be on her bad side if she feels left out. We can recall the rest of the performers once the Adams are ready to continue the show, but if their wife is alive, that may be a little longer."

Link runs his hand through Caspian's hair, and the shifter closes his eyes again, enjoying the feeling. I don't even think the two of them realize that they are being so affectionate with one another.

"Fine, I'll call the captain and Magenta as soon as I'm done with the call to Celestia. Let's aim to leave as soon as we can, okay?"

I'm impatient to see my wife, and with the way the two others scramble into action, untangling themselves, I would say they are too. I leave them to finish their own organization. Whistling under my breath, I move to the office to make the necessary calls. Today is going to be great.

Yesterday, I received a call from my aunt, telling me that my old clan had returned to Vilax and requested mediation. She said I had to present myself in person so the council could make their rulings. I assured her I would get there as soon as I could. Of course, with so many other things that need to happen right now, that could be a little longer than they think. I'm ecstatic about it really. Let those bitches wait.

CHAPTER TWENTY-SEVEN

Lila

The tension on our ship bound for Celestia is high, and everything is so damn awkward. I keep walking in on hushed conversations between Silac and Xavier, where they both clam up the minute I walk in the door. I know they are planning something, but they haven't bothered to share what or why. For all I know, they are planning to bump off Tirrian the minute his back is turned. Speaking of that asshole, he hasn't said another word to me despite admitting to everyone that his dragons have chosen me as his mate. And what does he mean, dragons? I mean, there's only one of them, so referring to them as plural is freaking weird. I'm almost certain I don't actually want anything from this man despite his banging body and pogo stick of a cock. My vagina and kraken mourn that we will never be able to take it for a spin, but oh well, that's life.

I spend the seven-day trip to Celestia practicing my other forms as much as possible. I'm still lacking knowledge of my Aquilian form, so I'm hoping once the guys arrive with the circus ship, I can use the empty Aquilian pool to practice everything I need to know. I wonder if they took all the sea life with them when they returned to Aquilia or if they are still on the ship. It might be fun to swim with Nikos's little friend, Sweetpea.

"Lila, we just arrived in Celestian airspace. We've been given permission to land on the planet, so it won't be long now." Xavier comes into the workout space, and I stop what I am doing. His eyes heat when he sees that I'm in my own warlock form, and he stalks quickly toward me, wrapping his arms around me and kissing me hard despite how sweaty I am.

I've been levitating the gym equipment to build up my strength, and it's hard work, but I'm finally getting there. I can now lift a whole weight bench, and these ones are a lot heavier because they are designed to withstand shifter and Vilaxian strength.

"You are so beautiful." Xavier looks down at me with a gentle smile.

"You're just saying that because I ended up with

marks similar to yours." I rest my head against his chest, physically and emotionally exhausted.

"No, *phoeall*, I loved you when you just looked like you and was the happiest man alive, knowing you were my intimate. It doesn't matter what form you are in, you are beautiful."

"Even in half kraken form?" I ask him, and he winks.

"Especially in half kraken form. How about we have a quick shower and freshen up for Celestia, and I can show you just how much I love every form?" he mutters as he presses little kisses all over my face.

"Even my Barcoa form?" I ask him, smirking, and the kisses trail off and he grimaces.

"Okay, I lied, not that form, and if you ever try to get me to suck that elbow cock, I will gag. It was all kinds of gross, but the look on Tirrian's face was priceless. I wish I'd thought to take a picture."

I chuckle as he leads me out of the equipment room and onto the flight deck of the small space craft. Silac and Tirrian are there. Silac smiles tentatively at me, but the dragon doesn't even turn around. I don't care, though, because filling the viewing window is the most wonderful sight in the world. It's the circus ship docked at a large space station orbiting Celestia.

"They are here," I whisper and turn to my warlock mate. "I want to shower in my room."

"Your wish is my command, *phoeall.*" He wraps his arms around me and looks at Silac. "I'll be back for both of you in a little while."

Silac nods, and I feel Xavier's mist cover us before the familiar lurch of teleporting. When the mist clears, we're in a large, unfamiliar living area, but it doesn't even matter, because sitting on the sofa with a beer in his hand is my kraken.

"Cas!" I squeal and throw myself at him. He just has time to put his beer down before he catches me.

"Lila." He mashes his mouth to mine, and we kiss like we haven't seen each other in years rather than almost two weeks. I straddle him and wrap my arms around his neck, grinding down onto his lap. My hormones scream with joy now that we are back within reach of all of our mates.

"Where are the children?" I hear Xavier ask, but Cas doesn't pull his mouth away from me. His hands roam my body, tugging at my shirt at the same time as I tug at his. His fingers find a nipple, and he tweaks it, swallowing the responding moan.

"They are asleep in their swim pods. They've only just gone down, so we've got a while. And Maxsim and Echo are in the lightning cat cave, so it's only the four of us." Link is the one who answers, but the familiar smell of marshmallows and chocolate tells me Saxon is in the room too.

"Well, how about we take this to Lila's bedroom

and you guys can show your wife exactly how much you missed her?"

That gets my attention, and I pull away from Caspian, blinking rapidly. "I'm finally getting an orgy?"

The guys chuckle, and Xavier nods his head. "If that's what you would like."

I scramble off Caspian's lap and hurry to where my bedroom used to be, hoping the others are on my tail. I screech to a halt when I open the door. Instead of my bedroom, there is a swimming pool where it used to be. It's nowhere as big as the Aquilian pool, but it's enough that Caspian, the babies, and I can all have a swim together in our kraken forms. I look around the room, and the whole area has been redeveloped.

"Holy shit. How did this happen? That looks deep."

"It is." Caspian slides in next to me. "While you and I were swimming beneath the ocean, waiting for our babies to come, the guys were all involved in the redesign of our living space. Originally, your grandpas were going to keep their suite on this level as well as the captain's, but when it became clear that you may end up with lots of mates, they decided to leave this whole level as the flight deck and your suite. We have swallowed up all the others and created a living space in which we are all going to be happy."

"There's the pool and an ice den for the cats. They are down in the old one retrieving their things and cleaning out Natalia's crap for when the other cats return," Link says behind us. "As well as a huge gymnasium designed to suit all of our requirements, with a large sparring space for Saxon. And look at this." Link takes my hand and drags me away from the pool. I hear one of the others close the door as we move down a long corridor. "That's the gaming and theater room just there." He points out another door. "We thought it would be a good idea to have our own. Our children will get in the way of the rest of the crew if we allow them to. This way the crew gets to have their own entertainment without having to worry about scarring fragile little minds."

I think about the different entertainment options available around the ship and decide it's probably a pretty good idea.

"We don't have a lot of families on the ship, do we?" I don't remember seeing children at any other time.

"No, most families return to their home planets once they are ready to have children, like the Aquilian pod." Before I can ask any more questions, Link stops at another door, and it opens wide. The smell of paper hits me in the face, and I feel a grin spread across my lips.

"A library. Awesome." I peer in and see it's a library to make a bitch swoon, with a huge fireplace, a comfy seating area, and a sliding ladder. "You win favorite husband today." I throw my arms around Link's neck and kiss him hard.

"Hey," I hear Saxon and Cas grumble, and I grin against Link's lips.

Pulling away, I look at the others. "So where are our bedrooms? Mine specifically." I'm impatient to get all of these men out of their clothes. I want their cocks, and I want them now.

"You know I hate to be the voice of reason, but shouldn't we heal John first and then have a celebratory orgy after?"

I glare at the warlock who, for the first time ever, is blowing off sex to be sensible. "Dude, shut your bleeping mouth. You're the one who had the idea in the first place. You pussy tease," I snap at him, and all four of them chuckle. Xavier holds his hands up defensively.

"I know, I wasn't thinking straight. I was overwhelmed by you and Caspian. Imagine if it was one of us waiting to be cured. I'm just saying."

Damn him for playing the angel on my shoulder when the devil on the other one wants them to make me see Jesus.

"How about we compromise? You need blood, so let Saxon join you in the shower while Link, Cas, and I make arrangements to teleport down onto the planet. Link can ready the flower for transport, and Cas and I can get the babies ready." Xavier is being the voice of reason, and I kind of want to shove my Barcoa elbow cock in his mouth just because, but he's right. The flower is back on the other transport ship with the snake and dragon.

"Okay, but the minute Grandpa John is up and well again, I am dragging you all back to this ship, and we will not leave the bedroom until I'm walking bowlegged."

The guys assure me they are down for the plan, and then we split up. Saxon takes my hand and leads me toward where I'm assuming our bedrooms are, while the other three go off to make the landing arrangements. I start sobbing uncontrollably the minute they are out of sight. My body is a flood of hormones, sadness, anxiety, and worry. I'm all over the fucking place. Saxon picks me up and races me through our living quarters, finally stopping in a large, beautiful bathroom. It still has a huge communal tub and a communal shower stall big enough for all seven of us to shower together. It's here that he puts me back on my feet. He slowly strips my body, his gaze not leaving mine.

"Never again, Lila. Never shall we be apart for so long. It was torturous for all of us. Each of us have been miserable and trying to keep a brave face so the babies don't know anything is wrong, but they are smart, and they knew we were sad, which made them sad too. There have been lots of cuddles and puppy piles between keeping them distracted and entertained. Being apart was not good for any of us."

"I agree a hundred percent." I hiccup, gasping for air between sobs. "I have felt longing and sadness too. Although I was busy, it was always in the back of my mind, and while Xavier did his best, he couldn't make up for the fact that you were all missing. Where I go, you all go too, and if there is anyone who doesn't like that, we will just sic Xavier on them in mist form. The all-powerful warlock is enough to make anyone crap their pants."

I reach for Saxon's clothes once he has me naked, his hands running all over my body, but I finally get him stripped down. His beautiful pale skin shines in the bright light of the bathroom, and his rock-hard cock makes my mouth water. I go to get down on my knees, because I want it in my mouth, but he stops me.

"Far be it for me to say no to having your gorgeous lips wrapped around my cock, but we need to be quick."

I pout, and he chuckles as he presses a few buttons and water starts to pour from the ceiling in a waterfall.

"Don't cry, my beauty. I will make sure all of your needs are taken care of for the moment, and later, when we have more time, I will make you choke on my cock as we work together until you are completely sated." He leans in and kisses me, his fangs piercing my lip, and then he licks the blood from it. A drop of his venom fizzes in my veins, distracting me from my sadness and sending my desire haywire.

He lifts me up, and I wrap my legs around his thick waist as he presses me against the wall, the warm water washing over us. He leans in and bares his neck to me. "Drink, my beauty, and gorge yourself until you are full. You must be starving."

I think back to my last meal. I haven't had to drink any since I took so much from the dragon. His blood must have some kind of magical properties, because despite using all of my mimic powers repeatedly over the last week on our journey here, I haven't needed to drink any blood from Xavier. I keep that information to myself, though, as my thirst comes rushing back to me and my fangs click into place.

"Fine, as long as you do the same. I missed feeling you inside me, and I also feel like my circulatory system is about to burst. I have an abundance of blood since you haven't fed in so long. I even had to ask Xavier to bag some because it became uncomfortable."

He smiles at my confession. "It makes me happy to know that my blood rose wants me to feed from her, and that I can feed my blood rose. It appeals to the primitive part of me like you would not believe."

Oh, I believe it, because I feel the same way—kind of possessive about feeding him even though I'm also happy and horny when he feeds from Xavier.

"And Sax? Please fuck me while we do," I beg, and his smile drops as his eyes bleed to red as he thrusts his cock deep into my needy pussy. My eyes roll back, and I gasp at the complete feeling of fullness as he pins me against the wall. Yes, this is what I want. I grab his wrist and bring it up to my mouth as I expose my neck to the predator before me.

He leans in and runs his tongue over the fat vein in my neck as I do the same to the one in his wrist. In sync, we strike as one before pulling away and feeding deeply on one another. Saxon's hips piston his cock in and out of my pussy, drawing out my pleasure much the same way he draws the blood from my body. It's exquisite, and it barely takes any time before I'm coming hard. My first orgasm thunders through my body, but neither of us let up. Together, we drink our fill while finding our pleasure until both of us are thoroughly sated.

A nap would be nice now, but we have a job to do and babies to snuggle. There is no rest for the weary, but it sure is a great state to be in.

CHAPTER TWENTY-EIGHT

Caspian

"Right, X, what the fuck has been going on? Your reply message to Saxon was vague and annoying," I demand the moment we are out of earshot of Lila. Thankfully Saxon will keep her busy while Link and I interrogate Xavier. I want us all to be on the same page before we go to the surface of Celestia. We don't need any surprises being sprung on us once we are down there.

When I look at the warlock, though, I can see dark circles under his eyes, and his exhaustion is suddenly clear. Okay, maybe he wasn't being deliberately obtuse. I guess he's probably been run ragged, trying to keep our wife happy and healthy, and he looks gaunt, like he hasn't been feeding properly.

"What is wrong with you?" I ask, and he grimaces and starts to shake his head in denial, but Link puts up a hand and runs it over Xavier's body, examining him from head to toe.

"You're exhausted, and you're starving." Link sounds incredulous as he pulls his hand away from the warlock, who collapses onto a sofa now that we've returned to the living room. His head flops back, and he closes his eyes against the glare of the artificial light. "How does one who feeds from emotions, which are all around us, starve?"

"Because the idiot is big on consent. All warlocks are, it's why they have harems, and if someone, say an asshole dragon and a confused snake, haven't given him consent, then he won't feed, and Lila on her own wouldn't have been enough to sustain him without their active intimate bond. Am I right?" I look down at the barely moving warlock and see his head nod minutely.

"I haven't really been able to feed since the gem market on Rilu, which was before our trip to the cavern and journey here. Lila is a riot of emotions, but because she's my intimate and she's upset, they are bitter and unpalatable." His words are barely audible. "The snake and dragon wouldn't allow me to feed from them, nor would they allow Lila to mimic them."

"What? Why the fuck not?" Link sounds agitated, which is a surprise because he's such an emotionally balanced being, unlike us shifters who are more primal with our feelings.

"So many reasons," he mutters, and I know if we don't do something quickly, then he's going to fall asleep.

"Well, you are always welcome to feed from me. Feed now," I instruct him, and he wrinkles his nose slightly.

"You're annoyed and worried, and so is the cyborg. It's unappetizing." Of course it is. He is into decadence and feeding from beings who are sexually aroused or stimulated in a way that is extreme. My worry must be as bland as Lila's sadness.

I reach out and haul the cyborg to me. Link has been my constant companion since Lila has been gone, helping me with our children and comforting me when my longing for my mate became extreme. We've been sleeping in the same bed for days now. I just needed the comfort of family, and he gave me that without question. I've grown quite fond of the doctor, and I am not blind. I can see what a delicious snack he is, and my kraken is in full agreement. I fuse my mouth to his, which drops open in shock, allowing my tongue access. I wrap my arms around him and pull his body against mine. I think I surprised him, and when it takes him a moment to respond, I start to panic that he isn't receptive to my advances. I've woken up to find myself wrapped around him the past few nights, and he hasn't complained a bit, so I thought maybe there was mutual interest. I'm just about to pull away when I feel his cock rapidly harden against mine, and his tongue slips out, caressing mine as his hands thread through my hair and hold me in place.

Holding Link is so very different from holding Lila. He's tall where she's small, he's wide where she's narrow, and he's hard where she is soft, but it is no less thrilling. Caspian the man is well and truly bisexual, and my kraken is now in complete agreement. Being mated to Lila is a hundred times better than finding myself locked into a mating with one person for the rest of my life. The fact that she is open-minded enough to let me play with her other mates is a blessing in itself, and having her participation will be the icing on the cake. If she had been against it, I would have been happy with just her, but I'm even happier now.

"Oh yeah, that's it. Fuck." Xavier almost sounds pornographic as he feeds on our emotions, and knowing he is getting something out of this carnal display as well makes it all the more delicious. Finally, I pull away, and Link blinks as he rubs a finger against his lips, his eyes hooded with desire.

"Was that okay?" I ask him, and he nods slowly.

"Yes, very much so."

I see guilt fill his eyes, and he glances around.

"Don't feel guilty, robot man," Xavier slurs, intoxicated from drinking the lust Link and I were putting off, and when we look at him, his pupils are blown, and he's got a very visible tent in his pants. "Your wife is a perv, you know that, and she would be fully into what the two of you just did. In fact, she would want to be the meat in that sandwich. You saw how she watched when I kissed you. She's greedy, and like a Pokémon trainer, she wants to catch them all."

What the fuck is he talking about? "Quiet, warlock, the adults are talking."

He just continues to mutter, so I roll my eyes and turn my attention back to Link, ignoring the now drunk but healthy warlock.

I cup the cyborg's cheek and press another short kiss to his mouth. "Thank you for doing that, and he's right. Don't feel guilty. She would love to see it, but I will wait until I can get her between us before we go any further. Plus, we have a grandpa to save, so this can be continued."

"I know Lila won't be upset, since she was very enthusiastic when Xavier and I gave her a blow job together…" He trails off and shrugs.

"It feels like cheating because she's not here?" I ask, and he nods, relief in his eyes that I get where he's going.

"It is fine, I completely understand, and it does a little bit. I would much rather have her very enthusiastic participation too. Okay, so how about you interrogate the warlock?" I suggest, backing away, and I see him relax minutely.

"Yes. I want to know exactly why she was so upset about Silac and Tirrian." We both turn to glare at the warlock, who had been rather tight-lipped when Saxon questioned why she had been so upset.

He sticks out his tongue and blows a fat, wet raspberry at us, and I glare at him. "Holy shit, man, get it together. Why are you reacting so strongly?" I reach down and give the warlock a little shake, and he startles. The fog in his eyes seems to clear slightly.

He clears his throat and adjusts the tent in his pants, a light blush warming his cheeks to a deep shade of lavender. "Fuck, I haven't reacted to lust like that since I was a teenager and had my first feed on it." Xavier shakes his head, trying to clear it.

Link hurries over to the fridge and grabs a bottle of Skarrian water for him before returning and holding it out.

"Thanks, man." Xavier takes it gratefully and pops the top, downing the contents within a few gulps. "Whoa, that was intense. Sorry, but thank you both so much. I was pretty much on empty. I'm so glad there were no enemies nearby, otherwise they would have easily been able to overpower me."

"Okay, well, we discussed it, and we don't think

it's a good idea for any of us to go off on our own anymore. With the orb rumor floating about, people are going to get curious, and who knows when one of us may be snatched up and interrogated? I'm assuming that's what happened to Liliana. I wonder what kind of state we will find her in." Link drops down onto one of the seats next to Xavier, and I take one across from them.

"Yes, Lila and I had much the same conversation on the journey here, not to mention how much she missed you all. She was practically despondent by the time we arrived here, and I'm not sure what kind of condition Liliana will be in when we finally find her. Zamala said we would need a petal from the flamegem and a carevasta bear to revive her."

I grimace, thinking about having to appeal to a carevasta bear for help. "That is going to suck."

"Big time, and as for the snakelet and the dragon, well, here is what happened." It takes Xavier about half an hour to give us the lowdown on both Silac and Tirrian. I'd known about Silac's arranged marriage, but I had no idea her family was the Bravalana basilisks. No wonder he is reluctant to break that arrangement. But Xavier assures me he is taking care of it, and very shortly, our naga should be available to pursue Lila to his heart's content.

I frown, uncertain about how I feel about that. Silac and I were once lovers, and I care for him deeply, but I thought that was all in the past. To know that we will now be sharing a mate is somewhat hard to wrap my head around. I'll have to think on it for a while and see where I stand on all of this.

"When you say Tirrian's dragons, what do you mean by that?" Link, of course, latches onto the one little bit of intrigue.

Xavier shrugs. "I have no idea. He basically didn't say another word to any of us once we left Rilu. I think Silac knows, but he's loyal to his friend and won't betray his secrets."

"No, he wouldn't," I agree.

"Do dragons have multiple forms?" Link asks, and I can tell that Xavier doesn't know. I certainly don't. Species interaction was frowned upon until recent times, and we certainly haven't been interacting long enough to know everything about all the different shifters.

"I guess it's back to the library for you, Link. Why don't you ask Corethea if you can access the royal library here? They would have an extensive species and race archive," I suggest, and Link's eyes light up adorably. He's such a nerd, but it's sexy.

Xavier is thoughtful. "They just need to have angry sex and get it out of their systems, but Tirrian is determined not to mate with Lila. I don't know what his prejudice is. It can't be the fact that she got Dylan kicked out of the circus, especially because he saw firsthand what a degenerate he is."

He told us all about their time on X69, and I cannot believe that they saw Dylan, or that she secretly mimicked a Madovian, but that is a problem for another day.

"I think he's scared," Link says quietly. "Scared to give himself over so completely to someone he barely even knows. It is overwhelming for many people. Statistics say it's one of the biggest fears that races with fated mates suffer, that the person fate has chosen for them will not be compatible, won't love them, and won't be interested in them sexually amongst other things."

"And because of the fear, he keeps any possible mate at arm's length, even the one that he knows would be perfect for him," I finish, and Link nods.

"You know, you might be onto something." Xavier rubs his chin thoughtfully. "We might have to play matchmaker, but let's put that on the back burner for now. They will be done in the shower soon, and none of us are ready. You still haven't gone and got the flower. I'll teleport you to the other ship."

"And I will go and wake our babies. They will be beyond excited to see their mother and Daddy X, and they are dying to meet Grandpa John," I tell Xavier, who smiles, and his hands start to clench and release, like he's dying to get them on our babies.

"Okay, we will hurry, because I missed the little buggers. I need my kraken kisses."

"Well, tag, you are it for the next twenty-four hours then," Link tells him. "The five of us are in desperate need of some real sleep, even Saxon and I who don't need all that much."

"It will be my pleasure. I have to teach them how to play tricks on Grandma and Grandpa Warlock because Lila said we will go to Westalin as soon as we are done here." Xavier is practically giddy with excitement. He's been so patient, it would be cruel to make him wait any longer.

"Alright, so meet back here in twenty minutes then?" I suggest, and the other two agree.

Xavier stands up, wobbling slightly, but he steadies himself before allowing his mist to seep out and around Link. They disappear in a flash of light, and I hurry in the direction of the babies' room. All three of their beds are in one large room, which already has two more cribs ready for Echo's babies when they come. There is a huge playroom attached to the sleeping area stocked full of toys and books and educational things to keep five rambunctious children occupied for ages, and it will allow for more if our family expands in the future, which I'm sure it will.

When they get big enough and need their own

rooms, there is still plenty of space on this level for it. That's why the grandpas and the captain moved down a level. Our family will be huge, and we need a lot of space. I also don't see us settling down on one planet anytime soon. Lila will eventually be in charge of the whole circus, and we will need to go where she does, so we are prepared for this now.

The nursery is quiet when I enter it, with only the gentle sound of the rolling ocean waves echoing out of speakers. Despite being put in their own beds, I find all three of them snuggled together in Calypso's bed. Jack and Cordy have worked out that if they change into their kraken forms, they can climb out of their cribs and into hers. I considered putting lids on them, but that just seemed cruel. I'm sure, like all siblings, they'll end up wanting their own space eventually, but for now, if they want to sleep together, why not let them?

A hand on my back has me spinning in surprise, but it's just Lila. Her hair is wet, and she smells like Saxon, but she looks better than she did when she first appeared. Just like Xavier, I think she was at her limit, but she seems to have recovered nicely.

I wrap an arm around her, and she leans her head against my chest as we look down at our sleeping children. "They are angels, aren't they?" She sighs with contentment.

"Yeah, while they are asleep, but I swear they are the warlock's kids when they are awake. Are you sure he didn't do something to you while you were pregnant? Because they are mischievous and sneaky," I joke, knowing full well what me and my own clutch mates were like as children.

"No, baby, that is all me and you there." I can hear how proud she is, and I puff up my chest, feeling much the same way.

"You know we could always go again," I say casually, my beast pushing against me, and she lifts her head and glares.

"Tell your beast that if he values his ovipositor, I better not see it anytime soon," she growls, and he quickly sinks down again. Now that Lila has her own kraken form, our mating dance is going to go a lot differently. I would say that getting her pregnant is not going to be as fun next time, but I'm sure he will keep trying.

"Mama?" Jack peers up at her, his eyes cloudy with sleep, but then a small smile spreads across his lips as he fully wakes. "Mama!" This time he shouts it, which wakes his two sisters. They don't appreciate being woken so abruptly, and both burst into tears while he scrambles up and holds his hands out for Lila. She lifts him and cuddles him close, sniffing deeply.

"God, they smell good. I never knew I had the capacity to love someone as much as I love these three. The only person I ever really loved before was Susie." Lila's eyes are cloudy with sadness, and

I hate seeing it there, but it soon clears when Cordy and Calypso hear their mom's voice, and the tears dry up as they hold their hands up for cuddles too. Lila passes me Jack and reaches down for both girls. We've become quite proficient at holding and cuddling multiple children at once.

"I'm sure once you get your memories back, you will realize you have loved way more than just Susie. Now how about we get these three dressed and ready to go down to Celestia? I bet you even have time for a quick visit with Susie. I'm sure she'd love to meet her nieces and nephew."

That chases away the rest of her sadness, and she hurries to find the girls cute outfits to wear. I never want to see that look in her eyes again, and I'm going to do my best to see that I don't.

CHAPTER TWENTY-NINE

Lila

W e're a big party as we transport down to the surface of Celestia. There are all six of my mates, plus my three children, as well as the dragon and the snake who didn't want to stay up on the ship. Broderick and Brannock, who had been living on the ship because he had nowhere else to go, chose to remain behind. Brannock's appearance still startles people, so he continues to wear his human glamor all the time. There is an air of sadness to him, and when I finally get five minutes to talk to him, I'm going to try to get to the bottom of it. Magenta was unreachable. When I last spoke to her, she was on Vilax with Hale and Velorina, but that relationship was coming to its inevitable conclusion. She's still not ready to bond with anyone, and I'm not sure if they would even want to bond with her. She refused to talk about it when I pushed her on it, and she would need to drink from the blood rose cup if they did decide to go in that direction. When we said our goodbyes, she was muttering about X69 just to have some fun with no strings. The life of an unbonded Skarrian must be exhausting.

When we rematerialize on the platform of the palace of Celestia, William and Eric are there to meet us. They look exhausted, but they have big hugs for me and the kids.

"You got the flower! And I see you got something else as well. New hairdo?" Eric lifts a strand of my sparkly silver locks. "You look like a My Little Pony." He chuckles, but the laughter doesn't quite reach his eyes, which is out of character for Eric. John's illness must be wearing on them.

My husbands assured me they love my new hair color, but I can't help but feel self-conscious about it. I asked Xavier to glamor me, and he refused to. He said I should wear it with pride. It is a sign of high status in Rilu.

"Yes, Link has it." They both turn to my cyborg, who is holding the bag with the flower in it.

"Let's not keep John waiting any longer, shall we?" he says, and Corethea approaches. She stayed back to give us a moment of privacy for our family reunion.

"Lila, you are looking much better than when I saw you last," she greets me, taking my hands. I bob slightly in a curtsy.

"Thank you, Your Majesty. It is lovely to see you again, and I don't know how I can ever repay you for what you did."

She squeezes my hand. "Nonsense. You brought me my boy back, and I hear you and his Susie are best friends. That makes us family as far as I am concerned, and family doesn't owe anything. Now, introduce me to your beautiful babies so I can have a quick cuddle before Tabbris and I heal John. He has waited long enough, but baby cuddles trump everything."

I introduce her to my babies, who are completely fascinated with the huge, white wings on her back, but I can tell by the way that Eric and William fidget that they have reached their limit.

"Would it be alright if we visited with Susie while you do your thing on John?"

"Of course. I will have someone show you the way to their quarters. Both my son and Susie have been impatiently waiting for you to arrive. I'm surprised they aren't here." Corethea laughs and gestures for one of their royal guards to escort me and the rest of our motley crew where we want to go.

"I'm going to stay and help. I would like to see the flamegem flower in action, and I want to see if my suspicions are right about the virus being a cyborg construct," Link tells me. We haven't told William and Eric the news about their wife yet. We wanted to wait until John was stable again and tell them all at once, but one of us needs to know how to use the flower, and Link volunteered so I can visit with Susie.

"How about just you and Cas go and visit with Susie and Mark. Having all of us there would be overwhelming. The rest of us can figure out something to do while we wait," Xavier suggests.

"Don't go too far. As soon as John is up and ready, we will make our way to Westalin," I warn the rest of my mates.

"We have a very nice bar for palace employees. How about I have one of the guards show you to that?" Corethea suggests, and the rest of the guys eagerly agree.

We split up, and Cas, the babies, and I are shown to Mark's wing of the palace. There are guards stationed in every hall we travel down. "Is it normal to have so many guards? Are there threats against the royal family?" I ask the one who is escorting us.

He grunts. "The royal family is being overzealous at the moment due to the return of their son. They are worried there is a credible threat to him since he was kidnapped. His reappearance halted any talks regarding changing from a monarchy to a republic. There are, of course, some people who are not happy about this."

"That seems reasonable to me," Cas says, bouncing Cordy and Cally up and down on his hips. "I would do the same if I thought my children were in danger."

Thankfully we can mostly control who gets access to our children on our ship. We've started using a more stringent background check after the Madovian incident, so hopefully we don't have any more issues going forward.

The guard stops at a door and lifts his hand to knock, but it opens before he can.

"Lila!" Susie screams and jumps for me, but she stops abruptly when she sees Jack in my arms. Her eyes soften and become misty. "You're a mother," she murmurs, running a finger across Jack's soft cheek. "Holy crap, they are not babies like I thought they'd be. Come in and tell me everything." She steps out of the way, allowing us to enter.

We visit with Mark and Susie and their new family for probably two hours. The children are fascinated with Mark's new set of royal blue angel wings. They keep trying to touch them until he plucks them each a feather of their own.

That kept them occupied for a good ten minutes, but Aura and the rest of their family had a blast keeping them distracted so I could fill Susie and Mark in on everything going on in my life, and they could share all their news, but we are eventually summoned to return to the throne room.

"Good luck on Westalin," she tells me as we hug, both of us reluctant to let go of one another.

"And good luck here. I hope it all goes well. When the royal family loosens the reins a little bit, you are all welcome to return back to the circus if you want."

She and Mark exchange a look. "We worry about Aura. They've been despondent since they lost the Pleasure Inn. This is the happiest they've been in weeks. We are hoping we can either establish a new one here or have our Earth ban lifted. We are working with the Galactic Council to see if they can intervene for us."

"I'll talk to the grandpas. They have some pull, and those charges were bogus. Agent Smith deserves to be investigated. He is very anti-alien, and he is not the right kind of person to be in his position, but unfortunately, we have a few more pressing issues first."

"Good luck with your grandma and meeting Xavier's family. The warlock royal family is no joke. They are feared by many. Mark and I have been having royal classes to get up to speed on important royal families in the galaxy for when we are invited to functions or have trade meetings."

A wave of nerves rushes over me, but I force a smile. "I'm sure it will be fine. My parents were friends with them, so they can't be all bad." I figuratively cross my fingers in hope.

When we return to the throne room, I'm thrilled to find John up and about. He looks pale and has lost a little weight, but he beams as Cas and I approach with the children.

"Lila, Cas." He struggles to get to his feet, and William helps him. "Look at you all. I can't believe so much has happened. A mimic in the family. I never would have guessed that. And look at these beauties." He's staring at my babies with wide-eyed wonder.

"This is Grandpa John," I tell them. They have heard all about him, of course. William and Eric made sure to tell them plenty of stories about him. Jack, my bulldozer, throws himself from my arms in a swift movement. Luckily John is close enough to catch him and does so with a surprised yelp.

"Whoops, sorry, that is one of their favorite moves—mostly because Xavier catches them with his powers if one of us doesn't react fast enough."

Jack snuggles into John as Cordy and Cally hold out their arms for Eric and William.

Corethea and Tabbris approach.

"Thank you so much," I say to both women.

"You are very welcome. It seems that the cavern chose you as its guardian. If we have need of the flower again, we will call you," Tabbris says in a soft voice, her pale, golden wings shimmering behind her.

"Of course, and if there is anything we can do for you, please let us know."

We take our leave and return to the ship. Broderick plots a direct course to Westalin, but it's time I share what I've learned about Grandma with her husbands. The guys take the children back to our living quarters while I escort my grandpas to their new ones on the deck below.

"You know you didn't have to give up your rooms for us," I tell them as we arrive at their new rooms.

William opens the door, and we follow him in. John immediately heads for the couch and sits down, exhaustion in his eyes.

"We know, but you need the space a lot more than we do, especially with two new little ones on the way." William goes to the replicator and programs in the vitamin drink that Corethea recommended for John to help get him back up to strength.

"Are you sure you're okay?" I ask him, sitting next to him and grabbing his hand. "I can shift into Celestian form and check over you again."

"Stop worrying, Lila. I just need some more

sleep and a couple of good meals, and I will be right as rain. Also, Saxon had a rehab program for me to help build up my muscle strength. There was a bit of wastage due to not moving, but with time, I will be completely back to normal."

William brings over John's health drink while Eric grabs him and William two beers, and me a rilaxious. I am finally allowed to drink again now that I'm no longer pregnant. The first sip of my drink goes down like a treat, and I must mutter something of the sort because the grandpas laugh at me.

"Okay, well, I have some more news I need to share with you. Are you sure your heart is okay?" I ask John, and he frowns and nods.

"Yes, what did you want to tell us?"

"Are you pregnant again? Whose is it this time?" Eric asks, laughing, and I flip him off.

"No, definitely not. There are no more babies in my life for the near future."

"We'll see," he mutters, and William raises an eyebrow.

"Another mate?" he guesses, and I shake my head despite what I know about Tirrian. I don't have any plans on announcing his rejection of me to my grandpas. They don't need any more added stress than the one I'm about to put on them.

"No, not another mate. This has to do with my trip to Rilu."

"Where you just happened to have bonded with the most elusive herd of larnuks on the whole planet. Not even an individual horse, but the whole herd," John says, chuckling and shaking his head. "Lila, I swear life is never going to be boring around you."

"Ah, no, that's not it. While we were there, I met Chief Zana's mother, Zamala."

"Is she still kicking around?" William sounds surprised.

"Yes, and she had a weird vision while I was there. Actually, all of us got weird, cryptic messages. The guys' were a little more vague, but mine was very specific."

"Zamala has a seer gift, but sometimes it works with glimpses of the future, and sometimes glimpses of the past. It is hit and miss when these visions appear to her, but very rarely is she wrong," Eric says, confirming what Zala had already told me about her grandmother's visions. I asked, because I was worried she was a crackpot like Zilla insisted, and I wasn't going to tell my grandpas anything if that was the case.

"Yes, well, there is no easy way to tell you this, but she gave me Grandma Liliana's location."

There's a loaded silence while the three of them process what I just said.

"Lili's alive?" Eric whispers like he's not sure if he heard correctly or not.

"Yes, until recently, she had been kept in the very cave I got the flower from."

"How? That cave is sacred. There is no way anyone other than the sacred family line should be able to access it," William argues.

"Where is she now?" John demands, all traces of his ordeal gone from his face in the light of this new information. He looks like he wants to jump out of his seat and hurry to her rescue, which is completely understandable.

"I asked the same thing about the cave, but we have no answers on how they got her there. As for where she is now, well, according to Zamala, she is in a stasis box in the middle of the death forest on Husadavia."

John blanches, and his already pale skin pales even further. "No." Eric and William swear up a blue streak, both getting to their feet and pacing back and forth.

"Yes, but before you get too worked up, on the trip from Rilu to here, Xavier and I tossed around some ideas, and I think we have a fairly solid plan, but we need to go to Westalin first, have my memories returned, and have our intimate bond sealed. That will increase Xavier's powers tenfold. Between him and the rest of the plan, we will have Liliana back before you three can blink." I reach for John's hand, giving it a squeeze. "I promise."

"Liliana's alive? I'd almost given up hope. Even

though we hadn't felt the bond break, I thought that maybe there was a reason for it." Eric sits down again, resting his elbows on his knees and dropping his head into his hands.

"Did Zamala say why? Why was she taken, and who took her?" William demands abruptly.

"No, I'm sorry. I have no more information than that."

"Well, it takes two weeks to get to Westalin. We better spend that time making sure you have everything you need to rescue our wife."

"Not to mention run the circus. If we get Liliana back, then there is no way I am wasting any more time running the circus. After my recent scare, I want to spend the rest of our lives letting her know how much I love her and how much she has been missed," John says quietly, and I can tell that both William and Eric are on board with this plan.

"Congratulations, Lila, you just got a promotion to ringmaster," Eric tells me with tears of joy in his eyes.

EPILOGUE

Lila

We're a week into our journey from Celestia to Westalin, and our little family is settling into life on board the circus ship. Cas and the kids are swimming in the Aquilian pool, Saxon is in the rec room working with John on his rehab, and Xavier, John, Eric, and Broderick are going over everything they can on the planet Husadavia. They set up a small war room off the flight deck with maps and information on the planet all gathered by halla harvesters.

Halla harvesters are made up of a group of different races who have perfected surviving on such an inhospitable planet. They are in constant contact with one of the leaders of the group who has been an immense amount of help. Today, Brannock was invited to join the group. I wanted to join it too, but my grandpas insisted that I learn how to work with the lightning cats so that the show is performable once the circus starts touring again. Xavier promised to fill me in on everything they talk about.

Link is doing research on the carevasta bears to learn what we need to know about them, and maybe some hint as to why we would need one with us.

I stand in the main ring on the circus pod, holding a glowing whip in my hand as Silac operates the console that changes the landscape from normal circus ring to lightning cat frozen tundra. I flick the whip around, trying to get a handle on the thing, and when I draw my arm up to lash it, the ends come around and slap me on the ass. A jolt of pain crashes through my body, and I drop to my knees with a sob. Oh fuck, that hurt. I just spanked my own ass with a laser whip. I wonder if I tore my pants.

I feel around with my other hand as tears well in my eyes from the pain. This is not as easy as Eric and William made it look. Maxsim and Echo rumble with displeasure and stalk back and forth around me.

"Hey, I'm okay, I'm just checking to see if I'm flashing my ass to anyone," I tell them, standing up. "Can you see?"

I wait as they both bound behind me, and then I feel a wet stroke of a cat's tongue across my ass, and I know that I have ripped a hole in my pants.

"You have got to be the worst whip handler I've ever seen," a dry voice says from the stands.

I hold a hand up to my face to shield my eyes from the glare as I try to see who said that. Well, I actually know who it is, since there is no missing that sarcastic drawl, but where is he?

When my eyes adjust, I find him sitting in the front row, that familiar glare of disdain focused on me.

I feel a dip in my stomach at the sight of him. I'm sad—sad that he refuses to acknowledge what I am to him, and sad that he refuses to take a chance on us—but also a little relieved at the same time. The dragon clearly has issues, and I have so much on my plate at the moment that I don't have time for all of his shit, and I deserve better. We both do. We deserve to be happy, and I deserve someone who is a hundred percent in, and that is never going to be Tirrian.

"Yeah, well, we can't be good at everything. I mean, they would do exactly what I told them to because they love me, but we need to put on a show, hence the whip." I hold up the blasted thing in my hand. "I was hoping I would run into you," I tell him, walking over to where he is. I think I surprise him, because he quickly scrambles to his feet like he doesn't want to get too close to me. I see his nostrils flare, and his beast flicks into his eyes before retreating or getting pushed down again.

"Why? So you could convince me why you would be the perfect mate?" Ouch, his hit hurts, but I just shake my head.

"No, Tirrian, despite what you might think, I don't want to force you into anything. I have enough people to love me, I really don't want to tie myself to someone who hates me, but I do have something for you."

I fish around in my pocket, looking for the thing I want to give him. When I told Xavier what I was going to do, he looked at me like I was stupid, but Link just smiled and nodded.

"Here." I find what I'm looking for and hold it out. I think I surprised him again, because before he can stop himself, he's reaching for the object. When I drop it in his hand, it's his turn to look gobsmacked for a change. "I thought you might like it for your hoard. You said you didn't have one, and that was the only loose one I saw on the entire trip, so I'm assuming you didn't manage to get one."

"You're giving me your gem?" he asks quietly, the shiny, opalescent gem shimmering in the stage lights.

"Yeah. I mean, I have this to remind me of it." I point to my hair, which is tied back in a bun to keep it out of my face to stop me from burning it with the whip, which I managed to do yesterday. Lesson learned.

"But why?" He still can't take his eyes away from the pretty shiny thing in his hand, and I smother a smirk.

"Because I think you're sad. I'm not sure why, but I hope that maybe that will make you feel a little happier inside."

He tears his eyes away from the gem and stares at me like he's trying to figure out a puzzle. Before he can say anything, though, an alarm starts to blare loudly, and red lights begin flashing.

"What's happening?" I ask as Silac leaves the control booth and hurries out to us, but he and Tirrian are new to the ship too and have no clue. I look at both cats, and Echo is cowering slightly, his paws over his ears as Maxsim shifts forms.

"We are under attack. Quick, we need to go to the flight deck. We don't have a full crew, and they will need help manning the guns."

We start running for the elevator to take us back to the main ship. I have to slow my speed for the others to keep up, and Silac notices. "Go, Lila, we will be right behind you," he calls, and I use my Vilaxian speed to get to the elevator.

I take it to the main ship and then use another to get to the flight deck. When I arrive, I'm barely breathing heavily. Everyone else is here. Cas, in half form, is dripping wet and has all three babies in their kraken form wrapped around his body.

"What is going on?" I ask, and I feel a lump of panic develop in my throat as I see what is outside the viewing window. It's a big black ship shaped like a manta ray, and it takes up most of the view. I can see that it is flanked by two more very similar vessels. "Who is that? And what do they want?"

"That is an Aquilian attack bird. As for what they want, they haven't said yet," Xavier replies, his whole body glowing with anger.

"What? That can't be right." William shakes his head. "We haven't done anything to cause the Aquilians to attack us. None of us have been anywhere near Aquilia."

"But Lila did see Nikos on Skarr, so maybe it's about that," Link suggests and worries his lip with his teeth. My cyborg husband looks like he knows something. Actually, when I look at all my mates, they all look like they know something, but before I can ask anything, we are being hailed.

"Lila Adams." The loud, robotic voice comes across the speaker of the flight deck. "You are hereby charged with crimes against the Aquilian royal family. Surrender now, or we will be forced to board and take you by any means necessary."

"Oh fuck."

GALAXY CIRCUS GLOSSARY

PLANET ICEEN

Lightning Cats

They are a shifter race that has two forms—a bipedal human form and their cat form. Their bipedal form is humanoid in shape, but they are covered in a soft downy fur except for the front of their torso and genital area. They have sharp teeth, big ears, and long tails in this form. Their animal form is similar to a saber-toothed tiger from Earth. They can shoot lightning from their tails, and it can be used for defense and attack.

They are a matriarchal society and live in family groups called streaks. They have alpha, beta, and omega distinctions, but there is always a female alpha who acts as head of the family.

Alphas have a rut and omegas have a heat. Only alpha and omegas can breed with one another, and betas can only breed with their own designation. There are male and female omegas. Both have breeding capabilities, but male omegas are rare. Most are killed once their designation is discovered to prevent competition with females for coveted positions within the streak.

The planet Iceen is a frozen tundra of caves and outcroppings, and the streaks usually have two dwellings—a cave for their animal form, and a dome-like, insulated glass building which they live in with their streaks.

Maxsim (Alpha Lightning Cat)

The leader of the streak of lightning cats that performs in the circus, despite it being a matriarchal society. Maxsim is a dark aqua blue that ombres out to snowy white in the legs, with black, tribal style markings across shoulders, chest, and arms. He has high cheekbones, cat ears, feline eyes, a tail, and fangs, which are bigger when in animal form, as well as a broad chest and well-defined arms. Fur covers his body when in humanoid form, except for a patch across his chest and down to his groin.

Maxsim keeps the rest of the streak safe from an aggressive Natalia.

Natalia (Beta Lightning Cat)

Only female in the group that performs in the circus. She is heir to her matriarchal streak, but is a beta designation. Natalia has pale blue fur all over, with long black hair, high cheekbones, cat ears, feline eyes, a tail, and fangs. She has small breasts, a slender, toned body, and a lean backside and legs. She has naked patch across her breasts and down to groin.

She wants to form a streak with Maxsim, Trace, Fuse, and Sim, but they are alphas and cannot breed with her. She took her omega sister's place, who was supposed to be the one performing with the circus.

Echo (Omega Lightning Cat)

He is a pure white lightning cat, with a smaller frame than Maxsim's, and built much more delicately. His designation is omega, and he has survived because he comes from a rare streak with a male omega. The streak, with help from the warlocks, protected him while growing up. They hid it, and he presents himself to the world as beta. He wants to form a streak with Maxsim, but not Natalia. She discovered he is an omega and keeps trying to kill him.

Other cats in the group
Trace (Alpha Lightning Cat)
Fuse (Alpha Lightning Cat)
Sim (Alpha Lightning Cat)

Mazlan Natalia's mother and Matriarch of the Lightning cats (Omega)

Sky blue fur

Minx Natalia's sister (Omega)

Shoshi Natalia's younger sister 10 yrs old (omega)

Jalin Echo's mother (Alpha)

Astrea Maxsim's mother (Omega)

Yalani

An abominable snowman type creature with shaggy white and gray fur. They are good at blending into their surroundings. It is a hunter-gatherer species that lives in caves on Iceen. Eight to nine feet tall, they are an aggressive species that will attack if they feel threatened. They live solitary lives unless mated and raising a family.

PLANET SKARR

This planet is the birthplace of the human race. The original humans were exploring Skarrians who crashed on Earth, and because they no longer had access to the magical waters, lost all their supernatural abilities.

Skarr looks much like Earth from above though the land masses are unfamiliar and the sea has a slight pink tint to it. I'm pretty sure that's got something to do with the two pink moons that shine brightly in the sky orbiting the planet

Skarrians are mostly polyamorous and have attraction marks that show up on both parties' bodies. If attraction wanes on either side, the marks disappear. Skarrians find themselves bonded to others after five rounds of sex, which requires them to orgasm simultaneously. Skarr is basically a sister planet to Earth in that it is made up of ten different land masses surrounded by pink oceans, but it has different species of plants and animals.

When reproducing, all bonded members of the family must participate to produce a child.

Lila Jenson (Liliana Adams) mimic and whisperer power

Orphaned at a young age, she moved from foster family to foster family, never really fitting in anywhere, though nothing terrible happened to her. One family put her into gymnastic lessons and self-defense courses to keep her out of trouble. She has no real goal in life, but has always thought there must be something more than working in a bar and having the occasional one-night stand.

She is average height, with a curvy figure, long chestnut hair with turquoise streaks, golden skin, and green eyes.

Lila discovered she has grandparents who are still alive, and they invited her to learn their family business.

Her mimic forms so far include Celestian, Warlock, Barcoa, Aquilian, Fire and Earth Elementi, Necro and Rilunese

John Adams, William Adams, and Eric Adams

Triplet brothers who appear to be in their late

forties, they possess chestnut hair, tall, slender builds, and emerald green eyes.

They have been searching for Liliana, also known as Lila, for years, and are thrilled to have finally found her. They are also the CEOs of the Galaxy Circus and guardians of the power orb.

William has a buzz cut and is gruff.

Eric has long hair, which he wears in a man bun, and is the joker and tease in the family.

John has short, tousled hair and is the kind and loving brother, but he is subject to spirals of depression.

Liliana Adams (Missing)

Lila's grandmother and namesake. She disappeared just before Lila's parents were killed. The Admas brothers haven't moved on because they haven't felt their bond break and they hope she's out there somewhere in the galaxy

Alina and Marcus Adams (Dec.)

Lila's parents moved to Earth in order to raise her in relative safety, but they were killed in a car accident. Alina had blonde hair and green eyes, and Marcus had brown eyes and the same chestnut hair as the grandpas and Lila.

Magenta

She is a performer in the circus. When on

Earth, she uses the circus silks, but on other planets, she uses her levitation powers. Magenta has bright pink hair and pale skin. She is mid height with a slim build and light blue, almost gray, eyes. She has been a lifeline for Lila when it comes to all things alien.

Broderick Potter (Bubby)

Captain of the mothership and Marcus Adams' best friend. He has red hair and a red beard with crystal blue eyes. He's rugged and well-built and thrilled to meet Lila.

Phillip and Fiona

They are Lila's twin cousins, but not on the Adams' side of the family.

Fiona has long, curly red hair, brown eyes, and freckles with a tall, slim build.

Phillip's red hair is cropped short, and he has brown eyes and freckles with a tall, slim build.

They oversee the dinosaur act. The dinosaurs were hand raised in the zoo on Skarr.

Captain Lester

Captain Lester is an alternate captain for the mothership and circus pod. He has an abrasive personality and a voice like he smokes two packs of cigarettes a day.

Terrans

Security officer for the circus pod and brother to Ferrans

Ferrans

Security officer for the main ship and brother to Terrans

Susie (A Night Most Wicked)

She is Lila's best friend, with dark, mahogany skin, melted chocolate colored eyes, and black corkscrew curls. She's a nurse and previously lived with Lila. Recently drank the waters from Skarr activating a dormant spark of power.

Vivian

The Adam's brothers sister in law. She is a member of the Skarrian council and a widow. Her own bond group died in a mysterious shuttle accident. She is Phillip and Fiona's grandmother and raised them when their own parents died. Detecting lies is one of her Skarrian abilities.

Oshan (mimic) The last known Skarrian mimic. He wears a glamor that has him looking like Dumbledore from Harry Potter complete with robes. Ib reality he is a blonde haired blur eyed man who looks about the same age of her Grandpas. He's hundreds of years old and has a large family.

Mimic's are immortal and their mates and partners also become immortal but any children from the pairings don't. Mimics can assume male or female form of whatever race is in their database.

Caspian and Lila's babies

Cordelia - purple when in kraken form, has pale blue skin and bright purple hair in her human form

Jack - blue when in kraken form has pale blue skin and blue hair in human form

Calypso - mottle blue, purple and pink in kraken form and in human form her skin is mottled blue and purple and she has longish pink hair.

PLANET FLUXX

Fluxx is a sister planet to Skarr, and its waters have magical properties too, but it gives its inhabitants the ability to shift into another creature. Fluxxians are animal shifters with three forms—humanoid while retaining coloration and some features of their animal, half form, and beast form. Fluxxians can use glamor to blend in and must do this when on Earth and in public. Fluxxians have fated mates, and their animal will dictate how they reproduce.

Caspian (Kraken Shifter, Lila's First Mate)

Caspian performs in the first act in the circus, shifting into half form and juggling multiple items with his tentacles.

He has mottled blue and purple skin, piercing stormy blue eyes, nipple rings, and vivid purple hair shaved on either side with a long section on top the drapes over one eye. His tentacles are purple and blue when in half form. Caspian's beast form is large. Male krakens implant their parents with their eggs via an ovipositor, and the womb then fertilizes the eggs, basically doing the opposite of a human. Fertilized eggs can lie dormant inside the female for a long time until she is ready to give birth. Drinking a large amount of the male kraken's cum tells the eggs that you are ready for babies. Four weeks later, they are born in kraken form. Two weeks after that, they are able to shift into their human form for the first time. Krakens can have anywhere between one and six babies at a time. Non-kraken mates will have their biology changed when given the mating bite. This allows them to carry a kraken's eggs for their partner.

Dylan (Dragon Shifter)

Dylan is in the first act of the show, which is a fire breathing act where he actually breathes fire.

He has ebony skin, wings, a metallic black shimmer to his scales, yellow and green reptilian eyes, and fangs. He also has sharp cheekbones, and his nose flattens slightly in half form.

Dylan is the man whore of the circus. He befriends Lila early on, only to betray her later and get kicked out of the circus for his act of aggression.

Silac (Naga Shifter)

Silac is one of the shifters who replaced Dylan in the first act. A Naga shifter, he has tousled emerald green hair in his humanoid form, with long, lean muscles and nipple rings. His eyes are orange and black. When he is in half form, he has a snake body from the waist down, with emerald green scales covered in horizontal orange stripes and black diamonds. Naga males have a hemipenis that hooks in to hold their partner close during copulation, and their mates give birth to live young.

Tirrian (Dragon Shifter)

Tirrian is the dragon shifter who replaced Dylan in the first act. Where Dylan was pitch black, he is more like an oil slick black. He has a shimmer to his skin that flickers from green and gold to pink and blue. He appears holographic depending on what angle you look at him from. In half form, his wings are the same color and his scales are holographic pink. He is tall, broad, and muscular. His hair is black with pink streaks in it, and his eyes are black with lines of pink in them. He's an asshole.

Dragons can only have young with female dragons or their mates. Once again, a mating bite will change a non-dragon shifter mate to allow them to lay eggs. Eggs are incubated by the couple for two months before being born. They must be kept at a certain temperature to ensure a live birth. Homosexual dragons can hire surrogates to help them with reproduction if they wish, and it is common practice for young dragons to offer this service as a way to start their own hoard before they wish to begin their own family. There is a website that can help facilitate this.

Caspian's family
Mother - Mira (kraken shifter)
Father - Murphy (kraken shifter)
Sisters all kraken shifters
Naia
Marin
Ocean
Neri
Marilla
Brothers - all kraken shifters
Morgan
Malik
Neptune
Fisher
Sister in laws
Saleny (dragon shifter) married to Morgan
Luxsim (Unisci shifter) married to Neptune
Brothers in law
Felix (wolf shifter) married to Neri

Unisci: Big cat shifter. Large like a saber tooth tiger, but has pitch black fur like a jaguar but it is long like a persian cat.

PLANET CYBERTRONIA

A technologically advanced planet inhabited by life forms that are half organic, half nanobot technology, allowing them to change their features at will. Reproduction occurs through intercourse, but parents program their respective organic matter with the traits and features they wish their babies to have. Once the baby is born, their source code is imprinted on a microchip, which is then deposited into a secret storage facility for safe keeping.

Pleasure Bot Industries is one of the main sources of employment for Cybertronia. They produce lifelike robots for sexual pleasure and are one of the galaxy's most popular purchases. Pleasure Bots are not like cyborgs, in that they are incapable of thoughts, feelings, or responses that have not been programmed into them.

Link Tesla/Digicon(Cyborg)

Link is the ship doctor for the Galaxy Circus and is one of Lila's boyfriends. His skin tone is peach with a shimmer. He has silver hair and eyes. He is built like a swimmer, with long, lean lines, a tapered waist, and broad shoulders, and he is able to change his body parts at will. Cyborgs can't lie.

Josa Spears (Cyborg Nurse)

Josa is the nurse to Link's doctor, but he was hired by Link's mom to spy on him and the circus. He was promised Link's hand in marriage and a share of the Pleasure Bot Industries fortune if he complied. He has the same shimmery skin tone as Link, with metallic green hair and eyes. He has a slender, feminine frame and a dirty attitude.

Deianira Digicon(Cyborg A Night Most Wicked)

CEO to Pleasure Bot Industries and Link's mother. She doesn't like to be told no.

Ricky (Cyborg A Night Most Wicked)

Sent to Aura as a gift from Deianira. Blonde hair, tanned skin and gorgeous body.

PLANET VILAX

Vilax is home to a race of blood drinkers, the sanguinistas. Much like Earth's legend of vampires, this race is strong, fast, and has heightened senses. They can fly, and are very hard to kill. Their bodies will regenerate as long as their body parts are close to one another. To kill them, you need to burn both of their hearts. They are a warrior race and one of the fiercest in the galaxy. Military service is mandatory for all Vilaxians.

Vilax only gets five hours of sunlight a day, so while they are not allergic to the sun, they do prefer the dark. Sanguinistas drink blood because their bodies cannot process their own red blood cells. They have a fated mate called a blood rose, but not everyone finds them. They live in family clans, and blood sharing can be a sexual thing, but with children, it isn't.

Saxon (Sanguinista)

Saxon is part of the aerial troupe in the circus. He has magenta-colored eyes and thick, short black hair that's long enough to run your fingers through. His body is muscular and broad, and he has pale skin and fangs.

Hale (Sanguinista)

He is in the same troupe as Saxon and is Saxon's best friend. He has blond hair, teal eyes, and fangs.

Radella (Sanguinista)

Estrella (Sanguinista)

Velorina (Sanguinista)

Xenos (Sanguinista)

Saxon's twin brother, his hair is longer and worn tied back.

Dante (Sanguinista)

Chocolate brown hair that falls in floppy curls over his forehead and lavender colored eyes. Tall and athletic

Kavita (Sanguinista)

Pin straight long red hair that falls to her ass

and dark eyes with red flecks in them and ruby red lips. Tall and athletic

Crimson (Sanguinista) A Night Most Wicked

Long red curly hair, tall, toned and lean. Crimson is antisocial and could never fit in with a sanguinista clan so once she finished her compulsory public service for Vilax, she got a job working at the Pleasure Inn so she would have a variety of options for feeding. Clients like being bitten during sexual relations. She was in a relationship with Savannah prior to Xane and Aura taking over the brothel. Aura bestowed a mating bite on her, permanently joining her in their group and she stopped seeing clients.

PLANET WESTALIN

This is the warlocks' home planet. Warlock powers include, but are not limited to, mind manipulation and control, teleporting, and manifestation. Powerful warlocks have harems to feed from because they are psychic feeders who feed from strong emotions. Weaker warlocks and other creatures make up these harems. Weaker warlocks benefit from it, as they are able to feed off the stronger warlock at the same time and get a temporary boost in power. Members of the harem receive a wage and a comfortable position within the warlock's household. Powerful warlocks are able to absorb powers and life force, but it is frowned upon and is only used as a punishment. Warlocks have soulmates they call intimates. When a warlock finds their intimate, they no longer need a harem to feed from.

Xavier Colest (Crown Prince)

Xavier is one of the most powerful beings in the galaxy, only second to his parents. He is mostly with the circus because he gets bored easily. He helps with glamor to confuse the humans. He has purple/blue eyes and long indigo hair. His body is lean and muscular, and he has piercings in his ears, nose, and eyebrow. His ears are pointed, and he has lavender-colored skin with silver markings.

Xylene Colest

Queen of the Westalins and Xavier's mother. She was best friends with Alina and Marcus Adams, Lila's parents.

Cronus Colest

King of the Westalins and Xavier's father. He was best friends with Alina and Marcus Adams.

Xane Colest (A night Most Wicked)

Nephew of the King and Queen and former Strike team commander. Mate to Aura Gasm, master of the Pleasure Inn and powerful warlock. He has long indigo hair, shaved at the sides exposing more silver tribal like tattoos on his skull, and is tied back and there's a top hat covering it. Silver rings line both ears, as well as in his eyebrow and his bottom lip. Sharp cheekbones with eyes that look to be purple and pouty lips. Rescued

Aura when they were enslaved on an illegal brothel ship.

Elyan (Warlock, Head Harem Girl in Xavier's Harem)

Nambra (Warlock, Harem Member)

She has red hair and a voluptuous figure.

Lexus (Warlock, Harem Member)

She has short dark hair and a petite frame.

Ara (Warlock, Harem Member)

Ara has pale pink hair, eyes, and skin.

Jastia (Warlock, Harem Member)

Jastia possesses buttercup yellow hair, eyes, and skin.

Sinath (Rasque, Harem Member)

The Rasque is a humanoid race that looks like an Earth grasshopper. They have segmented arms and legs with plated body structure. Their penis is covered by plated sections, which retract when manipulated. Once the penis extends, claspers lock the copulating couple together.

Mithus (Milobar, Harem Member)

He has a stingray-shaped head and body, with

arms, legs, and a barbed tail. Mithus has two penises, which both have barbs that activate during intercourse, locking them within their partner.

Zanorn (Morpheian, Harem Member)

A race of metamorphs, they are able to take any shape they desire. In natural form, they are like a blank slate with limited features and gray skin.

Topirey (Dionall, Harem Member)

Dionalls are plant creatures with two forms—one is an upright humanoid sentient form, and the other is a stationary plant form which is similar to the Earth's Venus flytrap, only a lot larger and it feeds on flesh. They have leafy foliage on their head and sharp teeth, and are able to grow their body parts at will.

PLANET AQUILIA

Aquilia is seventy-five percent water, and the Aquilians are an aquatic species with three forms—humanoid, mer, and beast form. In beast form, they resemble an Earth dolphin, but are scaled and have sharp teeth. They come in a variety of pastel colors. In half form and on two legs, they retain the pastel colors and cannot glamor. They require a glamor spell if they want to tour Earth. Family groups are called pods. Aquilians rarely leave their home planet, and if they do, they will return once they form a pod so that their young are born in their home waters.

Nikos (Aquilian Prince)

Nikos is one of the performers in the dolphin show in the circus. He is a member of the Aquilian royal family, but not in line to inherit. He is arrogant and horny. He has pastel green skin, and his scales are pastel green and gold. His hair and eyes are metallic gold.

Nixie (Aquilian princess)

Nixie is Nikos's sister and also a performer in the circus. She's friendly and fun and is interested in exploring the galaxy. She does not want to get trapped by being mated on Aquilia. Nixie is also open to trying relationships with other species. Her colors are pastel blue and gold, with metallic gold hair and eyes.

Galaxy Circus Pod Members
   Joaquin
   Nolani
   Marin
   Dorado

PLANET RILU

Rilu is a desert-like planet with small green oases dotted across its land surfaces. There are no above ground oceans or seas, but there are large underground ones which provide fresh water for the inhabitants of the planet. At each of the oases, which usually center around a small lake, are wells which provide fresh drinking water for travelers. Some of the larger lakes have permanent villages established for trade. The people of Rilu are nomadic tribes. They raise larnuks and are miners. Under the surface of Rilu are extensive gem mines, and the people of Rilu mine the gems for trade and to feed their larnuks.

Larnuks

These are creatures much like Earth's Pegasus, possessing both wings and a horn. They come in the same colors as the gems that are mined on their planet—emerald, ruby, sapphire, gold, and amethyst. They eat gems and spout fire, and they have sharp, vicious teeth. They are bred and raised by a larnuk mistress or master who will bond with their herd. The larnuk will bite them, and a lock of their hair will turn the same color as the larnuk's. The more streaks a master or mistress has, the more larnuks they control.

Rilax

Rilax are berries that grow in the mines alongside the gems. The berries are used to make rilaxious, a pink alcoholic beverage popular across the galaxy. It is slightly bubbly with a thick, creamy consistency.

Zala (Larnuk Mistress)

Zala is the larnuk mistress for the circus and is in charge of that portion of the show. She has exotic, Middle Eastern looks with darker skin and wavy, pitch-black hair with streaks of color in it from her horses. Her eyes are a pale blue, almost white, rimmed in kohl, and framed with long black lashes. She is tall and slim, and her body is covered in silvery scars from bonding with her horses. Five appear in the show, but she has more.

Chief Zana

Zala's father and reigning head Chief of Rilu

Zilla

Zala's sister and has a crush on Tirrian

Zamala

Zala's Grandmother and seer

PLANET MORLASH

Home of Morpheian race. They are shape shifters who can merge into any form, metamorphs. They are hermaphrodites and all members of the race have breeding capabilities. They usual assume a preferred form which is either male or female, Aura prefers to be both.

Morpheians are polyamorous and bestow a mating bite in their natural form to seal their mate to them. It is quite a painful process ensuring that the mate is genuine.

Aura Gasm Proprietor Pleasure Inn (A Night Most Wicked)

Aura was kidnapped by alien sex traffickers as a teenager and forced into an illegal brothel where she was regularly abused to keep her in line. Developed Stockholm syndrome and tried to defend her captors when the ship was raided by a warlock strike force led by Xane. Xane, besotted by Aura nursed them back to health and have been together ever since.

PLANET CELESTIA

Celestian are what humans would call angels. All Celestians have wings and powers. Powers tend to be emotive in nature, healing is one of the powers, as is being able to manipulate emotions. Celestians glow with heightened emotions, the color their glowing tells what emotion they are feeling. Lavender is horny.

Celestians are also polyamorous and reproduction involves a magical process that combines everyone's DNA ensuring the child is a part of all mates before depositing the embryo into the chosen carrier.

Savannah (A Night Most Wicked)

Tall and voluptuous with a long mane of blonde curls, and silver eyes. Savannah is a product of rape and forced breeding which should be impossible with the way Celestians breed. She was cast out by her mother as a baby, never fitting in anywhere, teased and ridiculed. She made her home the Pleasure Inn as a way to make herself feel good. Crimson taught her she did need to have sex with someone to be loved.

Mark (Marcus Aurelias) (A Night Most Wicked)

Stolen from his parents by unknown assailants. Needs to go through an activation ceremony. Mark is Susie's boyfriend. He has black hair and gray eyes, and worked as an emergency room doctor. Mark is also bi.

King Jotan Angelis
One of Mark's father and fierce King who has hung onto the monarchy while his mates have been mourning

Queen Corethea Angelis
One of Mark's mothers, blonde with large white wings, and a talented healer

Queen Tabbris Angelis
One of Mark's mothers and also a talented healer

PLANET RECCEDEA

A lush, foliage-covered, tropical planet with frozen poles on either end. It is the birthplace of the dinosaurs found in the circus. Many species of dinosaurs that once roamed the Earth continue to survive and thrive on this planet.

Vigolash

Viggy is a red and black tyrannosaurus rex. He was trained from a baby, and acts just like a giant, overgrown golden retriever.

Htaed

Htaed is a yellow and orange velociraptor, who was also trained from a baby, but is unruly and kind of crazy.

PLANET AAZ'AX

The leadership of this race was cruel and vicious and wanted to use the orb to conquer other lands. They possessed it momentarily and laid waste to a number of planets, but the Unas were able to take it back. By then, the Aaz'ax weren't doing well. A mysterious illness had taken most of their women, and women of other races wanted nothing to do with the men. Their species has been on the brink of extinction and were finally able to dispose of their tyrannical leadership. Remaining survivors scattered to planets far and wide. The Aaz'ax are distant ancestors of the Vilaxians. Although they do not require blood, they can consume it, but it acts much like alcohol and drugs to a human. They have the ability to glamor, and they have two natural forms, their warrior form which is humanoid, but their shoulders and backs are covered in ridges and their body looks like they are covered in thorns. With their green skin and blood-red hair, they resemble a rose. And their everyday form which is again humanoid but he is covered in spikes, long and short. Comparable to an Earth's lionfish. The long spikes have sheer membrane draped between them. They don't have hair, just a crest of spikes, but it's their color that is stunning. They look like an opal, all greens, reds, blues, yellows, and pinks. Originally people thought they were two separate races because of how different they look.

Brannock

Hiding on Earth. Escaped there with his unit over a hundred years ago when the Una's and Aaz'axian war finished. Move every thirty years and change identities. Uses a glamor to blend in. Can't hold his glamor when intoxicated.

PLANET ELEMENTAL

A race of beings capable of controlling the elements. Four different varieties Earth, Fire, Air and Water. Humanoid in shape and features. They do have fated mates, but they are rare and only found within their own kinds so usually it will be a life partner pairing with no cosmic and divine intervention. However, it isn't forbidden to have sex outside of their own kind, it is frowned upon to choose a life partner of a different elemental and any children born from a non matched union will result in the child taking on only one element of it's parent. Those kind of pairings are often seen as outcasts in the community. In fact on the planet Elemental there is a whole city made up of odd parings as they often get shunned by their birth families.

Elementi need to breed with Elementi. Children won't happen with another species.

Earth Elementi

The earth Elementi have antler style horns, a tail with the end fanning out like a leaf. They have dark green wings that are also leaf shaped and double fanned and their skin tone is mottled shades of green. They are fine and almost fairy like in stature with long lithe limbs and a shorter stature.

Abilities include They can manipulate, reshape, and control earth elements at will. Including all crystals, metals, and minerals. Make and command gollums which gives them access to an entire army of beings at their command. Create tunnels in the ground to transport themself by. They have the ability to create, control, and manipulate volcanoes, lava, and magma which is something the share with a fire Elementi.

They have a second larger form that's like a bear, but green with antlers, wings and the tail. They are also herbivores.

Fire Elementi

Come in a range of solid colors, red/yellow/orange and amber bat like wings that have a smokey shimmer to them. Horns on the head, kind of look like molten lava and their tail has flames on the end of it. The wings will flame up when you use them and their bodies can withstand any sort of flame or fire. They also have a second form, the wings, horns and tail stay the same but they get a lot bigger and more gray in color and have cracks in the skin that look like lava. They are meat eaters, they can eat vegetation, but prefer meat.

Abilities include create, control, and manipulate anything fire and heat related including plasma. As well as the volcano ability they share with the earth Elementi. Generate and control a magical fire that will do their bidding. Control of fireworks and the ability to teleport through fire. Self detonation - phoenix like powers were they can blow themself up and then reform unharmed. Fire breathing.

OTHER ALIEN RACES

Unas

A race of highly intelligent, peaceful, powerful beings who created the power orb that the Galaxy Circus protects. The now extinct race had powers that were fueled through sexual energy. They didn't have mates or partners, it was just a free-for-all orgy.

Their war with the Aaz'ax dwindled their numbers until there were only a handful left. Their energy was absorbed into the orb when they turned it over to the Adams brothers. They used the Adams' ancestors' blood to link it to them, and if it leaves their line, anyone remaining will be absorbed too.

The power orb was supposed to be a clean, free source of energy capable of powering planets across the galaxy. It can be used as a weapon of mass destruction, but cannot be destroyed because the galaxy would implode.

Utaz - Oshan's son. Pure Una and he would like Lila to meet him in the hope they will return the Una race to the Galaxy. Lila is reluctant.

Darklarkian (Planet Elos)

Elf-like race identifiable by their pointy ears and black skin, and green snake-like eyes.

Snarkle (Planet Cereabosto)

Humanoid bodies with two heads. Each head has a mouthful of sharp teeth

Pistadon (Planet Laxo)

Bird like creature similar to a pterodactyl. Sharp beaks and beady eyes, they have no feathers, look like a freshly plucked chicken. The only feathers on their body surround their cloaca. Red and yellow spike-like feathers circle this opening protecting it from unauthorized penetration.

Seiomann (Planet So)

Magic race with subjugating powers. They can make it so a being cannot access their powers. They also have the ability to freeze a person in stasis. They appear floating draped in a dark cloak with only discernible features are three red eyes.

Telazions (Planet Telaz)

They sold the tech for the iPhone to Steve Jobs.

Nengh

They perform as clowns in the circus. They have detachable limbs and are able to adjust their body's size and mass. They are humanoid in shape, but they are orange with feathery tufts instead of hair. They use a glamor provided by Xavier to appear human when on Earth.

Jelliads

A race of purple gelatinous amorphic creatures. They are sentient and communicate via telepathy. They feed from the atmosphere of their home planet but they can also feed on orgasmic energy. They can change their shape and the breed asexually.

Bacalacian

From the planet Bacalac they are humanoid in form in that they walk upright and have two legs but they have a red armor plated outer shell, bright red when on high alert, orange at rest. They have two pincers in place of arms that are razor sharp and dangerous. Their torso is triangular with two eyes on stalks sticking out of the top and a mouth opening with a single pair of teeth on top and bottom which grind food between them.

Dodarran

A demon counterpart to the Celestians.

Gilani: member of the circus. In the first act with Caspian one of the jugglers. He's got red leathery looking skin and big horns and his own set of large bat-like wings.

Filani

A race of being that can be likened to succubus and incubus. So beautiful they can seduce with their looks and can absorb someones life force during sex to feed.

Madova

This race has only females and they have two forms. Humanoid with hypnotizing gaze, snake like appendages for hair, fangs, nose slits, wings. A snake-like appendage that comes out of the vagina and penetrates the male to lay eggs. They have sex through an x like opening in their stomachs.

Animal form, shifts into a serpent like dragon with wings that spits venoms and bites the head off the male they have sex with once the babies are ready to be born. Babies then consume the remaining body.

Tutva

Four armed humanoid race. The women have three breasts and two vaginas and the men have double cocks and only one nipple in the middle of their chest. Tall and built with trusts and horns. Kind of like orcs. The come in various shades of green gray and brown

Tully and **Sully** are sisters who run Orion's Belt

Vengii (Planet Sotda VX)

Tinka - No legs -mushroom style base long spindly arms with mauve skin. Round back skull like a human but the front half tapers down into a snout. Black beady eyes, no hair, ridges and bumps all over the back of their head. Snout ends in pouty lips. Seamstress and fashion designer for the Galaxy Circus.

Flobberstums (Planet Flor)

No human like features what so ever. They are a large flat and wide worm like creature, with brilliant colors and patterns covering the back of the bodies while the front is a smooth black. There are no discernible features. Flobberstums are neither male nor female but both, and they cock fight to see who will bare their young each year. Three prong trident penis that must pierce the opposing Flobberstum implanting their seed into the other and the loser is responsible for carrying their clutch to term."

Barcoa (Planet Barc)

Barcoa are slightly primitive warrior race, that is big and beefy. They kind of look like rocks but the texture of their skin is more like leather. Not all that intelligent but good at following orders and almost indestructible. They are often used as security guards for high profile people. Humanoid in shape but they have a centralized mouth situated on their stomach and they eat moss. The thing that makes them good security is they have several decentralized eyes. One on their hand, one on either side of their head, and one on the back of their knee. It gives them three hundred and sixty degrees of vision. But their sexual organs are in their elbows. Both male and female, they have a vagina like slit on one arm and a penis which is retractable on the other."

Carevasta Bear (**Planet Carevasta**)

Information to come.

DICTIONARY

Phoeall (fo-all): Warlock for...

Vigolash: Obedient one in Aaz'axian

Sandar worm: native to the planet Westalin, they are large creatures that turn soil over in their paddocks between crops. They eat all organic matter left from past crops, leaving it free for farmers to plant the next crop.

Silax worm: Native to Rilu, it lives in the mines and is a pest. Their secretion kills the rilax berry plant. They are trapped, and their secretions are used to make achom.

Achom: A drink that is like a blend of coffee and chocolate with a chili vodka kick. Made from the anal secretions of the silax worm, found in the cave system of Rilu

GIN: Galaxy Information Network.

Karta monster: A large, kaiju style creature the size of an elephant.

Cirillion: Little bundles of fluff with big eyes.

Lastovian hog:

Saturn's Rings: A restaurant on the Galaxy Circus mothership.

Edalaxion Space Station: A space station with dodgy bars and meeting spaces for the dregs of the galaxy.

Celesian Brothel: A popular brothel if you want to have sex with living beings as opposed to sex bots.

Jaxa bird: A bird native to Westalin, it looks like a cross between a peacock and a phoenix. Its tail is a fanned bloom of fire.

Kala mouse: A marsupial found on Westalin.

Coolmy shell: This is a crustacean found in Aquilian waters.

Farlucks: A creature from Westalin similar to an Earth fox with three tails and pink fur. They are an aquatic mammal.

Husad Mead: From Husadavia, an uninhabited planet in the Kavar system. The planets and animals on it are carnivorous and lethal and it takes a special kind of being to harvest the fruit from the Halla bush. It's quite popular and quite potent

Mitavin: rodent found on space junk and in space stations. Skeletal beings with a tail like a beaver and body like a racoon

Treason: board game like monopoly but you invade planets

Toosook Flowers: shimmery pink and purple blooms shaped very much like a cross between hollyhocks and tulips. A special coral that grows deep within the ocean. They get their color from a species of fish that brush against them to keep clean. The shimmer is from their scales. They will also never die. If you put them in a vase at home and top the vase up with ocean water every few days, they will live continuously. Found only in the oceans of Fluxx

Lemug: Round smooth and blue about the size of a marble, they are very much like a pearl from Earth, in the they grow inside the shell of a sea creature. Found only in the oceans of Fluxx

Catava grain: similar to Earth wheat used to brew beer on Fluxx.

Suva : A red fluffy moss substance that grows only on the cliffs next the Capsians
parents home. USed to make a recreational drug that gives a similar high to coke but is not addictive. Mira and Murphy sell it to drug manufacturers all over the galaxy.

Catsuva beer: A beer brewed from catava grain and suva moss. Has a high alcohol content and gives a burst of energy in the drinker

Whathefucorcadiles- a cross between a crocodile, orca and a great white shark. Hungry aggressive predators.

Mallac bear - From westalin. Large stocky scaled beast with plates like an armadillo. Size of a hippopotamus with a mouthful of fangs that drip a paralyzing toxin.

Station X69 - Popular recreational and trading station

Saluktat beans - A bean used to make a beverage similar to coffee from Westalin

Earth Alien Aliiance (EAA) Located in Area 51. Keeps track of all aliens on Earth and assures they are adhearing to the visa laws

Galactic Council. One member from all planets in the Galaxy ensuring smooth relations between all member planets

Lollecado - Black banana shaped fruit found in the thermal caverns of Rilu. It is solid as a rock until cut in half. The inside flesh is seedy like a dragon fruit but blood red in color and steaming hot. Grows in lava pools, and is harvested by dragons or Riluense wearing special gloves. It's coveted by dragons because it makes their cum taste like the fruit.

THANK YOU FOR READING!

I know I know. Lexie what are you doing? How can you leave us hanging like that? Well the answer is easily. ROFL .

Why on Earth is Lila wanted by the Aquilians? Well you won't have too long to wait because the next book will be out soon.

I hope you enjoyed the book. It would be super awesome if you could leave a review wherever you bought it, because I love to hear what you thought of the story.

I'll be putting up a preorder soon for the next one so keep an eye out for it.

In the mean time why don't you check out one of my other series. You can find everything you need to know here.

www.lexiewinston.com

ACKNOWLEDGMENTS

To my cover designer Jessica, of Raven Ink Covers. Thank you for making the covers exactly what I envisioned, you nailed it and all of them.

Thank you to both Jess at Elemental Editing. My book is pretty and readable thanks to you.

My ever reliable and faithful beta reader Kerry… You da bomb xxx

Galaxy Circus is a real passion project for me. I love writing it and I hope to keep working on it for a little while longer. There will be at least 1 more book. Keep an eye on my Facebook Group - Lexie's Ladygarden for news of when it will release.

Thank you to Kirsty Ellis whose creative brain came up with the Elementi.

And lastly to you guys the readers. I love what I do, and probably would do it regardless if anyone read them or not, but you guys make it that much sweeter so thank you.

Until next time, happy reading